I0603985

A Requiem for the Sanctuary

Michael Taylor

Copyright © 2024 Michael Taylor. All rights reserved.

No portion of this book may be reproduced in any form without permission from the publisher, except as permitted by U.S. and UK copyright law. For permissions contact: Michael Taylor michaeltaylorbooks@gmail.com

A Requiem for the Sanctuary and The-Passage-Between-The-Worlds series is copyright to Michael Taylor

This novel's story and characters are fictitious. Certain long-standing institutions, agencies, and historical figures are mentioned, but the characters involved are wholly imaginary.

For my wonderful children. Every single day you make me proud.

PROLOGUE

"Can't you hurry up?"

For a long moment, there is silence, until the man turns and grunts. "I told you it will take a month."

"Cornelius, it's been five weeks already!" she complains, but he merely shrugs and turns his back, intent on his task again. The girl gives a *tsk* of annoyance and returns inside. She knows the spell is a difficult one, the wizard has tried to explain its intricacies until her eyes glazed over, but five weeks, *really?*

The sun is setting behind the distant Welsh mountains before Cornelius has finished for the day and the girl feels a twinge of guilt at her earlier petulance. He looks exhausted and she hurries to sit him down, making sure he's comfortable before rushing to the kitchen of the ancient inn and putting on the kettle.

When she returns and hands him a huge mug of the tea he loves, he takes a long sip, slurping unashamedly, and closes his eyes briefly in satisfaction. "It is almost finished," he observes suddenly, trying for nonchalance. She glances involuntarily at the mug. "Not the tea, the spell."

"Oh." She feels a sudden surge of panic. "So soon."

"It was five weeks, remember?" he says drily, then becomes serious. "Catrin, are you certain you want to do this? There is still time—"

"No!" she exclaims. "I will not back down now." Tears fill her eyes and she wipes them away angrily. "Since grandfather died, I…"

"Does Gruffydd know of your quest?"

More guilt, stronger this time. "No. And don't you go telling him, he'll only try and stop me. And don't you persuade me not to go either." She looks at him defiantly. Gruffydd was her childhood friend and it had long been assumed they'd marry. And so it had come to pass – almost. It had been at their betrothal ceremony that the Dark Wizard had committed his greatest crime yet, the spawn he had created bringing death and destruction to their village.

Catrin's grandfather, Ffranc, had been just one of many murdered that day. Since then, she had known she could never settle down to the provincial life of the village and that she must find a purpose of her own, something that would make her grandfather proud.

"I'm not trying to stop you," he reminds her gently. "I've spent more than a month opening the portal for you, haven't I?"

"Is it ready?" she asks eagerly. "I mean, can I just step inside and walk into the land of shades?"

The way she describes it, as if she will merely take a stroll down the lane…

*   *   *   *

"Anyway, I'll have Rosalind to guide me."

It is the next day and they are walking, arm in arm, to where Cornelius has opened the portal. It is complete and he has no more excuses to delay her, even though he's been doing so for a month now. Opening the portal had taken only a week; creating it had taken him a decade.

"Only to the gates of the land of shades. Beyond those, *if* they even allow you inside, you'll be on your own."

"Oh, don't be an old fusspot, Landlord." She laughs, using the name by which he is usually known hereabouts. "I'll get inside somehow." And suddenly he yearns for those innocent, carefree times when Catrin was a child, before the weight of her grief had nearly crushed her.

They hear a shout behind them and wait for Rosalind to catch up, then the three of them walk on together until, abruptly, the Landlord stops. "Here it is."

"Where?" Catrin looks around. "I can't see anything."

"Well, obviously," he says, a little tersely, then lays an apologetic hand on her arm. "Can't have just anyone finding the portal, can we? That would be something of a disaster. Probably."

"So…?" Catrin raises an eyebrow.

"You ready?"

She nods.

He takes out his wand, says a brief incantation, and immediately a door appears. It is an ordinary-looking door, painted dark blue with a black handle, but it looks very incongruous, standing there in the middle of a field.

"So we just turn the handle and walk through?" Rosalind looks at him, suddenly nervous.

"Yes. Perhaps I'll come with you to the gate after all." He nudges Catrin.

"Landlord, *stop* it. I'll be fine!"

"Yes." Rosalind lays a hand gently on his sleeve. "I will take care of her, Cornelius." With that, she takes hold of Catrin's hand, turns the handle, and the door swings open. They step through, and then they are gone.

As the portal closes, they are plunged into a green semi-darkness. Catrin looks back, but the entrance is already hidden in the gloom. It feels uncomfortable to be cut off from her world and she is hit with the realisation that the entrance would also be their exit. *If we can find it again,* she thinks, half wishing the Landlord had come after all.

They are on a narrow path lined thickly on both sides with tall trees that rise far into the sky. There is no hint of daylight to be seen through their branches. *Perhaps it's always nighttime here,* Catrin wonders.

Rosalind takes out her wand and mutters softly. An intense glow shines from its tip, illuminating the way ahead. Although neither can discern a breeze, the trees sway gently, as if disturbed by the brightness. The pool of light gives comfort yet it makes the blackness beyond its edges seem darker and more menacing. Catrin stays close to Rosalind, drawing strength from the witch's presence.

Yet on this intimidating path, there is beauty – the ground between the trees is a carpet of flowers, woodland animals peek warily at them before scuttling quickly away, and fireflies hover above their heads or zip, lightning fast, between the trees. Catrin squeals in delight when one alights on her hand and she momentarily forgets her fear. Rosalind smiles; fireflies do not usually inhabit these parts but she knows Cornelius has arranged it, somehow.

"Don't you think it's strange there's such abundant life when we're on the path to the dead?" Catrin whispers.

"Yeah, I suppose." To Rosalind, it seems irrelevant but she understands the girl's need to break the eerie silence. "Why are we whispering?" she whispers.

"I don't know, it's just the kind of place where you feel you should," Catrin whispers back. Immediately, the branches of the trees sway with greater intensity and their leaves take up the refrain, *whisper, whisper, whisper...* The noise becomes a cacophony and, frightened, the fireflies disappear. The trees lean inward, so the travellers have to stoop and then stop altogether as their way is barred.

"Stop it!" Rosalind commands sternly, but their tormentors only press closer so that soon they are hemmed in on all sides.

"I'm glad you have your wand. I don't like—" begins Catrin, when suddenly a thin branch with long twig fingers whips forward and snatches Rosalind's wand from her hand. Immediately there is a tree-ish howl of pain as the wand protests and emits a jolt of power that sets its fingers ablaze.

"Let us pass," Rosalind orders calmly as she retrieves her wand, and after a pause, during which angry mutterings can be heard, the trees obey and retreat, if only a little.

Nervously, they continue on their way, Rosalind leading with Catrin following so close behind she keeps tripping over the witch's feet.

"Don't worry," Rosalind hisses. "Look, the path is widening." And sure enough, the trees have retreated and now they make good progress, Catrin skipping almost happily at Rosalind's side, chattering nonstop.

"Anyway," she says, after they've walked for a couple of hours without incident, "I guess the trees have stopped hassling us." She nudges Rosalind playfully in the ribs. "It's plain sailing now." Rosalind grunts noncommittally and receives another dig in the ribs. "Lighten up, I'm telling you…" They round a sharp bend and Catrin stares with horror at the path before them.

"It seems you spoke too soon," says Rosalind grimly, looking at the gaping crevasse that dissects the path, disappearing deep into the forest on either side. They walk carefully to the edge and look down; there is no bottom to be seen. "Any ideas?" asks Rosalind, when they've stood staring for several minutes.

"I suppose we could go into the forest and see if there's a way around?" Catrin answers, doubtful.

"Not tempting," she says, and Catrin doesn't argue. They sit at the edge of the crevasse and wait, hoping inspiration will come.

"It's hopeless," says Catrin at last. "Couldn't you just, like, use your wand and chop down a couple of trees to make a bridge across?"

"You want to antagonise them further?"

"Well, what's the alternative? We can't sit here forever until we grow old and join the dead ourselves!"

"Do not make such jokes," Rosalind warns in a soft voice. "Not here. It isn't wise. Now hush and let me think."

There is a tinkle of laughter from somewhere in the trees and it is taken up until it seems the entire forest is laughing at them.

"Make it stop!" wails Catrin, hands over her ears. "It's horrible. I hate these trees!"

"I don't think it's the trees," Rosalind replies slowly, "it's the dead, making fun of us. But I don't think it's malicious, and you've given me an idea." Standing, she levels her wand at the trees and begins a melodious chant. Almost immediately, leaves start to fall, dozens at first, then in their hundreds, and the trees growl, but they are powerless to resist the spell.

Rosalind ignores their anger and when the air is thick with the susurration of the leaves, she commands them to lay a carpet across the crevasse. "Quickly! Do not hesitate, the spell will not last!" She takes Catrin's hand and together they run toward the carpet.

"I can't!" Catrin shouts, frightened. "We'll fall!"

"We won't, trust me!" They reach the edge of the crevasse and Catrin closes her eyes tight, allowing Rosalind to drag her across. As they run, the leaves behind them drift away into the void, but in seconds they are safe, collapsing to the ground, panting and nearly sobbing with relief. Behind, the crevasse has disappeared, as if it were never there.

They walk on, wondering if this interminable journey will ever end, and as if paying them back, the trees crowd in once more. A huge oak moves across and blocks their way and at the same time others shift to create a new path; the travellers are being shepherded away from the main one and are now at the mercy of the forest.

"Don't worry," whispers Rosalind, "I sense no malign intent. It's almost as if they are merely toying with us."

"Some joke," complains Catrin. "I'm already lost and goodness knows how we'll find the path again."

"We'll find it." She squeezes the girl's hand reassuringly, sounding more confident than she feels. But after an hour of wandering, the witch has had enough. "This is no good," she says loudly, making sure the forest can hear. "We must make our own path."

"Go into the forest, you mean?" Catrin gulps nervously and eyes the seemingly impenetrable shadows. "But then we'll *really* be lost. We don't even know what direction to take."

"Nevertheless, we must try," Rosalind says firmly, "and it's... this way." She sets off into the trees, leaving Catrin no choice but to follow. The trees, as if taken by surprise, part before them, making no effort to interfere, and after only a few minutes Rosalind laughs. "I told you they didn't wish us harm. Look – we were never far from the path after all!" And, sure enough, there it is before them.

Catrin yells with relief, and as they hurry along the trees thin quickly, as if tired of the game. Soon they are in the open countryside at last. Catrin flings herself down onto a patch of grass and stretches luxuriously, letting the hot sunshine warm her. She lays there for a few minutes, Rosalind sitting next to her, when suddenly she sits up. "I don't feel hungry," she announces, "but we were in that forest for *hours*. I should be ravenous!"

Rosalind smiles. "I don't think we were, actually. It felt like hours, but I suspect it was only minutes, an hour tops. Time is strange here. Just as I reckon weeks have passed in the real world."

"How do you know?"

"I don't know how I know, I just… know. It's a witchy thing."

"Well, anyway, it's been easy so far," Catrin says blithely. "I wasn't worried at all in there." She waves at the trees, which are now far in the distance.

"Really?" Rosalind grins knowingly.

"I wasn't!" Catrin protests, then grins back. "Well, maybe just a little."

"Come on." Rosalind pulls her to her feet. "Time we were going."

They are in no hurry now, the sun is too hot for haste, yet soon they approach a narrow stone bridge covered in green moss and yellow lichen. Beyond is a long, cobbled pathway and, in the distance, what looks like a huge pair of stone doors.

Eagerly, Catrin runs onto the bridge, sliding on the slippery moss, and is halfway across before she realises Rosalind hasn't followed. "Come on," she says, impatient, but Rosalind shakes her head.

"I can't," she says, "look." And as she tries to walk on the bridge, an invisible barrier prevents her.

"Can't you use your wand or something?"

"I could try," Rosalind says, "but, somehow, I don't think it would do any good. I think this is where my journey ends. You must go on alone."

"Oh!" Catrin runs back to her, suddenly scared; she has forgotten Rosalind cannot accompany her into the world of the dead. "I don't know what to do."

"You'll be fine." Rosalind hugs her tightly. "Look, the doors are opening for you." Catrin turns and, sure enough, the doors are open and she can see a small figure standing, waiting.

"Courage," Rosalind says, giving her a slight push. "I'll be here waiting when you come out."

The girl nods then turns and, without a backward glance, marches across the bridge.

"Forgive me,"—the figure smiles as she approaches—"you've had quite a fright, but you were never in real danger. We have to make it difficult or *everyone* would be seeking their dead friends and relatives."

She is a witch, Catrin senses it immediately, and very old, yet her face shows the remains of the great beauty she must once have been. *And her eyes are kind,* she decides. Behind her stands another witch, ancient-looking, with deeply lined skin and sharp, angular features. *Her eyes are not kind.*

"Hello," she answers politely, "my name is Catrin, and—"

"I know who you are," interrupts the witch, and the smile leaves her face. "Now, why do you intrude here?"

Taken aback at the sudden shift in mood, Catrin falters. But after a moment, she remembers her courage. "I've come for the potion," she replies boldly.

PART ONE

Chapter 1

On the first floor of the Sanctuary, in a dimension apart from that of the mortal world, is a bedroom; one of many rooms in that secret place. It is just an ordinary bedroom, neither small nor large, with a bed, drawers, and a wardrobe; the usual things. And in that room lived a young woman. She was a prisoner there.

At that moment, Cissy was calm, staring out of the window, as she did for much of the day, looking out across London and wondering, confusedly, why her friends had deserted her.

Sometimes she was still aware of her friends; her boyfriend Luke who, in her more lucid moments, she remembered she adores; Molly, the sometimes irritable but kindly old witch; Morgan, the powerful wizard, whom she had replaced as leader; and Wallace, taciturn but always loyal. And the Landlord, of course, scatterbrained, slightly crazy but utterly loveable. But that was in her lucid moments, which were few. Most of the time she viewed them with suspicion and hatred. Because Cissy was insane, made so by the sliver of evil lodged close to her brain.

At a knock on the door, she stiffened, then turned slowly as someone walked cautiously into the room. "Hello, love," Molly greeted her warily. "How are you feelin' today? Do you want to chat?" Occasionally, Cissy did talk a little, but these were always stilted conversations, filled with caution, and Molly yearned for the headstrong, friendly girl to return to them.

Nowadays Molly was always alert and rarely ventured far into the room. Today Cissy was silent, watching her keenly. Receiving no answer, Molly placed the tray of food on the table and backed slowly toward the door; it was then that Cissy pounced. The witch, though very old, still had the reflexes of a cat, and her wand was in her hand instantly, firing a blinding bolt of power, which hit Cissy in the chest, strong enough to stop her in her tracks but weak enough not to hurt. A second later, Molly was back in the corridor, the door slammed shut and the locking spell in place. She breathed heavily for a few moments, then trudged sadly away, the guilt at her inability to find a cure acute as always.

Lucy waited further down the corridor, hoping today would be the one where she could finally hug her daughter. Her shoulders slumped when she saw Molly's dejection, and when the old witch gave a brief shake of her head, she turned away with tears in her eyes.

When Cissy had been damaged and rendered insane, Lucy had insisted on staying at the Sanctuary to be nearby, should there be any improvement in what she thought of as Cissy's *illness.* Sympathetically, Morgan had agreed, knowing that without a cure she would never recover. Nor was one likely to be found; Molly, the most skilled of healers, had scoured the library of the Sanctuary without success and searched deep within her mind for the knowledge taught her by the ancient witch Siwaraksa. But there was nothing; nothing at all. Now, she thought of going after Lucy but didn't, knowing her clumsy attempts at comfort would be unwelcome. Anyway, Molly knew she was failing Cissy and she never could get used to that look of accusation in her mother's eyes.

Inside the room, Cissy stared at the door and grinned wolfishly; it had been close this time. *The old witch is getting slow,* she thought. *Eventually I will escape my prison and join him.* In her fractured mind, she imagined herself in love with the wizard who had caused her this harm – Anarkus.

Chapter 2

For more than a decade, Anarkus had lain deep in a coma, hidden inside the Dark Wizard's mansion while his body repaired itself until, gradually, his slumber had lessened and he awoke to feel magic surging through his veins once again.

Now he stood, clothes caked with dust, hair matted with cobwebs, and fingered the scar near his heart, caused by the

Knife of Chiang. A wave of anger engulfed him as he thought of the disastrous end to his attack on the Sanctuary, one that had almost ended with his death. If the knife had been just an inch to the left…

All at once he realised he was ravenously hungry and, thrusting his anger aside, he leaped up the short flight of steps from the dungeon and into the kitchen. Flinging the fridge door open, he was met with a glutinous mass of green mould that slopped to the floor near his feet. He jumped back with a cry of disgust and slammed the door shut, then began opening cupboards, searching for something, *anything*, that would assuage his hunger.

It soon became clear there was nothing and, to Anarkus, this was just another example of how utterly useless the Dark Wizard was. For a moment, he wondered where he had gone, then remembered that Logan was now a prisoner, trapped in the Chasm of Nothingness. Unless, of course, the witch and wizard council had rescued him, in which case they'd have killed him by now while he, Anarkus, slept.

Unable to ignore his gnawing pangs of hunger, Anarkus ventured outside to look for food but, of course, in this dimension of London there were few people, particularly so close to the Dark Wizard's mansion, which all knew to avoid. Walking briskly, he soon reached the alleyway, with its brick wall at the end and windows set high up. Taking a run, he leaped up the wall, through the window that opened to admit him, then dropped down into present-day London.

At once his nose wrinkled at the disgusting smell of dirt, exhaust fumes, and mortals, and for a moment he wondered why he'd ever wanted to rule this place. But then he remembered the loneliness of his own planet, that solitary existence he'd tolerated for millennia. All at once a different smell reached his nostrils, this one tempting and delicious, and he felt saliva jetting into his mouth. It was an aroma he recognised, and he hurried towards it. *Onions,* he remembered it was called, with a long piece of meat shaped like a finger, all stuffed inside a big chunk of bread. *And that stuff they put on top,* he thought, trying to recall.

Turning a corner, he saw the food van up ahead and ran to it, glaring at a young woman who was about to get there first. She sensibly turned and went in search of food elsewhere. "Give me one of those," he demanded, pointing at a photo on the glass window.

"Mind yer manners, mate," said the man inside, irritated. "A please don't cost nuffink."

Equally irritated, Anarkus twitched his wand and the man's eyes glazed over. "Certainly." He smiled. "Best food in London, this is. You want ketchup on that, mate?"

Ketchup, Anarkus remembered, *that's what it's called.* "Yes," he replied, "and lots of it." He walked away without offering to pay – not that he had money anyway – but the man didn't object. Anarkus sank his teeth into the hotdog and closed his eyes, revelling in the taste and munching quickly. It was finished all too soon and, dissatisfied, he scrunched the paper wrapper, threw it high into the air, and muttered a few words.

It unfolded, transformed into a paper airplane, and flew back to the hotdog van where it waited patiently for another to be supplied.

Anarkus plucked it from the air as it flew back, then wandered in no particular direction until his feet took him to Westminster Bridge. He smiled, remembering the chaos he'd caused when he'd almost taken over the mortal world, but his mood soured as he again thought of the Sanctuary and how they'd thwarted him.

They won't stop me next time, he thought as he walked through the gothic entrance of the Houses of Parliament. *I must go and see Portia.* That last thought surprised him; he had no idea where it came from, yet suddenly it made perfect sense. He spent a full minute turning slowly around on the spot, gazing intently at his surroundings. *What fun I had that day.* He grinned as a young woman approached, suspicion etched on her face.

"Can I help you, sir?" she asked politely. "You look a little lost."

"Lost?" He raised an eyebrow. "Oh no, I know this place very well."

"Okay..." She paused, but Anarkus caught her surreptitious glance toward the security guards.

"Don't worry, my dear, I'm not here to cause trouble,"—he winked—"not today, anyway. Tell me, is the Prime Minister home?"

"Well, the Prime Minister doesn't actually live here." She fingered the security alarm at her belt, wondering whether she should push the button.

"What a pity!" He laughed loudly. "He and I are *old* friends! Still, perhaps we will cross swords again one day. The last time he almost started a nuclear war, you know!"

Was that a security threat? she wondered as she watched him leave, unsure and not wanting to risk being mocked in her male-dominated occupation. Some of her colleagues were complete wan—

"Who was that?" She jumped as one of them approached silently from behind. She glanced at him; he was one of the better ones, but still…

"Nobody," she said firmly, hoping she was right. "Nobody at all."

Anarkus continued his rather aimless wanderings, thinking about Portia and wondering just how he might find a portal to reach her. Frustrated, he shelved the idea for another day and decided to try out the mortals' subterranean conveyance, which had always intrigued him. Soon he was sitting on the Tube, squashed between an old, extremely fat mortal who smelled faintly of fish, and a young mortal who sat on his mother's lap and burrowed a finger deep into his nostril while staring at him incessantly.

Disgusted, Anarkus drew a breath and muttered one word, deep and sonorous, *"Leeaaaave."* At once, everyone crowded to the exit door and got off at the next station and, although the platform was crowded with mortals, not one entered his carriage. Anarkus swung his feet up and relaxed, able to enjoy the ride now, apart from the dreadful, lingering stink of mortals. Presently though, he grew bored and decided to get off, glancing at the blue, white, and red sign that said Southwark Station, before leaping up the steps and into the fresh air; fresh in the sense that it didn't reek so much of mortals.

It was getting late now and there were fewer around anyway as he turned in no particular direction and allowed his feet to take him where they wished. A quarter-hour later, he walked onto Southwark Bridge, deserted except for someone at its centre, sitting on the balustrade. As he approached, he recognised her instantly.

Chapter 3

The Dark Wizard had never been one for self-reflection; he'd breezed through his long life confident in his pursuit of evil and consistent in his hatred for his brother. But even after ten long years trapped in this hellish place, Logan still couldn't understand why Morgan had saved his life when they'd been enemies for so long. But as each year passed, his hatred became less certain, until now, when it seemed pointless.

For many hours each day, he roamed this Chasm of Nothingness – there was little else to occupy his time – but despite the passing years, he'd still only traversed a fraction of that dark, mysterious world. He stopped, suddenly aware of being observed, as had happened many times over the years. Although he'd never identified the observer, its malign intent had always been clear. He'd always suspected it to be Anarkus, or perhaps the witch and wizard council, making sure he hadn't escaped. But today was different; whoever watched wished him no harm and he scanned the horizon eagerly.

Kamontip, queen of the goblins, sighed. As always, she was unable to fully comprehend her feelings toward the Dark Wizard. That he was deeply flawed was clear, yet there was a vulnerability about him too. And there was goodness within him, she was certain; buried deep perhaps, but there. And many times, she had silently thanked Morgan and Cornelius for his deliverance from certain execution by the witch and wizard council, even if the price he had paid was ten long years imprisoned in this thankless world.

She had stood here often, observing him, and not once had she allowed herself to be seen. But she was becoming impatient and today it had made her careless; she realised Logan had sensed her presence.

Sometimes she had considered rescuing him; it would be easy, she knew, and foolish – it would result in reprisals against her kind, and that she couldn't risk. But her senses were finely tuned, even more so perhaps than those of the wizard Cornelius, and today she was aware of a change in the air. Some evil was approaching, as yet unclear, but it would place all of them, including Logan, in danger. Kamontip was certain and she sighed again then turned away. *Soon, Logan, I will come. Soon.*

Chapter 4

Despite the cold, she wore only a thin tee-shirt and the scars on her arms shone brightly in the moonlight. After years of psychotherapy, tests, prodding, and poking by doctors, Amelia was well, or so they had told her. They agreed that her medication would prevent her from relapsing and that there was nothing further they could do; it was time she made her own way in the world.

Her first act upon leaving the hospital was to throw the bag of medication with which she'd been, as she saw it, thrown out of the door, into the nearest bin. Her second was to seek out the hostel where she would stay until she *found her feet,* as the well-meaning social worker had called it.

But Amelia was far from well, for how does one cure the damage done by a powerful, evil wizard? She'd waited so long for him to come for her until the realisation had dawned that he never would. Gradually, her yearning had turned into a cold, burning desire for revenge. But she'd learned cunning and had hidden her madness, until now. Here she was, free but alone in the world and with no idea how to find him. After almost a year of struggling to survive on the meagre welfare provided by the state, each day a battle to survive the torture of her demons, she found herself sitting on Southwark Bridge, legs swinging as she stared down into the roiling water of the Thames.

Desire for revenge could only sustain you so far, and she knew she could never find the wizard who had ruined her. So what was the point of living? Amelia leaned forward, bracing herself for that final, irrevocable leap into the cold London fog and oblivion.

"That water looks *awfully* cold."

Startled, she turned to see a tall man standing behind her. She hadn't heard his approach. "What the hell do you want?"

"Oh, nothing. It's just that if you jump in there,"—he indicated the freezing water below—"you'll never have the chance to find him."

"Find who?" She eyed him suspiciously. "What do you mean?"

"Why, the wizard, of course. The one who scared you so long ago. The one who destroyed your *mind.*"

Fighting to hide her inner shock, she stared at him. *How does he know about that?* "No idea what you're talking about." She glared. "Now, if you don't mind…"

"He's a little difficult to reach right now," Anarkus admitted. "However, he and I are great friends," he lied, "and I'm sure he'd want me to look after you. He feels bad about what he did." Another lie.

"I do not need looking after." She scowled. "And I still don't know what you're on about."

"Yes, you do," he said without heat, "your need is palpable. The question is, do you want to know where he is. Amelia, isn't it?"

Another shock. *Who is he?* "So tell me where to find him, then get lost."

"As I say, it's not that simple, you have to get through the lamppost for starters. Why are you so anxious to find him anyway?"

"Because I'm going to kill him."

"Really? Well, I dare say he deserves it." There was silence for a while. "Well, if you change your mind," Anarkus said at last, "you know where to find me. When you reach the alleyway, I will come for you. Come and stay with me if you like!"

As he turned away, Amelia saw that each footstep left a faint silver glow in its wake; a path she could follow.

"You want me to come and stay with you?" she called after him. "What are you, some kind of dirty paedophile?"

He looked back and laughed loudly, the sound echoing in the fog that now drifted across the bridge, enveloping them in its wispy tendrils. "No, but you interest me. Your encounter with Logan — that's his name, by the way — has left you with certain powers. Limited of course, raw and untested, but let's just say you'll make a satisfactory disciple."

"Disciple? You've gotta be kidding me, you weirdo. Now get lost!"

As he left, he grinned, knowing she would come.

Chapter 5

Penelope looked longingly from her tenth-floor office window and wished fervently that the weekend would hurry up, so she could see her friends again. She watched as purple-black clouds scudded across a stormy sky and jumped slightly as lightning forked and lit up the city before her. She loved the rain and almost laughed aloud as it clattered against the window, wishing she could open it and let it caress her skin.

She loved the lightning too and, in her daydream, she imagined it came from the wands of witches and wizards as they protected the world from evil.

"Penny…"

What if the lightning was to strike this building, reduce it to rubble, so we could all go home… she thought fancifully.

"Pen…"

But I wouldn't want anyone to be hurt, she added, lest her wish somehow came true.

"Pen!"

She jumped and straightened guiltily; she had been resting her elbows on the narrow window ledge, chin cupped in her hands.

"Sorry, Tom." She flushed, wondering how long he'd been there. "Did you need something?"

"I was asking if you were busy on Saturday. Maybe we could go for a drink or something? There's a really good live band playing at the pub down the road, or we could go somewhere quieter if you—"

"I'm sorry, Tom," she interrupted, trying to keep the irritation from her voice; this was the third week running he'd asked her out. *Couldn't the guy take a hint?* "I'm a bit busy this weekend."

"Same as you were last weekend, and the one before that, and the one—"

"Yeah, sorry," she repeated, and turned once more to the window, hoping that was a hint he *would* take.

She was not unused to male attention, for she had grown from a pretty child to a gorgeous young woman. And some of the guys at work she did like, although Tom wasn't one of them; he was far too aware of his good looks and so-called charm for her taste. But Kane, for instance, who worked in the accounts department, and Mikey, the office junior who never failed to bring her coffee as soon as she walked through the door each morning and who quite clearly had an enormous crush on her; *they* were nice.

She liked both of them, was always happy for an excuse to stop working and chat, but that didn't mean she was attracted to either of them; she couldn't actually recall being seriously attracted to any man. Anyway, she knew Kane was gay and had a boyfriend; no way did he think of her in *that* way. In any case, her weekends were far too important for her to consider any kind of relationship; they brought escape from the boring mortal world and into the exciting one of the Sanctuary.

Seeing that Tom had gone off in a huff, she turned her attention once more to the computer on her desk, wishing the day would end.

After the demon war, and at Morgan's request, Charles and Lucy Hamilton had agreed to look after Penelope, just for a few weeks, which had then somehow become permanent. They quickly became very fond of the child, and now that Lucy spent most of her time within the walls of the Sanctuary to be near their daughter, Penelope was a comfort for Charles in his world so suddenly filled with pain.

And she grew to adore Cissy's kind and gentle father, who was so laid back and generally cool, not least because he allowed her to spend so much time at the Sanctuary. He even insisted on taking her there each time, although he would not accompany her beyond its secret entrance, no matter how much she pleaded. He would fob her off with some feeble excuse every time, thinking, *never again will I set foot in that terrible place.*

Penelope would have loved to spend her entire life at the Sanctuary, fighting demons and saving the world, so she was furious when Molly turned up unexpectedly one day to speak with Charles about her education. To Penelope's immense disappointment, he had not only sided with Molly but suggested she should go on to college and get a job in the real world.

She'd rebelled almost immediately, frequently skipping her new school, misbehaving when she was there, and even, on one occasion, running away from home. This continued until Charles nearly despaired, and that was when the Sanctuary intervened in the shape of Luke and Molly. At first, she was angry at their criticism and sat silently, arms crossed defensively, a mutinous look on her face.

But after a while, she felt ashamed, particularly on seeing the worried expression on Luke's face, who she adored. But it was when Molly said she *couldn't bleedin' believe the girl who'd practically saved them all from the demons could behave in such a way,* that the girl finally realised how badly she'd behaved and broke down in tears.

After that, there were no more problems, and as she grew older, she began to appreciate the wisdom of her elders, for Penelope would never be a true witch. She'd been taught all kinds of minor spells over the last ten years, useful spells but nothing too dangerous. She even had a wand, but one of very limited power that would not consume her.

At first, her disappointment had been overwhelming – how she longed to be a witch like Molly and Cissy – but it was clear from the outset that she had no talent. Usually, no ordinary mortal would be allowed to even own a wand, but all knew the debt they owed this girl who'd saved the Sanctuary, and thus the entire human race, from the might of the demons.

The week passed slowly, but Friday afternoon came at last, and Penelope sat at her desk, all pretence of work long gone, and watched the clock tick slowly round. Kane dropped by and they spent a pleasant few minutes chatting, although she had to tell a few white lies about her plans for the weekend. When she glanced at the clock again, it had hardly moved. She spotted Mikey looking surreptitiously at her from his desk at the other side of the room and waved, smiling as he ducked his head and blushed.

Another thirty, painful minutes passed until she had an idea. She stood and caught Mikey looking at her again, but this time he turned away before he could see her wave, no doubt blushing madly again. She went to the staff room, made two cups of coffee, and took them to his desk.

"Hi, Mikey." She smiled reassuringly. "Thought I'd return the favour." She put the coffee next to his mouse mat, pulled up a chair, and sat.

"Th… thanks," he stammered, not meeting her eyes.

"Are you looking forward to the weekend?"

"Yes,"—this time he managed to look at her—"thanks." She waited expectantly for more, but clearly that was the limit of his conversation and suddenly she felt guilty. She'd thought it would be fun to tease him but now she saw she was being cruel.

"Mikey," she said gently, "look at me." She took his hand and squeezed. "I know you like me but,"—she hesitated—"well, I'm kinda… unavailable."

To her surprise, he squeezed back. "I know," he admitted, "but I still like you and,"—he turned extremely pink—"you're the coolest one here."

"Cool? Me?" She laughed, momentarily stumped. "I'll tell you who's cooler. You know Patricia from the floor below? And she likes you." Penelope had no idea if it was true, but Patricia was just as shy as he was; they'd be a good match.

"Really? She's so pretty."

"Yeah, she told me she does." Now that was a lie, but she had her fingers crossed tightly so it didn't count. "And you're right, she's sooo pretty." Penelope stood and bent to kiss his cheek. Curiously, this time he didn't blush. In fact, he seemed somewhat distracted, and she smiled. "Have a fab weekend, Mikey, and promise me you'll send her a friend request."

He nodded and smiled back. "I will."

Glancing at the clock, she was pleased to see only five minutes remained, and she grabbed her coat, ready to dash out; she knew as soon as it hit five Tom would be running down the stairs from two floors above, trying to cut her off. At last, the minute hand clicked round and she was gone, with an excited, "See you Monday, everyone!"

As she left, she heard footsteps clattering down the stairs and, as expected, the shout of, "Penny, wait!"

Mentally she showed him her middle finger, then crashed through the exit door, heading for the nearby station. Ten minutes later, she was on the tube for the thirty-minute journey home.

"Hi, Dad!" she shouted as she entered the house.

Charles looked up from the book he was reading and grinned at the excited young woman. "You're full of beans. Doing anything special tonight?"

"Oh hush." She laughed, flinging her arms around him and kissing his cheek. "You say that every Friday."

"So I'm boring now?" he deadpanned.

"You," she said, "are the least boring person in the entire world." She poked his chest. "And you're the coolest."

Feeling curiously pleased, Charles smiled as he watched her dash upstairs to her bedroom. Then he thought of Cissy and his mood soured. Sighing, he heard the shower starting up, then sat and returned to his book. In a remarkably short space of time, she was back, and he nodded approvingly. "You look great."

When Penelope went out with her friends, she dressed elaborately but with style; a white top usually, leather jacket, and a leather skirt that in Charles's opinion was far too short, although he would never have dreamed of saying so. Add to that black boots, which added at least ten centimetres to her already tall frame, skilfully applied eye make-up, nearly always crimson or purple, lipstick, and a hairstyle he had no idea how she managed to achieve, she always looked stunning. Now though she was dressed simply in a baggy tee-shirt, skinny jeans, scruffy white sneakers, very little make-up, and hair tied back in ropes. To Charles, she looked equally, if not more, lovely.

"Thanks." She smiled, before noticing the sadness in his eyes and wrapping her arms around his neck. "She'll be cured eventually, and I'll send her your love." As always, she felt a twinge of guilt at leaving him by himself.

He hugged her back and then stood. "I'll get the car keys. And, Penny,"—she raised her eyebrows questioningly—"you've no need to feel guilty, just have a good time, okay?"

He really is so cool, she thought, wishing for the millionth time he really was her father. "I will," she promised, "and no need to drive me, I'm a big girl now!" She was already opening the door, but she ran back and kissed him again. "See you Sunday night!"

And then, like a whirlwind that had briefly entered the house, she was gone.

Chapter 6

When Anarkus disappeared into the fog, Amelia turned her attention back to the river below her feet. But it no longer looked inviting; now it just looked cold and scary. She swung her legs back onto the bridge and, for the first time, noticed the bitter cold. Shivering, she set off on the long walk back to the hostel, but then remembered the strange glow she'd seen from the weirdo's feet. The fog was thick now and she had to kneel to find them but, yes, there they were!

Not that she intended to follow him. *He's probably waiting round a corner to abduct me,* she thought, fingering the knife she always kept hidden at her waist. *Well, just let him try.* Still, she kept a watchful eye on her way back to the hostel. The few people she did encounter gave her a wide berth, sensing something wasn't quite right with this girl who, though still pretty despite her rough-shorn fair hair and old, scruffy clothes, exuded an aura of menace.

In the following days, Amelia hardly left her room at the hostel. There was a communal dining room but she never used it, preferring to eat in her room. On the few occasions she had ventured there, the room had emptied pretty quickly, all eyes avoiding hers as they hurried out. Her few overtures of friendship had been rebuffed or ignored and now she didn't bother, telling herself she was better off on her own. Mostly she believed it, but occasionally it was bravado; not even in the hospital had she felt so alone.

The days passed and her depression deepened further, enveloping her in a cloak of hopelessness. She began to think of the water again, how inviting it had looked, and the wish to be rid of her useless existence became a longing once more, quickly turning to a compulsion. Fighting it, without quite knowing why, she turned her thoughts instead to the stranger at the bridge, *the weirdo* as she thought of him.

I wonder what he wants with me, she mused. *Nothing good, probably.* Again, she felt the river inviting her. *But he said he could help me find the monster who did this to me. What was he called…? Logan.* She felt a flare of anger and it surprised her; it was rare for her to feel any emotion, had been for a very long time. *He has to pay; he ruined my life!* Making her decision, she stood abruptly and left the hostel.

It was a long walk to the bridge and she was hungry. Sunk in the pit of depression from the moment she'd awakened, she'd missed the calls for all the meals. *Now it must be around six,* she thought. Across the road was a convenience store and she approached it, cautiously peering inside. *Not too busy, only one security guard as far as I can see.* She nodded with satisfaction and walked confidently inside, smiling sweetly at the guard as she passed. She disappeared quickly, but not so quickly as to arouse suspicion, into one of the aisles, and within a minute she'd stuffed two sandwiches beneath her thin jacket and three chocolate bars into her pockets. She was heading for the drinks section when the guard stepped out from nowhere.

"Excuse me, miss," he began, but Amelia lunged forward, already drawing her knife and aiming for his eyes. Instead, she gave him a nasty gash on the cheek. As she ran from the store and into the road, she made the mistake of glancing backward and cannoned into a cyclist, sending them both flying. Most of the things she'd stolen were strewn across the road but she had no time to retrieve them; already, outraged customers and shop staff were heading toward her. She stood and grabbed the bike, kicking the cyclist in the stomach when he tried to rise and prevent her, and pedalled away, wobbling slightly and going through a red light, causing a cacophony of car horns and shouted insults.

Of course, the police were called, and when they reviewed the CCTV, the upturned face of the thief was framed in the centre of the screen. But its features were smudged into a grotesque caricature, like an artist had taken a palette knife and scraped it across a still-wet oil painting. Although still recognisable as human, one of the officers summed it up best when she described the image as demonic.

With her new transport, Amelia reached the bridge within a few minutes, dumped the bike and patted her clothing, discovering a tuna-mayo sandwich and a Snickers had survived the crash. She cast around for the weirdo's footsteps, relieved but not surprised to find they were still there. Munching hungrily, she followed them.

After a half hour, she was getting fed up and cursing that she'd not thought to bring the bike. *I'll give it another ten minutes, then I'm going back to the hostel* – she never thought of it as home – she told herself, knowing she would not. Presently, she came to a busy intersection and was forced to wait for the lights. Glancing idly to her right, she felt a curious desire to go that way instead, one she found impossible to ignore. She looked at the footsteps. *They'll still be here when I return,* she thought, then turned away, noticing as she did so the black and white street sign on the wall; Old Kent Road.

Old Kent Road followed the route of the Roman Watling Street and it was long, about five kilometres, stretching from Elephant and Castle to Peckham, in the Southwark area of London. As Amelia walked slowly along, she felt a kind of pressure building inside, a mixture of excitement, anticipation, and trepidation. It was when she passed the bus stop that she stopped and turned, her senses screaming, *this is the place!* Curiously, she brushed her fingers across the Perspex windows, the metal frame, and the plastic seats of the bus shelter, but no, that wasn't it; all she felt was metal and plastic.

Abruptly she swung round and stared into the large glass window of a shop and her memory shifted, still indistinct and elusive, but fractionally closer to solving the puzzle. Suddenly she fancied there was an image in the glass, faint but discernible and familiar. *Me and my mother?* she wondered, the pressure almost unbearable now, and the image sharpened into focus, showing a young woman, pretty but her face careworn, and a small girl with blonde hair, pretty like her mother, wearing a bright red coat.

Oh my God, what's happening? She was frightened now as she whirled and forced her eyes to look across the road. And there it was. She stared at the lamppost, knowing it was important, but why? That final piece in the jigsaw of her memory refused to click into place. She ran across the road, dodging the traffic, which was lighter now. *What had the weirdo said about finding the lamppost?* Her hands pressed onto its ornate metal, searching for a clue. She spotted the tiny door near its base and knelt, pulling at its tiny handle but it was stuck or locked. Then behind her, a voice spoke.

"What are you doing?"

Chapter 7

Anarkus had been certain the girl would come and her absence was more than a minor annoyance, for his pride was hurt. *How dare she defy me,* he thought sourly. *Surely she noticed the trail I left?* He dismissed her from his mind, for he had more pressing concerns. *Now, where is that portal?*

Of the many dreams he'd had during his long sleep, there had been one recurring theme, a desire for revenge against the Sanctuary. But for them, he would have succeeded in his quest to rule the mortal world, and he would make them pay for their interference. But Anarkus was not delusional, he knew that last time he'd had the Queen's Wand, and still it hadn't been enough. Now, powerful though he was, he knew he would need help, and for that, he needed Portia. And he had a strong feeling he would get it.

Certainly, it was a risk; the last time he'd been in the castle of the witch and wizard council, he'd murdered Liias, their leader, and barely escaped with his life. But somehow, he didn't think he was in danger; he'd long ago sensed something dark within Portia and he was curious to see what was happening with the council these days. She had always hidden her lust for power, but he'd known. He'd always known.

But the portal, where was it? He'd sensed its presence in the days when he'd roamed the mortal world, destroying the minds of its inhabitants and using other portals to reach their presidents and dictators all across the planet. But he'd taken little notice at the time, much to his current chagrin. How difficult could it be? He closed his mind to all other thoughts and allowed a map of London to form.

Holding his wand in front, much like the ancients used sticks to divine water, he walked through London, oblivious to the curious looks of passersby. Almost at once his wand twitched to the side, but he ignored it; that portal led to the large country, with its president who, he remembered, had been so very loud. He soon passed another, and another, dismissing each one in turn. Occasionally he came upon a portal that brought back particular memories. This one had taken him to a country with a dictator who was *really* crazy. Even Anarkus, who'd been a little crazy himself at the time, had recognised that one wasn't quite right in the head.

After traipsing around London for an age, Anarkus was fed up and in need of coffee. He entered a café and, since it had worked so well the last time, twitched his wand; the girl behind the counter handed over the drink without requesting payment. He sat at a table and savoured the taste. It wasn't as good as the coffee on his home planet, which was heavily spiced, but passable.

The map in his head retreated, and he was thankful to let it go for a while as he gazed idly around, allowing his mind to wander. The mortal at the next table was looking at her communication device and next to her was a child sitting in some kind of chair with wheels; it was staring at him with rapt interest. Anarkus stared back and stuck out his tongue; the child giggled. Frowning, he raised his eyebrows to a slant and made a passable impression of a demon; now it laughed aloud and Anarkus sighed. Why was it that mature mortals were afraid of him, while their offspring were not? He noticed the mortal was looking at images on her communication device, dozens of them. He shuddered and wondered what the point was. Mortals were universally stupid, he decided.

It was a habit he'd noticed before; mortals took numerous pictures of themselves. Why? Didn't they already know what they looked like? *Pictures,* he scoffed inwardly. *Who needs pictures…? Pictures…* The idea was so obvious he could hardly believe he'd not thought of it before. Quickly, he summoned the map and allowed Portia's image to form. Almost immediately, a single bright light lit up on the map and he grinned, finished his coffee, and left.

It was a long way off and he was forced to take a bus, which he bore, he thought, with great fortitude, and soon he was standing at the portal. He stepped through and found himself instantly surrounded by lush, green countryside, next to a large forest. Before him was a castle, an exact replica of the one on the old planet, and he smiled. He knew exactly where to find Portia.

Chapter 8

Penelope approached the lamppost with her usual bubbling excitement, so she was put out to see someone standing right next to it.

Who is that? she thought, annoyed. *Why is she hanging around my lamppost?* Penelope was rather proprietorial about the entrance to the passage-between-the-worlds and tended to think of it as her own. After all, she was the only one who used it these days.

Now she's pulling at the door! she thought anxiously. As she drew nearer, Penelope could see it was a girl, perhaps about her own age, or a little younger.

"What are you doing?" The girl jumped to her feet, startled, and looked at Penelope, who took a step backward as she felt an intense rush of attraction. *Her eyes,* she thought, *such an amazing shade of blue. And that hair, she's gorgeous!*

"Doing? Nothing!" Amelia realised she sounded guilty. "I just like old things like this," she improvised.

"Really?" Rarely had Penelope been so tongue-tied.

"Yeah."

"Right." They lapsed into silence, neither knowing what to say next.

"I'm—"

"My name is—"

They both laughed as they spoke together. "You go first," invited Amelia, wondering why she'd taken an instant liking to this girl. She couldn't recall ever liking anyone. *Except for my mother,* she supposed. *I must have liked her.* Amelia sheered away from the thought of love.

"I was going to say my name is Penelope." She put out a tentative hand.

"Amelia." She took the hand; it felt nice, warm and soft. It was the first human contact she'd had in years. "So where were you going?"

"Me?" Penelope laughed nervously. "Nowhere special. I only stopped because I thought you had a problem."

"Problem?"

"Yeah, the way you were tugging at the door," she explained.

"Oh, I see." Amelia thought frantically. "I was just curious to see if it would open."

"No, it doesn't," Penelope began, then stopped, horrified. "I mean, it probably doesn't," she amended, "being so old and all."

Amelia nodded, then realised they were still holding each other's hand. She withdrew hers hurriedly, embarrassed, and they looked at each other self-consciously.

"Okay, well, see you around," Penelope said at last as she looked again into the girl's eyes and shivered sensuously. She walked away down the street as if that had been her destination all along, hoping the girl would say something to stop her. But Amelia just watched her leave, trying desperately to think of something to say that might prolong the meeting.

What are you thinking! Penelope scolded herself. *You can't just let her go!* Turning, she blurted, "Would you like to get a coffee or something?"

Amelia grinned with relief. "Yeah, sure." The idea of *getting a coffee* with someone was a novel one. And she was cold and still hungry. "Do you know a place?"

"Oh, sorry! I… er… I didn't mean now; I have to be somewhere. Sorry!" Penelope's face burned with embarrassment. "But perhaps tomorrow? No, not tomorrow either, I—"

"Yeah, I get it. You have to be somewhere. Look, if you'd rather not—"

"No! I want to, a lot," she interrupted, aware she was sounding way too keen. "Monday evening? If you're free, that is. There's a Starbucks just round the corner from here."

"What's Starbucks?"

Penelope stared at her curiously. "You don't know?"

"Oh, yeah. Of course." Amelia realised her mistake. "I didn't hear you properly. 'Bout seven?"

"Great! Well, see you then." Penelope wished she could pluck up the courage to kiss her cheek but told herself it might seem a little strange. Anyway, Amelia was already walking away and she watched as her newfound friend disappeared around a nearby corner. Then, glancing round to make sure nobody was watching, she took out her wand, muttered an incantation, and tapped the tiny door of the lamppost. It opened and, within seconds, Penelope had oozed inside, the door closing behind her.

Watching from around the corner, Amelia stared in amazement. She had expected Penelope to walk away and had wanted one last glimpse. *Who is she?* she wondered. *Was that a wand?* She recalled the weirdo's words again and now they echoed loudly, painfully around her mind. *You have to find the lamppost, you have to find the lamppost, you have to...* Amelia pressed her hands against her ears, trying to make it stop, but it grew even louder. *You have to find...* Suddenly the memory of *that day* clicked into place and Amelia began to scream softly. *You have to find the lamppost...*

"Are you alright, dear?"

Amelia jumped with fright at the man who was looking at her with concern. She gasped, her chest heaving, unable to catch her breath as panic overwhelmed her. In her tortured mind, the man transformed into the tall, dark stranger and she could see the demons inside his mouth, waiting to get out. Waiting for her. She screamed, loud and piercing this time, before she stumbled away.

It was morning before her panic faded and she made her way, exhausted, back to the hostel.

*　　　　*　　　　*　　　　*

After sleeping all day Saturday, Amelia woke on Sunday full of anger. *He's damaged me enough,* she thought. *I'm sick of it and he's going to pay.* Imagining the revenge she would visit upon Logan satisfied her until she reached the footsteps, where she'd abandoned them to walk down Old Kent Road. *The weirdo can show me magic, then it's payback time,* and the image of the Dark Wizard lying in a pool of blood at her feet made her grin wildly.

An elderly lady who happened to be passing smiled back. "Good morning, dear, it's a beautiful day."

Amelia looked at her, bemused, wondering what it felt like to take pleasure from something like a beautiful day.

Presently, the footsteps led her to an alley, and when she was halfway down, Amelia stopped uncertainly as she realised how dark and lonely it was. *Why has the weirdo led me here?* she wondered. *Perhaps I should go back.* But she dismissed the thought and walked determinedly on. Anyway, she had her knife, she would stick him if he tried anything. But when she reached the high brick wall at the end of the alley, all her doubts returned.

Anarkus had already sensed her approach, and after Amelia had stood there for five minutes in an agony of indecision, one of the three windows near the top of the wall was flung open and he appeared.

"You're here at last!" he called cheerfully, startling her. "I'd almost given up on you." He withdrew, then a second later two long legs appeared over the edge of the windowsill and he jumped down, landing catlike even though the window was several meters high.

"You look like…" Anarkus took in her gaunt cheeks, her lank hair, and the dark shadows beneath her eyes. "What's the word you mortals use?"

"Yeah, I get it," she snapped, "thanks." Ignoring his smirk, she asked, "How did you get here?"

"From up there." He pointed. "You watched me, remember?"

She ignored the sarcasm. "And where is *up there*, exactly?"

"It's a gap between dimensions." He moved a few steps from the wall, took a short run, then leaped lithely up and sat in the window again. He indicated she should follow.

"What? How?"

"Trust me, Amelia."

No chance, she thought darkly, but she did as he asked and was amazed when her legs, quite beyond her control, took her up the wall to sit beside him. She stepped into a very narrow corridor with identical windows on the opposite wall. "Where do they lead?"

"Well, into the other dimension, obviously."

Not really understanding, she pointed to two doors, barely visible in the gloom, a few meters down the corridor in each direction. "And what about those?"

"I have no idea," he admitted, "nowhere important, I should imagine. Now, come on." He took her hand and leaped through a window, pulling her with him. She yelled with fright but landed easily and, to her surprise, without injury into an identical alleyway on the other side.

They walked in silence as Amelia looked around curiously. But when they reached the old mansion, she shivered, suddenly wishing, for the first time ever, she was back in the hostel. *It's so creepy,* she thought. *Is this where he brings his victims?* But she didn't really think he was going to murder her. Hadn't he said something about her having some kind of power?

"Now," he said, his satisfaction evident, "here at last. Come, it's time to begin your education."

"What is this place?"

"It used to be Logan's, now it's mine."

She stared at him, horrified. "Are you mad?" She looked around nervously. "Is he here?"

"Of course not." He laughed at her discomfort. "He's a prisoner somewhere far away. Well, maybe not too far away, but in another dimension."

"I'm not sure about this." Suddenly her bravado fell away and she was very frightened. "I've changed my mind." She tried to hide her fear. "I want to leave."

"You *could* leave." He nodded. "Although you can't actually get back to your own world without me."

"So I'm your prisoner?"

"Not at all," he replied, suddenly bored. "I can take you back if you really want me to, I've no desire to keep you against your will." He was surprised to find this was true; he had far too much on his plate to be bothered. "But,"—he dangled the carrot—"you'll never find Logan without me. You still want revenge, right?"

Chapter 9

Goblins are a long-lived race and Kamontip was already many centuries old. A mere ten years to her was as the passage of ten minutes to a mortal. Yet nearly every night of those years had been troubled with dreams of the Dark Wizard, alone in the Chasm of Nothingness, his prison. Now, back in her own world, she was deep in thought and had been for three days, barely eating and with a deep furrow across her brow. At last, her master wand maker, Gnerx, approached with a tray of food and drink.

"I said I wasn't to be disturbed," she said irritably, and the old goblin smiled.

"You did," he agreed, "and I have disobeyed. What will you do, cast me in chains?" This was delivered in such a deadpan manner that Kamontip couldn't help smiling.

"As ever, my friend, you keep me grounded and admonish me when I am too imperious. Now, I have been doing a little thinking."

"For three days actually."

"Yes, and the path is clear to me. Gnerx, I want you to make a wand."

"Of course, my lady. May I ask who it is for?"

"You remember the Dark Wizard who visited some time ago? It is for him."

"Ah." Gnerx smiled. "So you'd like it to be of poor quality." He chuckled, remembering the last time he'd made a wand for Logan.

"No." She shook her head. "This time it must be the finest you can make." Gnerx looked surprised. "Not now." She held up a hand as he prepared to speak. "First, please bring Maisey and Myla; I will explain to the three of you."

When they were gathered, she outlined her plan, and the reaction she received was not unexpected. Myla and Gnerx went rigid with shock but Maisey jumped to her feet.

"You can't!' she exclaimed. "You absolutely can't bring him here!"

"I will overlook your lapse in manners, Maisey," Kamontip admonished mildly, "but it is exactly what I intend to do."

"But he is evil!" argued Myla, remembering those unfortunates she and Maisey had freed from the Dark Wizard's dungeon. "And I barely escaped with my life!"

Forbearing to point out that Myla shouldn't have been there in the first place, Kamontip nodded. "I understand," she said gently, "yet I believe he has changed. Or," she admitted, "can be persuaded to."

"But why? Why free him?"

This was the difficult part and Kamontip hesitated, wondering how they would react. "Because I sense an evil has awakened, one that will put us all in grave danger. Logan is a powerful wizard and—"

"And not to be trusted," Maisey warned.

"Perhaps," she acknowledged.

"What kind of evil, my queen?" Gnerx asked. "Surely with your power and our wands we can defeat any foe?"

"Yes, our skill at making elite wands is renowned among all races. For thousands of years, the most powerful have sought us out, knowing our skills cannot be matched. And yes, there is the Queen's Wand, the most powerful of them all..." She hesitated. *Let them believe for now that this is true.*

"Yes?" Gnerx persisted.

"Yet it is my belief that this threat is like no other we have ever faced; not just we goblins, but other worlds too."

"How do you know, Kamontip?" asked Myla.

"I don't. Not for certain. But this feeling I have, it is an assault on my senses. I am… frightened."

Sobered, the three were silent for a while; their queen had always seemed invulnerable, and if she was frightened, so were they. "But the Dark Wizard is just as likely to join with this evil… *thing* and work against us," Maisey said at last. "And if you give him an elite wand…" She left the sentence unfinished.

"There is risk," Kamontip admitted, "yet I believe it is worth taking. Logan is a very powerful wizard and may be vital in helping us fight this evil. And I do not think he will betray me."

"I wouldn't be so sure," Myla muttered, unconvinced.

"The matter is closed," Kamontip said firmly. "Gnerx, away and begin your task – remember, it must be the finest wand you can make, but do not delay; we do not know when this evil will strike." As the old wand maker hurried away, she turned to the two young goblins. "Now, there are preparations to make and you two will be responsible for making sure they are carried out. Here is what I want you to do."

Chapter 10

In the old council chamber at the top of their castle, the witch and wizard council had gathered. "Thank you, everyone, for assembling at such short notice. I have an important announcement to make." Portia, their leader, paused and looked around the chamber, still weighing up how she would break the news to the more resistant among them. "As I was saying—"

She was interrupted as the door opened and a tall, lithe figure stepped confidently inside. Some of those present gaped in shock, others appeared quite unfazed. But only one looked angry; Agnes, the witch who'd voted against the execution of the Dark Wizard and had been viewed with suspicion ever since.

"Ah, Anarkus." Portia beamed. "You pre-empt my news. Welcome to the council, we were about to begin today's proceedings." She gestured to an empty chair further along the table. "You may take a seat there for now until we debate your rightful place in the hierarchy of the council."

Until recently, the chair had been occupied by a stately old wizard, revered by most of his compatriots due to his great age. He had mysteriously disappeared only a week prior and had yet to be found. Portia had shown great concern and been most assiduous in organising the searches, which still continued.

"What is he doing here?" Agnes glared at Anarkus, hatred shining from her eyes.

"Well, we are one short," Portia replied.

"Yes, how convenient! Your timing is impeccable!"

"Be careful at what you are suggesting!"

"And what exactly am I *suggesting?*" Agnes said scornfully. "That you murdered that old man so you could bring him here?" She swept her gaze around the council members. "How can you all be so *blind?*"

"Oh dear." Portia shook her head in mock sorrow and looked round the table. "It seems our friend here is against us!"

She shot a piercing look at the witch. "Are you against us, Agnes?"

Agnes jumped to her feet. "If he is to be allowed here, you're damned right I am!" she shouted.

There was a long silence, but Portia was smiling. "Such a shame," she said in a low voice, "but I've long suspected your treachery. Guards!"

But Agnes was already leaping through the door and, as the guards came running, she barged them aside and raced down the corridor. One side was lined with tall windows, each masked with heavy brocade curtains, and Agnes leaped to grasp one of the burning torches set along the other wall. She swept it along each one as she ran, adding a little magic so they burst instantly into flames.

As thick, black smoke billowed behind her, she felt fire licking at her back and heard Portia's desperate shout, "Get after the traitor! And kill her!" But now she'd reached the top of the stone spiral staircase that led right down to the castle drawbridge. Although how she'd get past the guards was a problem she'd solve when she got there; *if* she got there.

These thoughts flashed through her mind in an instant as she raced down the steps, almost losing her footing, such was her speed. She ducked as a bolt of wand fire hit the wall above her head, then sent one of her own over her shoulder, which, by sheer fluke, hit one of her pursuers. Winded, he crashed to the floor and those following close behind tripped over him, all of them ending up in a comical heap of bodies. It gained Agnes precious seconds but others had leaped nimbly over the writing mess and were sending streams of wand fire that ricocheted off the walls around her, some coming perilously close to hitting their mark.

She passed an open doorway that led to a large eating room for the lesser witches and wizards but she discounted it. There was no escape that way, and she continued her mad race down the stairs, more than once nearly falling head over heels, dizzy now and leg muscles screaming in protest.

All at once she heard footsteps coming up the stairs and she groaned. *Oh, for goodness' sake!* she protested as she pirouetted dangerously, still at full speed, and ran back up the stairs. Those coming down were almost upon her and she ran desperately through the doorway into the eating room, her heart quailing, knowing she was trapped.

Some of the diners had heard the commotion and were moving cautiously toward the doorway; she waved her wand wildly at them and they scattered. Others were intent on their food and glanced at her only with mild curiosity. One rather stout wizard froze when he saw her rushing toward him and, unable to avoid the collision, she crashed into him, sending sausages, eggs, beans, and the rest flying everywhere, mostly all over the pristine whitewashed walls.

"Stop!" came shouts from behind, but her pursuers were hampered by the presence of innocent bystanders and they could not use their wands. Still, there was nowhere further to run and Agnes found herself backed up against a wooden wall filled with small, paned windows that overlooked the balcony outside. She held her wand defiantly against the line of witches and wizards who now confronted her. Her heart sank further when she saw they were led by Suluhura, Portia's second in command and a man with no morals whatsoever. She knew he would show no mercy.

"You have nowhere else to go." He grinned. "Lower your wand, submit and you will live. Refuse and you will die, here and now."

"Never!" she spat, knowing he lied and she faced certain execution if captured. "You cannot murder me in front of all these witnesses!" She indicated the score of bewildered onlookers.

Suluhura glanced behind him and sneered. "Oh, they will see what they are told to see. Now, you were about to surrender, I think?" Suluhura was enjoying himself immensely.

"Not a chance," she said. "You won't kill me here." As she spoke, she sidled along the wall, knowing she was only delaying the inevitable.

"Your choice." Suluhura shrugged dismissively. "Seize her!" As they approached, wands held high, Agnes felt something hard press into her back and excitement surged inside her. *The door onto the balcony!* With a silent prayer that it would be unlocked, she groped behind her and twisted. The door opened and she stumbled backward, but as she fell, she sent a bolt of wand fire into the ceiling.

Her pursuers were enveloped in large chunks of plaster, stone, and dust, giving Agnes the chance to leap to her feet and run. The balcony traversed each wall of the castle and as she turned the corner, she heard footsteps behind her. She ignored the bewildered faces pressed against the windows, enjoying the excitement. Instead, she peered over the balcony wall as she ran, searching for any kind of handhold in the sheer rock face, knowing there were none.

Agnes knew some of her pursuers would have run the opposite way around the balcony and that scant seconds remained until she was trapped. She briefly considered jumping to her death – *anything* was better than being captured and executed – yet the instinct to survive was too strong. But sure enough, as she turned the next corner, she saw three of her enemies, as she now thought of them, running towards her and, glancing back, two more. They slowed to a walk, knowing their quarry had nowhere to run.

Desperately, Agnes jumped onto the balcony wall. Water glistened far below. *The lake*, she thought, *it's my only chance.* Then, as her enemies raised their wands, she leaped into the void.

Chapter 11

"Well, I guess this is goodbye," Penelope said, already looking forward to when they would next meet. "Wanna do it again?" She spoke with a casualness she didn't feel.

They'd kept their date at Starbucks, meeting outside and smiling shyly at each other until Penelope led them inside. Amelia had been shocked at the price of a simple hot chocolate and nervously fingered the coins in her pocket, money she'd found left carelessly lying around in the hostel office, and hoped she'd have enough.

It had been close, but Amelia had been spared embarrassment, then they'd passed a pleasant hour chatting about nothing, their shyness gradually fading.

"Yeah," Amelia said, suddenly unsure. She'd survived alone for so long that the thought of sharing even a tiny piece of herself, of trusting someone, was terrifying.

"Okay." Penelope took out her iPhone. "What's your number?"

"My number?"

"Yeah, your number, silly." She waved the phone in Amelia's face. "So we can keep in touch. Maybe I'll text you when I get home."

"Oh, right." She flushed. "I don't have a phone."

"Really?" Penelope laughed, incredulous, failing to notice the sudden change in Amelia's expression. "Everyone has a phone!"

"Well I don't!" She stood abruptly and leaned forward, her face close to Penelope's. "I don't have much money, okay?" she spat. "We can't all be little rich kids!" She headed angrily for the door without a backward glance and was out on the street as Penelope caught up.

"Look, I'm sorry!" She took Amelia's arm but it was shrugged off. "Amelia, wait!"

But the girl was hurrying away, quickly disappearing into the gloom. Her first instinct was to follow but she stopped, suddenly angry. *Oh, for goodness' sake!* she thought resentfully. *What an overreaction!* She spent a minute telling herself she didn't care anyway, then turned to trudge sadly away, glancing through the window and looking wistfully at the table where they'd sat only a few moments before.

A voice spoke behind her and she whirled.

"Amelia!" She flung her arms around the girl's neck, startling her, and instantly the knife was out and held millimetres from Penelope's stomach. But then Amelia felt a hand behind her head, pulling her gently forward, and lips against hers, tentative at first but becoming more insistent. After a moment's hesitation, Amelia slipped the knife back into her pocket and surrendered to the kiss.

When they pulled apart at last, they both ginned, a little shyly. "That was nice," Penelope breathed, "really nice."

Amelia's heart was pounding; she'd never experienced anything like that before. "Yes," she agreed, "it was."

Penelope walked home with her head in the clouds, thinking of the kiss, already wishing the days would pass quickly until they could meet again. She jumped over the garden gate and into the house where Charles was emptying the dishwasher.

"Hi, Dad!" She flung her arms around his neck and hugged him tightly.

"Wow! Someone's happy." He laughed. "What's going on?"

"Oh nothing." She shrugged. "Just that I've met someone I really like."

"Great! What's his name? When will I get to meet him?" Charles smiled, enjoying her happiness. Sometimes he thought she was far too serious for a young woman.

"*She's* called Amelia, and I thought I might bring her around one evening next week."

"Oh! Right!" He coughed to cover his embarrassment. "Well, yes, that would be great, you can bring her around for tea."

"Tea? Really? Dad, this isn't the 1950s!" She grinned and turned to dash up the stairs but he called her back.

"Pen,"—he cupped her cheeks in his hands—"I'm really happy for you, and I'm looking forward to meeting her."

*   *   *   *

Amelia didn't go home – not that she thought of the hostel as such. She had other plans. She was already regretting the kiss, or rather the feelings it had evoked; she had let her guard down and she knew from bitter experience that was never a good idea. Now she was eager to see Anarkus again, to delve more deeply into that enticing glimpse of the magical world he had shown her.

By now she knew the way to the deserted alley and she waited, wondering if he would sense her presence and come. Sure enough, she'd only waited a few minutes when he appeared.

"There you are." He grinned; it was not a nice grin. "Been getting cosy with your new *mortal* friend, I see."

Amelia shook her head, wondering how he knew. "She's just an amusing diversion," she said, sensing right away that he wouldn't believe her.

Anarkus laughed scornfully and then once again took her through the portal and into the dimension beyond. Soon they were back in the Dark Wizard's mansion. "I know things about that particular dirty mortal that you don't," he said, eyeing her slyly to gauge her reaction. "I'll be needing you to spy on her."

"Spy?" She was far too canny to let her emotions show on her face; she'd had a lifetime of hiding them. "I'll probably never even see her again."

"Oh no, Amelia,"—his voice was low and dangerous—"you will see her again. And you will tell me *everything*." He clapped his hands and smiled, adopting his usual, mocking tone. "Now, back to your lessons!"

Chapter 12

Several weeks had passed since Catrin and Rosalind disappeared into the land of shades but the Landlord wasn't worried. He knew time was different there and that only a day or so might have passed.

But as the weeks continued, he became aware of a tension in the air; it felt heavy and ominous, somehow not quite right. Frustrated, he searched deep within his mind, trying to determine its source, but for once his instincts were as baffled as he was.

"Trouble is coming, boy." He looked down at Oscar, who stood close, pressed against his leg. The Landlord suddenly realised the dog hadn't left his side for days; that, if nothing else, told him that something very bad indeed was going to happen.

His first thought was for the protection of the village, home to Catrin and Gruffydd, and where he had many old friends. He had made it his purpose to protect them from evil, a task he'd done successfully for thousands of years. The Demon King, the Necromancer, and many before them had all tried and failed.

Those threats had always come from the seventeenth Century side of the old inn but now, as he looked out onto the twenty-first side, he sensed this new menace would come from there. If whatever it was defeated him, they would have free rein to destroy the village. What he needed was a barrier.

Now that the Landlord had fetched his wand and was actually doing something, Oscar felt free to leave his side for a while. The first foundations of the barrier had already been completed when he was interrupted by the sight of the little dog running toward him, a rabbit firmly held in his jaws.

"Oscar." He rolled his eyes. "Not again."

It was a game the dog liked to play and he never actually harmed the rabbits. This one, cheekier and more daring than some of its friends, liked to tease Oscar. She often got too close and this wasn't the first time she had been captured. The dog grinned and barked sharply, allowing his prey to fall nimbly to the ground. She swiped him smartly across the chops with her paw, then gambolled happily away.

"Serves you right." The Landlord laughed. "Now behave and let me get on." It took the rest of the day and most of the next before he was satisfied. The barrier was invisible and very strong; he was confident it would deter the most vociferous of invaders.

*   *   *   *

Meanwhile, in the land of the faeries, the queen and king were deep in conversation.

"Will we intervene?"

Ana, Queen of the Faeries, looked at her husband and shook her head, her long golden hair sending sparkles of glittering dust into the air. "No, of course not. The affairs of mortals are not our concern."

"Yet we did so once before."

"We did," she agreed, "but that was different, the prophecy originated with our race. We were duty bound to ensure no mistakes were made."

They referred to an ancient prophecy that foretold of someone with great power who would come to the aid of the Sanctuary in its direst need. But when not one but *two* candidates unexpectedly arose, Velveteena and Moth had been sent to make sure the right one was chosen. This had proved not to be Luke, as had been supposed, but Cissy.

"I know," her husband mused, and they lapsed into the silence. "The girl was ill-used though," he continued at last, "by Anarkus, I mean. She has not yet had the opportunity to prove her worth, locked inside her insanity as she has been."

"It is still not our concern," Ana replied gently, with the easy confidence of one who knows her own people are not threatened. She was not uncaring, but the faerie world had existed long before any other, and she had seen the devastation that war brings; she would not allow it to enter her realm. The entrance to the faerie world was not easily breached, unlike the primitive barriers between dimensions fashioned by the old witch and wizard council. Anyway, Portia would have to be monumentally foolish to make the attempt, and Ana knew she was not.

There was laughter from outside and the queen moved to the window and smiled at the antics of their two children playing. They had woven beams of sunlight into a tightrope and were trying to outmatch each other, seeing who could keep their balance the longest. It had been hours already but neither were willing to concede.

Seeing her mother watching, Velveteena grinned and waved. Taking advantage of her distraction, Moth gleefully pushed his sister from the rope and quickly summoned more strands of light. Before she could fly away, he sent them spinning around her so that, trapped, she could only tumble helplessly to the ground.

The faerie king joined his wife at the window and they watched the antics of their children with a deep pleasure.

"You do know they'll want to go," he observed wryly.
The faerie queen sighed. "I know."

Chapter 13

As far as the council knew, there was only one portal from their world to that of the witches, and Agnes ran toward it at full speed, the sounds of pursuit fading behind her. But when she could no longer be seen, she veered in a different direction becuase actually there were two portals; Agnes had created a second centuries ago as a precaution, should she ever need to escape. So, as her pursuers headed for the original, Agnes entered her own world unseen, where she was welcomed with great joy and celebration; many remembered she had once, long ago, been leader of the village near the waterfall. Gradually she cast away the strain and stress of the last few centuries, from being constantly viewed with suspicion and even hostility by certain members of the witch and wizard council.

For so long she'd suspected Portia of not being quite what she appeared and now, with Anarkus on the council, she was certain of it. And then there was her narrow escape; they'd tried to kill her! Something must be done, she knew, but what? She couldn't think clearly, she was so tired…

But it wasn't in Agnes's nature to remain passive, and after a week or so relaxing and doing nothing, she began to worry. *At least when I was there I could keep watch,* she thought, *and now that Anarkus is back…* Making up her mind, she got up early one morning, before the village stirred, walked the short distance into the woodland, and gave a low whistle.

Before long there was a gathering of birds and woodland animals, all delighted to see her. She was reminded of a time, long ago, when, with a similar gathering, they had plotted and freed the wizard Cornelius and his beloved Mitra, enabling them to escape the malice of the witch Racine.

Although Agnes explained there would be great danger, there were many volunteers for what she proposed and she was touched by their loyalty. After much deliberation, she chose a young pigeon for the task.

Since then, she'd left the village every few days, saying she had business elsewhere. Many were curious what she was up to but none dreamed she was secretly returning to the land of the witch and wizard council. There she would walk stealthily around, looking for signs of wrongdoing, while the pigeon entered the castle grounds, sometimes the castle itself, watching and listening.

Now she stood near the portal, waiting apprehensively for the pigeon to return; it had been gone much longer than usual and Agnes feared harm had befallen him. When nightfall came, she returned, anxious and dejected, back through the portal to the village.

She returned the next day and every day after, waiting until the sun was low in the sky until, eventually, after many days, she accepted the pigeon was lost, perhaps dead. Sadly, she turned toward the portal, dreading the moment she must tell the woodland creatures.

Chapter 14

It was Friday and, unwilling to wait until after the weekend to see Amelia again, Penelope took the day off work. As it was raining, she splashed out on a cab into central London.

"You still haven't told me where you live," Penelope said idly. They were walking hand in hand through Green Park, sheltering beneath the trees to dodge the frequent showers.

"No." Amelia removed her hand and moved away. "I know."

"So, where is it?"

"Just leave it, okay!"

"Sorry!" Penelope flashed back. "Forgive me for being *interested!*"

"No, it's me who's sorry. It's just that the area I live in is pretty gruesome and my… apartment is even worse. I guess I'm a little ashamed."

"Amelia, that's silly," said Penelope earnestly. "It's you I like. I don't care if you don't have much—'

"Like I said, just leave it." They walked in uncomfortable silence for a while, neither reaching again for the other's hand, but presently the rain stopped and the sun appeared. Leaving the park, they approached the imposing magnificence of Buckingham Palace.

"Wow!" Amelia stared. "Would you look at that!"

Penelope gave her a puzzled glance. "You've never seen it before?"

"Never! Who owns it?"

You live in London; how could you not know? How could you have never seen Buckingham Palace? "It belongs to the queen. It's where the Royal Family lives." *Who are you?*

"Of course it does." Amelia nudged her playfully in the ribs; she had seen Penelope's glance. "I'm joking."

"Right." Penelope was unconvinced. "Good joke." They walked silently for a while, both feeling ill at ease, but then the rain began again, more heavily this time. "Look, this is no good, we're gonna be soaked. Why don't you come back to mine for a while, my dad would love to meet you."

"Are you sure?" Amelia asked, uncertain and suddenly nervous. "He won't mind?"

"Of course not, you'll like him." Penelope grinned. "Come on." She took her hand and they ran to the nearby Tube station. As soon as they were underground, Amelia gripped Penelope's hand tightly, frightened by the loud echoing announcements and the thundering roar of the trains as they went by.

"You okay?" Amelia nodded, tight-lipped, and didn't answer. Once on the crowded train, they were forced to stand and she instinctively moved close to Penelope, her eyes squeezed shut, trying to block out the almost painful sensations of noise, heat, and people crowded close around her.

"Hey, it's ok." Penelope hugged her tightly. "You should have told me you were claustrophobic; we could have got a cab home."

As they emerged into the rain, Amelia heaved a sigh of relief and smiled sheepishly at Penelope. She hated showing any kind of weakness but that had been a truly horrible experience. "I'm not claustrophobic," she explained, "or at least I don't think I am. I've just never been on a – what did you call it – a Tube before."

"Never?" Penelope looked at her surprised. "How is that even possible? What, have you been locked away somewhere for all your life?" She'd also noticed Amelia's uncertainty over the name *Tube,* and once again wondered who this girl was. But she was totally unprepared for what happened next.

Amelia's carefully maintained mask slipped and she glared ferociously at Penelope, eyes blazing and her teeth bared into a snarl. "What do you know?" She gripped Penelope's arm roughly. "What makes you think I've been locked away? Tell me!"

More angry than frightened, Penelope wrenched her arm away. "I don't think that, obviously. What's wrong with you!"

Amelia realized she'd blundered and took Penelope's arm again, gently this time. "Look, I'm sorry," she said, earnestly, "I just have a bit of a temper sometimes."

"Yeah, I noticed," Penelope said, but she didn't remove Amelia's hand. "Forget it, come on it's not far."

"So where do you disappear to every weekend?" Amelia asked, changing the subject. "You're very mysterious."

Now it was Penelope's turn to be wrong-footed. "Oh, I'm not really." It was a question she had dreaded. Amelia waited expectantly. "I just visit… friends."

"That's great, perhaps we can all get together sometime."

Wishing she would drop the subject, Penelope remained silent, but for the first time, she felt uncomfortable in Amelia's company.

"Do they live in London, these friends of yours?" Amelia persisted.

"Yes, er, no… Well, sort of."

"You *are* mysterious! Well, I'll get the secret from you one day!" Amelia couldn't fail to see the flash of panic in her girlfriend's eyes.

"There's no secret!" Penelope burst out, her reaction confirming that there was. "It's just a... family thing," she finished lamely.

"Okay, okay,"—Amelia held up her hands in mock surrender—"if you say so."

* * * *

Charles was sitting at the kitchen table with his MacBook, attempting to write a novel, for which he had many ideas, and was typing furiously. When they entered, he stood and shook Amelia's hand as Penelope introduced her. She noticed he withdrew his hand again quickly. *He doesn't like me,* she thought, wondering why. She felt uncomfortable in his presence, sensing that this man was no fool. *Does he suspect me? He could be dangerous.* She needed time to think.

"May I use the bathroom, please?" she asked politely.

Penelope directed her, and when she was gone, Charles turned to Penelope. "You haven't told her about the lamppost have you?" he whispered.

"Of course not!" she hissed back. "I'm not stupid!"

"Pen, I don't like her. There's something not right there."

"What?" Penelope was incredulous and anger took over. "It's because she's a girl, isn't it? I never had you down for a homophobe, Charles!" She glared at him with a rare hostility.

She only ever used his name on the few occasions they argued and he became defensive. He realised he'd overstepped the mark and certainly chosen the wrong time, with the girl in the house. "Of course it's not that," he whispered, "it's just—"

"What! Her clothes? Because they're a bit worn and she clearly doesn't have much money, is that it? You're such a snob!"

Upstairs, Amelia took the opportunity to snoop a little. One door was ajar and she looked inside. It was a bedroom, neat and tidy, and from its contents, Amelia could see it belonged to Penelope. Curiously, she stepped in and walked around, lifting an ornament here, a bottle of perfume there, before replacing them gently. On the dressing table was a framed photo of a younger Penelope, flanked by two teenagers, a girl, and a boy. Idly she wondered who they were. Then she heard shouting and, spooked, she left the room quickly.

Relieved to find nobody had come looking for her, and hearing more raised voices from the kitchen, she opened another door, which turned out to be Charles' bedroom. It was of no interest and she closed the door again softly, mindful she'd already been upstairs for several minutes. Opening the third and final door, she entered a small room, containing a bookcase, desk, and little else. On the desk was a wallet and, quickly checking the coast was still clear, she opened it, surprised to see it was full of ten and twenty pound notes, as well as a couple of credit cards.

Excitedly, she removed the money, wondering how much she could safely steal. She had a feeling Charles would notice if she took too much and settled for twenty pounds, smiling as she stuffed it into her jeans pocket. *He'll never notice such a small amount,* she thought as she withdrew. She went to the bathroom and flushed the toilet, then ran the tap in the basin for a few seconds.

When she returned, the argument had stopped but Amelia couldn't fail to notice the tension in the room. "Everything okay?" she asked.

"Everything is fine," Penelope said shortly. "Come on, we're going. I'll walk you home."

"Oh, I don't want—"

"Fine! Part of the way then! I need to get out of this house!"

Charles winced as the door slammed behind them.

They were silent for a while until Amelia put a hand on her arm. "Hey, slow down, we're practically running!"

"Sorry." Penelope smiled weakly. "I kinda lost it a bit there."

"What happened, it sounded intense?"

"Nothing," she said quickly, hoping Amelia hadn't heard the argument. "Dad can be an idiot sometimes." It wasn't true and Penelope was upset and puzzled by his attitude. She wondered if she should go back and smooth the waters.

"So, you seeing your friends this weekend?"

"Yeah," she said distractedly, "yeah I am." She realised they were approaching the entrance to the Sanctuary.

"We're near that lamppost again."

"Really?" Penelope feigned innocence. "Oh, so we are. How weird!"

"Isn't it?" Amelia smiled sweetly. "You can leave me here if you want."

"What? Oh, yes, okay."

It wasn't until she had reached the passage-between-the-worlds that Penelope realised they hadn't kissed goodbye. Nor had they arranged where they'd meet next.

Still hardly believing what she was seeing, Amelia returned to the lamppost after Penelope had disappeared inside. Again, she pulled at the door, cursing when it wouldn't open. Across the street, a woman stared at her.

"What are you looking at!" Amelia shouted, taking a few steps into the road. The woman hurried away and she smiled maliciously. But as she walked away, Amelia felt a strange sense of loss, knowing the day hadn't gone well. *I like her a lot,* she admitted to herself, before thrusting the thought aside. *Don't be so weak, Anarkus is the only one you need. Only he can show you the way to Logan.* She smiled when she imagined the shock on the Dark Wizard's face when he saw her, when she slid the knife between his ribs.

*   *   *   *

"Hi, love, how are you?" Molly took Penelope in a bear hug, squeezing her tightly. "I've been cooking, it should be ready…"

Before Penelope could question the wisdom of Molly going anywhere *near* the kitchen, the old witch stopped and cocked her head, as if listening. "Someone is hanging around the lamppost," she said, puzzled. "Did anyone see you?"

Amelia, Penelope thought, panic-stricken. *Did she see me?* "No." She shook her head. "Of course not."

Molly sensed the girl was lying. "What's wrong? You're not yourself."

"Nothing." But tears brimmed inconveniently. "I just argued with Dad."

Surprised, Molly lifted an eyebrow; Charles was the least argumentative man she knew.

"Over my girlfriend; he doesn't like her."

Molly wasn't the most tactful of witches but she nevertheless held her tongue. Charles was a perceptive man, plus he was part wizard. *Well, a failed wizard really,* she admitted to herself, but he could still sense wrong in people.

"So was that your girlfriend hanging around the lamppost?"

"No!" But she avoided Molly's piercing look. "I don't think so. She doesn't suspect anything."

Or did she? Suddenly Penelope was filled with doubt.

Chapter 15

Early one morning, before the sun had cleared the horizon, Portia slipped quietly from her bedchamber and down a narrow, little used stairway to a small door at the bottom. She pulled it open and cursed under her breath as it creaked loudly, but then she was through and into the overgrown ground at the back of the castle, where nobody ever came.

"Are you here?" she whispered loudly, and a tall figure stepped out from an overgrown thicket of brambles.

"It's freezing," complained Anarkus, stamping his feet to keep warm. "This secret of yours had better be good."

"Oh, you won't be disappointed," she said brusquely. "Now stop complaining and follow me." She strode past and led the way along the path to the lakeside and a small boat. "Get in," she ordered, "you can row."

Anarkus gave her a sharp look but didn't argue. He took hold of each oar and, with much splashing, managed to get them away from the bank. But it was a windy morning and the water was choppy. Having never even been in a boat before, let alone tried to steer one, Anarkus found it quite impossible to get the oars to dip into the water at the same time. Soon the boat was drifting around in circles, refusing to do what he wanted.

"We're supposed to be going across," Portia hissed and pointed, "over there. You're taking us near the front of the castle; someone will see us!"

"It's not as easy as it looks, you know," replied Anarkus, unperturbed. "Why don't you have a go!"

"Oh, honestly, Anarkus," she said, "this is hopeless. Put the oars back in the boat." She took out her wand, muttered an incantation, and the boat straightened and moved steadily in the right direction.

"Why didn't you just do that to start with!" Anarkus complained.

"Hush!" she whispered. "Sound carries over water. And I didn't want to use magic in case somebody senses it." As they glided across the lake, Portia cast anxious glances at the windows of the castle, but soon they were across and clambering onto solid ground. They didn't speak as she led the way uphill and into the dense forest that covered much of this world. After an hour, Anarkus was thoroughly disgruntled – usually he'd be just waking up to a delicious breakfast at this time, rather than clambering up a muddy hill at silly o'clock in the morning. He was just about to give up and go back when they entered a small glade.

"Here at last," announced Portia.

"Where?" Apart from a ramshackle building in the centre of the glade, Anarkus could see nothing special about it, although the morning sunshine was welcome after the cool of the forest. "You brought me here to see a building that's falling to pieces?"

"Stop moaning!" She grasped his hand and led him to the door of the cottage which, unlike the rest of the place, looked whole and strong. She flicked her wand toward him and his ears were filled with a loud, piercing shriek. Quickly, she muttered the spell and unlocked the door, then turned, grinning. "Sorry," she said, laughing, "but the opening spell is secret. Not that I don't trust you…"

"Fine," he muttered sourly as the shrieking ceased, and he followed Portia through the portal.

As the door closed, the pigeon slipped in, unseen, behind them.

The first thing Anarkus noticed was the immense heat and he immediately broke out in a sweat, his clothes sticking uncomfortably to his skin. Looking around, he saw they were surrounded by desert, rolling dunes of sand stretching to the horizon. Above, the sun was a huge orb, much larger than it appeared on the world they had just left.

"Where is this?" he asked, but Portia shrugged.

"It doesn't have a name. It was too inhospitable for use by the old council, but I have found a purpose for it. Come." She led the way through the shimmering air until they reached a group of small buildings, where they were greeted obsequiously by a man with sun-darkened skin, wearing a long, flowing white robe.

"Welcome, mistress." He bowed so low his nose almost touched the ground. When he straightened, he didn't meet her eyes but stood with head bowed.

"My servant," she explained, nodding curtly. "Prepare refreshments." The man scuttled away. She led Anarkus around the buildings to the edge of a small cliff, where he looked out over the plateau and gaped in astonishment. "I've spent a thousand years building this army."

"Impressive," Anarkus said at last, "but why?"

"Because being leader of the council is a token, meaningless! I've spent too long listening to their petty disagreements!" She realised she was shouting and lowered her voice. "I exist on that lonely planet while the mortals have one that is rich and full of possibility. Can you understand,

Anarkus? I want to rule somewhere I can use my talent and power. I want to enjoy my life!"

"Right." Anarkus nodded; this was something he could relate to. "But a thousand years? Why so long? Why haven't you acted sooner?"

"I'm a patient woman, Anarkus, and while for a long time now I've had the numbers,"—she waved a hand across the valley—"look at them, there are hundreds of thousands! They make the army of the old demon, Kanzser, look like a mere rabble, don't they!"

"They do," Anarkus agreed, impressed by the scale of her vision. "But you were saying?"

"Yes, I had the numbers, but my army was never quite fierce enough, and our enemies are not without significant power. Building an army that cannot be conquered takes time, a thousand years of time, but now I have it!"

Anarkus looked across the hordes that covered the entire plain before them. Most were humanoid in form, but all horribly, monstrously deformed. "What do you call these creatures? Are they demons?"

"Demons?" Portia threw her head back and laughed. "No, Anarkus, there are no demons because Cornelius's damned blood moon *melted* them all. No, they all came from the mortal world." She smiled at his surprised look. "You've heard of the animatus spell, of course."

"I have, but it's almost impossible to master, it hasn't been used for thousands of years!"

She nodded. "True, yet I have mastered it. And used it many times." She was silent for a while, reminiscing. "Ah, there are rich pickings to be had there," she said at last. "You see, Anarkus, the mortals are unique in their love of one thing, war."

"I don't understand."

"Don't be dense. These,"—she looked proudly at her army—"are the reanimated corpses of the dead. It took less than a hundred years to make—"

"You said it took a thousand years," he cut in.

"Do not,"—Portia looked at him sharply—"interrupt me." She smirked, knowing the rebuke would sting. "As I was saying, it took a century, but then I realised my mistake." She sighed. "Most of the dead were simple souls, forced into war, and none of them particularly bad or evil. I was forced to discard nearly all, and since then I have chosen only the most depraved; murderers, sexual deviants and the like. *That* is why it has taken a millennium."

"I see." Anarkus nodded approvingly. "Does anyone else know? Suluhura, perhaps, or other members of the council?"

"I told you, Anarkus, nobody can know." She levelled a steely gaze at him. "If you are thinking of betrayal, your life will end here."

He laughed and patted her arm condescendingly, although he knew she had the power to carry out her threat. "Of course not, I was merely curious. Suluhura, for example, is completely loyal to you."

"He is," she agreed, "but he's also rash and hot-headed. I could never trust him with a secret like this."

He nodded again, seeing the sense of this. "So what are your plans? Defeat the Sanctuary, get rid of those do-gooding idiots? Take over the mortal world, perhaps?"

"Anarkus, Anarkus." She shook her head, as if disappointed in him. "I never thought you capable of thinking on such a small scale!"

"So?" He grinned. "Tell me."

"Well, I still haven't worked out the finer details, but it will go something like this." She indicated for him to sit and motioned to the servant. When food and wine had been served, she signalled him to leave, then began to speak. As she did, the pigeon flew down and settled on the table, pretending to scavenge for crumbs. Portia brushed it away and it flew to a nearby ledge where it stayed, head cocked, listening.

She spoke for nearly an hour, then stood abruptly. "Come, we should return before our absence is noted."

"By the way, what do you call these creatures," Anarkus asked as they walked back to the portal.

"In the old tongue, I call them my *rue*."

"Your *unlucky ones*." He laughed. "Cute."

"Thanks," she replied dismissively. "You know, Anarkus, it's a pity Agnes couldn't be persuaded to join me; her skills would have been useful when the battles begin. And it's more of a pity that she escaped."

"Yes, that was careless of you, if I may say."

"You may." She refused to let him see her irritation — he'd always been able to do that, and it was always deliberate. It was a timely reminder that he answered to nobody and that once she had achieved her aims, he would need careful watching. If he survived the battle. *Which he might not...* she mused.

As they approached the portal, the pigeon followed, eager now to return to his own world. But his eagerness made him careless and one wing brushed against Anarkus' hair. Instinctively the wizard lashed out, knocking the pigeon to the ground, where he lay stunned. The last thing he heard as the portal entrance opened and then closed again were their voices, faint now.

"Think of it, Anarkus! With all of them dead, there will be nobody to stop me!"

"Stop us," he reminded her lightly.

Chapter 16

As he sat on a rocky outcrop and stared across the valley, Logan was troubled, and he didn't hear the soft tread of footsteps behind him.

"Hello."

Logan turned; he wasn't surprised she had come. "What are you doing here?"

"I was just passing; thought I'd drop in."

"You took your time."

Kamontip shrugged. "Ten years doesn't seem so very long."

"Try spending it trapped in here!" he flared, before lapsing into silence.

"You sense it too, then, the disturbance?" she asked after a while.

"Anarkus has returned."

"No, that's not it. Even he doesn't have the power to cause a disturbance such as this."

"I have sensed it, Kamontip, and his evil knows no bounds."

She didn't really think Logan was in a position to criticise anyone about their evil doings, but wisely hid the thought. "Alright, but if he is responsible, he is not working alone."

He shook his head. "You didn't see him almost transform himself into the Necromancer. He has enormous power."

"No, Logan, no matter how talented a wizard or witch may be, and Anarkus is certainly talented, they are still governed in some part by the wand they hold."

"He used the Queens's Wand."

"Ah, I wondered about that." She nodded. "But he no longer has it."

"Who then? Where does the threat come from?"

She narrowed her eyes, wondering if she could truly trust him, and decided to wait. "I cannot be sure yet," which was true, although she was becoming more certain.

"But you have an idea."

"Perhaps."

"Anyway, you weren't just passing. Nobody just *passes* this place, they avoid it like a disease."

"I've come to offer you a way out." She looked around with distaste at her surroundings.

"You have?" Logan frowned, suspecting a trick. "Why?"

"Because… because…" She frowned, unsure of her motives. Yes, there was a battle coming, but she suspected they'd manage without him if necessary. "Let's just say we have unfinished business."

"And why should I trust you?"

She laughed at that. "Why wouldn't you? I have done you no harm."

"When you left me in the passage-between-the-worlds,"—he paused, surprised to find the hurt was still strong—"you sent me home."

"I don't see what that—"

"I was captured by Portia's henchmen as soon as I entered the mortal world."

"And you think I had something to do with it?"

"I've… wondered."

His paranoia was one of the things that really irritated her and she wondered if it had been a mistake to come here.

"That isn't my style, Logan. If I'd wished you harm, I would have done it myself. Anyway, you must know I like you."

That last sentence hung like a heavy weight between them, but as ever, Logan was unable to conceive of anyone feeling anything but hatred toward him, and he chose to ignore it. "Yet you didn't attempt a rescue."

"No," she said simply, "I didn't."

"Why?"

Why indeed? she thought, having asked herself the same question a thousand times. "Logan, I have lived alone for so long…" She stopped; it wasn't what she was trying to say. "I didn't… I mean, I thought about it." She paused again, frustrated. "I told you I like you," she finished lamely.

"Not enough to stop me being executed, it seems."

"Oh, stop sulking!" she flashed. "There's not a day went by that I didn't think of you in this place, wondering if…"

"Wondering if what?"

Wondering if you ever thought of me. "Nothing," she said, "it doesn't matter."

"You said you would get me out of here."

"I said I would *offer* a way out."

"You want me to help you fight this menace."

She smiled; nobody could accuse Logan of being unintelligent. "Yes."

"I'll do it!" The lie came easily.

"You're still thinking like the old Logan," she said, sadly. "I'd hoped you'd changed."

"What? I will help you, I swear it. Just give me the chance!"

"Don't lie to me, Logan!" she spat. "Never to me." And softly, so he wouldn't hear, "Please, not to me."

"I'm not—" He stopped, surprised to find he didn't want to lie to her again.

"Just for once," she said patiently, "think about what your actions can do for others, not yourself. Something horrible is coming, Logan, many will die. You can betray me and skulk away home, I won't stop you. Or you can…" *Or you can do it for me.*

He didn't reply and Kamontip remained silent, knowing he looked within himself.

Logan searched for a long time until, all at once, her words made sense; always he had only ever done what benefited him, had never put another's wishes first. *But do I really want to put myself in danger?* he thought, curious at his new uncertainty.

They remained quiet until he looked at her; looked with his heart for the first time, not just his eyes, and she met his gaze and smiled. Logan felt a rush of warmth such as he'd never experienced, and instinctively thrust it away as weakness. *Stop doing that!* The thought forced its way in and would not leave. *Just stop.*

I don't want to lie to her, he realised at last, unconsciously moving closer, and they sat, not speaking. Presently, she rested her head on his shoulder and together they watched the sun go down.

*   *   *   *

Anarkus had taken Amelia into the mortal world but so far would not answer her excited questions. At last, they stopped and he took out his wand. "Watch."

Over the next thirty minutes, he performed a variety of spells. Nothing too bad – that would come later – but more for the amusement of annoying mortals. Changing the traffic signs and road markings around Marble Arch, causing chaos and more than a few bumps and scrapes. Making people's clothes suddenly disappear so they ran around, frantically trying to cover themselves while others stared and sniggered. But after a few more silly spells, he was soon bored.

"You have such power!" Amelia was genuinely impressed, but he laughed dismissively.

"This is nothing, mere tricks." He looked at her speculatively, wondering if he should say more. "The fate I have in store for the mortal world is far worse than this. But for now, I should remain inconspicuous and keep my plans secret."

"What plans?"

"Later," he hedged, but she protested.

"I thought you trusted me, Anarkus. I am your protégé, after all."

"Alright," he said at last, "when we return to the mansion, I will tell you everything." And to himself, he thought, *but if you think to betray me, I will kill you.*

Walking under a nearby tree, he scouted around for a moment before finding what he wanted, a small, straight branch, little more than a twig. Taking out his wand again, he infused it with magic.

"My very own wand." She grinned. "Thank you!"

Anarkus smiled cynically. The wand was basic and would allow her to do very little damage, except perhaps to herself. He certainly wasn't going to give her any real power; he wasn't so stupid.

Chapter 17

Penelope spent an uncomfortable weekend in the Sanctuary. It was the first time ever she'd not enjoyed being there, filled with doubts about Amelia and speculative looks from Molly.

Monday at work was no better and she spent most of it staring idly into space and watching the clock grind slowly round. Home at last, she forced down a hurried snack, putting on a show of normalcy for Charles, then hurried to the Starbucks. It was the only place she could think of that Amelia might go, and she kept her fingers crossed that her girlfriend – if she even still was her girlfriend – would be there. She wasn't.

It was the same on Tuesday and Wednesday, and now Charles couldn't help but notice something was wrong. But Penelope remained tight-lipped amidst all his questions, and on Thursday there she was again, in Starbucks, hoping against hope that Amelia would show up. She waited an hour, then another, before she stood and prepared to leave. Then her spirits soared as a familiar figure came hurrying through the door and flung herself into her arms.

There were looks of disapproval from some, who looked askance, even in these modern times, at the sight of two women kissing. A couple of teenage lads stared, mouths open at the sight of the two beautiful girls, but looked hurriedly away when Amelia glared at them. But most ignored them and two older women sitting in a corner table smiled lovingly at each other; one took the other's hand and kissed it.

"I didn't think I'd see you again." Penelope grinned, excited that perhaps all was not lost after all.

"I had to come." Amelia hesitated. "There's something I need to know, something you have to tell me."

"Oh." Penelope felt a little deflated. "You didn't come because you miss me then?"

"Of course I missed you," she replied earnestly, her blue eyes fixed on Penelope's.

"So what do you want to know?"

"Not here." Amelia looked around. "It's too crowded. Let's go."

"So?" Penelope said after they'd walked for a few minutes. Neither had taken the other's hand; there was a tension between them now.

"I saw you!" Amelia blurted suddenly. "At the lamppost. You went inside!"

Penelope's stomach lurched and, panic-stricken, she denied it. "What are you talking about?" She laughed, but she could hear how nervous she sounded. "How would that be possible?"

"Don't lie to me!" Amelia's voice took on an angry, threatening tone, and Penelope stepped back.

"I'm not, Amelia, you must have imagined it." Unaccountably, she found herself feeling guilty at the lie, but there was no way she could admit the truth. "Can't you hear how ridiculous that sounds?"

"So that's it then?" Amelia fired back scornfully. "You say you like me but then keep secrets from me?"

"Oh no, don't you dare." Penelope was suddenly furious. "Don't you dare lay a guilt trip on me. You might be my girlfriend but you don't own me!"

"You think I'm your girlfriend?" Amelia's mocking laughter was aimed to hurt. "I'm just using you!" She gripped Penelope's arm and dragged her along the street; the lamppost was already visible in the distance. "And you *will* show me the secret or you'll be sorry!"

Penelope was no weakling, but she was powerless to release the grip, and in no time at all, they were standing by the old, wrought iron lamp. "Now, get on with it," Amelia hissed, "and no tricks."

Penelope rubbed her arm, which she knew would soon bruise. She was shocked at the turn of events, a little scared even, but she was not intimidated, and she was thinking hard. "Okay," she said at last, "you win."

"Whatever. Just get me inside!"

"And where will you go then? There are people there who will not stand for any of your nonsense," Penelope taunted.

"It doesn't matter. Just open the lamppost and do whatever it is that you do!" Penelope's words had struck hard, and for the first time Amelia felt uncertain. She'd not considered who she might encounter once inside, nor where she would go from there. All she knew, or suspected at least, was that it would bring her closer to finding Logan.

"Okay." Penelope sighed theatrically. "You asked for it." She reached inside her coat and withdrew her wand, which she always carried.

"No tricks!" Amelia repeated and took out her knife. "I'll stab you if you try anything."

Penelope stared at the knife, truly shocked now. *Oh, that's the final straw,* she thought. *It's going to make this so much easier.* Although she hadn't been taught anything really powerful, Charles had been adamant in showing her some useful tricks for protection on the dangerous London streets.

Without hesitation, she jabbed her wand at Amelia, shouted a few magic words, and sent her flying backward, a dozen meters at least, into a wall, where she lay dazed for a long moment.

"Don't you dare *fuck* with me again!" Penelope rarely swore and the word sounded incongruous to her ears as she strode quickly to where Amelia lay. "And don't you ever come near me again." She held up the wand threateningly, but Amelia was already losing consciousness.

Penelope was still shaken but her anger sustained her on the short walk home. As soon as she saw Charles, she fell into his arms and the tears came. "You were right, Dad," she sobbed, "so right. I'm sorry I didn't listen to you."

"It's okay," he breathed, kissing the top of her head. "It's all okay, everything will be fine."

He couldn't know how wrong he was, but for now, Penelope was comforted.

Chapter 18

"Concentrate!"

Amelia forced herself to pay attention to Anarkus' teachings but thoughts of Penelope kept flashing into her head, and she was having difficulty thrusting them away. *Stupid bitch,* she thought, *get out of my mind, you are nothing to me.* Yet she knew it was a lie and that she was finding the incident with Penelope strangely disturbing.

"What is wrong with you?" Anarkus said, annoyed at her distraction. The girl had been doing well and he knew she would make a useful companion in the wars to come. He already planned to use her as a shield to protect himself; better she be the one to perish if it came to it. But today she was unable to listen to anything he said.

"Nothing," she replied curtly.

"Ah, it is the dirty mortal girl." He laughed. "You like her."

Amelia said nothing, declining to remind him she herself was a mortal.

Anarkus gripped her arm painfully. She tried to pull free but he was far too strong. "Listen to me," he hissed, his eyes boring into hers with frightening intensity. "You are my disciple, and you know too many of my plans." His grip loosened slightly. "Either you are with me or against me, choose now, Amelia."

"Of course I'm with you." She pulled her arm free. "I'm just using the mortal girl; I will discard her when she has outlived her usefulness." But Amelia didn't think mortals were dirty, herself perhaps, but certainly not Penelope. *No,* she thought, *Penelope is beautiful.*

"Yes, use her as much as you wish," he agreed, "but I will decide when she has outlived her usefulness. Then you will kill her."

"Of course." Amelia shrugged nonchalantly. "It will be my pleasure," she lied.

"Good. Now try the spell again, and this time, concentrate!"

"I need to get my things from the hostel. I've made my decision and I want to stay with you and learn as much as I can." Tentatively, she took hold of Anarkus' hand, though it made her feel sick to do so. "I want to help with the war you're planning."

"Why?" He looked at her, ever suspicious.

"Because then you will reward me." Her eyes shone into his with all the honesty she could muster. "You will show me where the Dark Wizard is hiding." It was a half-truth; she still dreamed of exacting the worst possible revenge on Logan, but not if the cost was harming Penelope.

"Good." He nodded, and his eyes bored into hers hypnotically. "Because it's time for you to learn some of the darker spells, those that do real harm. You'll need them if you are to murder Logan."

Amelia felt a surge of excitement as she stared into those eyes. *At last!* she thought. *This is what I've wanted!* A wave of disgust at her feelings for Penelope over the last few weeks engulfed her and it all suddenly seemed trite and unimportant. Worse, it felt weak!

What was I thinking, getting involved with her, behaving like a lovesick child? I've never needed anyone before, I'm a survivor!

"I see the prospect pleases you."

"It is everything I want."

Anarkus smiled inwardly. *So easy*, he thought, *so very easy*. "And the girl?"

"The girl means nothing to me. I am your loyal pupil." This time, Amelia meant every word.

Chapter 19

For almost a fortnight, Portia and Anarkus plotted and schemed until at last they were ready to face the council. There was silence at first as plans for the destruction of the Sanctuary, domination of the mortal world, and the conquering of the hidden worlds were described.

She'd been speaking for only a few minutes when a witch stood abruptly and headed for the door. Taking courage from her action, another witch and a wizard joined her.

"No doubt you'll have us killed," one of them said, turning accusingly to Portia, "but I'll hear no more of this."

"You dishonour me," she replied, injecting as much sincerity into the statement as she could. "You are, of course, free to make your choice." She turned to those remaining and spread her arms expansively. "As are you all!"

The three of them exited, knowing they walked to their deaths. Portia spoke for another few minutes before two more witches, naively believing her promise, stood and left.

That's okay, she thought as she looked around at the remainder and received nods or smiles of support. *It leaves six of us, me and five wizards; more than enough.*

"I have a question. More of a complaint really," Suluhura announced suddenly.

"A complaint?" Portia turned to him, unsurprised. She'd noticed he'd been unusually quiet, sulky almost; he usually had far too much to say. Trying to keep the boredom from her voice, she forced concern into her eyes. "It pains me to know I have offended you, dear friend."

"You haven't!" he exclaimed. "It's just him!" He nodded but didn't meet Anarkus' cold glare.

"You object to Anarkus' presence on the council?" Even Suluhura recognised how her tone had lowered, becoming dangerous.

"No!" he exclaimed, too quickly. "I'm delighted he is here." He looked at Anarkus with what he hoped was a sincere smile. "It's just, I have been here much longer than he." He shrugged. "I would have hoped you'd entrust me sooner with your plans."

"You know I trust you, Suluhura," she soothed, "you are my most valued companion. I'm sure you understand there was need for secrecy, but it hurt me terribly to keep this from you."

She gave him her sweetest smile and, of course, Suluhura was completely fooled. Yet, when her aims were accomplished, she would not discard him, she had already decided; he was stupid but loyal. *But the others,* she thought, smiling round at them, *they will have to go.* She switched her gaze onto Anarkus. *And him, certainly.*

*   *   *   *

Like many desert places, nights could be bitterly cold, and the pigeon might have perished but for the kindness of the servant. He had lay stunned for several hours before limping toward the shelter of the buildings, too bruised to fly. There he had fainted, and by the time morning arrived, was near to death.

He awoke later that day to find himself wrapped in a scrap of cloth, toasty and warm, the servant feeding drops of milk and bread into his beak. The pigeon gulped hungrily until he was full, then, raising his head with difficulty, pecked his hand gently in thanks, not wanting to reveal he understood everything the man was saying.

By nightfall, the pigeon had recovered his strength and, before flying away, he made a decision. In his clear, trilling voice, he spoke to the servant. "I thank you for my life and that of countless others. Because of your kindness, I can give warning of this treachery." He nodded to the huge army encamped on the plain below. "Many lives will be saved." He hopped onto the servant's shoulder and nuzzled it for a few moments. Then, with a cry of farewell, he was gone.

The servant, mouth gaping, could only stare in amazement.

But a few minutes later, the pigeon was back. "The witch and her companions will return soon, I am certain of it," he said gravely.

"How… how can you talk?" the servant stammered.

"I come from a world where all living things can talk." If he could have smiled, the pigeon would have done so. "In the witch's world, all beings are considered equal. Oh, it is a beautiful place." He sighed wistfully, suddenly full of longing. "If you should ever go there, I will ensure you are made welcome."

"I thank you,"—the servant shook his head sadly—"but I fear this accursed place will be my home until I die."

"No," the pigeon said urgently. "That is why I returned, to warn you."

"Warn? This place is not so bad, except for the heat and the sand." He grimaced theatrically. "And the lack of water and decent food."

"Listen," the pigeon urged, "you must *listen!*" He hopped onto the servant's hand and pecked it, not so gently this time. "Soon the witch will return for her army, and when she does you will have outlived your usefulness."

"You think she might allow me to return to my home in the village? There is only me now, I have no family. But still, I would like to go back."

"No!" The pigeon was becoming agitated. "You don't understand. She will have you killed!"

"But what can we do?" The servant looked around fearfully, as if expecting his demise to come there and then.

"I intend to escape," the pigeon replied, nuzzling and kissing his neck to help him calm. "I will slip unseen into the portal when it is opened, but you cannot. You must go now, hide as far away as possible, and hope the witch doesn't come looking."

"Yes," he said, nodding, "I can do that. It means I will be trapped here forever, but at least I will be alive."

"When the witch is defeated, I will come for you. Remember, you are welcome in my world, should you so wish."

"You think the witch and her army can be destroyed?" he asked, doubtful.

"I do." The pigeon nodded and, as he flew away, he muttered, "I have to believe it, for the alternative is chaos." By the time he reached the portal entrance, the servant had already gathered his meagre possessions and was running as fast as he could across the dunes.

The pigeon didn't have long to wait until the portal opened. As Portia, Anarkus, and the other four wizards stepped through, he slipped inside unseen and was enveloped in darkness once more. There he perched, trembling with excitement at the thought of escape.

An hour later, they returned, and the four wizards who had witnessed the vast army for the first time were chattering animatedly. Anarkus was silent, not bothering to hide his irritation at their wittering, and Portia was also quiet, seething with anger at the servant's desertion and promising she would find him and enact the severest punishment she could devise.

As the portal opened again, nobody noticed the pigeon slip out after them. Now, as they made their way back to the castle, taking care not to be seen, he flew away, his mission almost complete. But when he reached the portal, Agnes wasn't there and, with no magic of his own, the pigeon could only sit, helplessly waiting and hoping she would come.

Chapter 20

Back in her room at the hostel, Amelia was lying on her bed, thinking about Penelope, when there was a knock at the door. Instantly alert, she sat up and checked her pocket to be sure the knife was still there.

"You've been thieving," barked the manager without preamble as she entered. "Money's gone missing and I know it's you!"

"It is not!" Amelia leaped to her feet. "You can't prove it, you bitch. And anyway, that's slander!"

Whether she had expected Amelia to be repentant, or whether it was the threatening tone or the dangerous glint in her eye, the manager took a step backward. "Well," she huffed, "somebody took it."

"It wasn't me, now get out!"

When the door had closed, Amelia lay back down and smiled, enjoying the feeling of power the encounter had brought. *That'll teach her,* she thought gleefully, and then the most delicious idea came to her. She peered at her right hand, turning it palm down and then back up. *Can I do it?* she wondered. *Could I really do it?* An hour later, she knocked softly at the manager's office door.

"What do you want? If you've come to make trouble—"

"I've come to say I'm sorry," Amelia interrupted meekly, lowering her eyes.

"So you admit to stealing that money?"

"Yeah." Amelia looked at her earnestly. "But I promise I'm gonna pay you back."

"How?" the manager said suspiciously. "And when?"

"Oh,"—she grinned—"it will be very, *very* soon." She held out her hand. Warily, the manager took it and gave a limp handshake.

"Well, I must say, Amelia, this is a pleasant surp—" She paused as a strange tingling sensation invaded her hand and spread quickly up her arm. "What?" She stared at the girl. "What did you do?"

Amelia laughed. "Told you I'd pay you back!" She stepped quickly round the desk and opened one drawer, then another. Finding the purse, she drew out a handful of banknotes and stuffed them into her pocket.

The manager was too distressed and panic-stricken to care as she stared at the lumps beneath her skin that now moved up her arm as if they were alive. "Please! Help me, Amelia, please. I'm sorry!" Weeping now, she looked imploringly at the girl. Several of the lumps had reached her shoulder and were moving across her breast or round to her back. She could feel them scraping her ribs as they passed through. "Make it go away!" she screamed. "I don't care about the money, just make it stop!"

The only reply she received was that of Amelia's mocking, cruel laughter as she ran back up the corridor to her room.

Finding almost two hundred pounds in her pocket, Amelia was delighted but strangely disappointed at the magic. *Shame I couldn't have done some lasting damage,* she thought. *She'll be okay in an hour. Anarkus has to teach me better stuff than that.*

Still, it had been fun, but there was no time to dwell on her success. The police could be arriving any minute. She grabbed her bag with its meagre contents and headed out the door. She flagged down a taxi, deciding to travel in style, and soon she stood in the alley, staring at the windows and wondering if Anarkus would know she was there, like last time.

Back at the hostel, an ambulance had arrived, closely followed by the police. But truthfully, with resources stretched, the theft of a few hundred pounds was never going to be seriously investigated. As for the manager, there was nothing wrong with her, and the ambulance crew, annoyed at having their time wasted, put her experience down to some kind of hysteria.

Amelia's social worker was concerned for a while at the girl's disappearance, but she had so many other people to look after, there really wasn't the time. Eventually, Amelia became just another statistic in a file, in a drawer, in some forgotten room.

Chapter 21

Agnes was with one of the young witches, fetching water from the well. The day was hot and they perspired freely, stopping frequently to rest.

"Tell me what it was like in the old days, Agnes," the witch asked, a little shyly, for Agnes was something of a legend in their world. What she really meant, Agnes suspected, was, *tell me how you rescued Mitra and Cornelius.*

"I'm sure you've heard the stories many times," she demurred. "Surely you're bored with them by now?"

"Oh no," the young witch said vehemently, "I could never be bored. It must have been such an exciting time."

Agnes sighed and motioned for them to sit on the grass. Truthfully, she was glad of the break from carrying the heavy pails. "Alright then,"—she smiled at the eager young witch—"what would you like to know?"

"Well, I've heard a lot about how you rescued Mitra and Cornelius from certain death."

"With the help of the woodland creatures," Agnes reminded her.

"Yes, of course, but…"

"Yes?" Agnes smiled encouragingly. "What is it?"

"I've always wondered about the witch Racine," she said, hesitating, for she knew that name was no longer mentioned in this place. "I mean, why did she get so bad, what made her do the things she did?"

Agnes felt a jolt in her stomach. Even after so many centuries, Racine's treachery still hurt. "It's not something to dwell on," she said softly, "it belongs in the past." Suddenly the warmth had left the sun and she felt depressed.

"I… I'm sorry," her companion stammered. "I didn't mean—"

"It's fine," Agnes cut in. "Really, it is." She took the girl's hand and squeezed gently. "It's just that—" She stopped and her head whipped around to face the east.

"What is it?"

But Agnes held up a hand, listening intently. *Yes, there it is again!* Instantly she was on her feet and running in the direction of the sound.

"Where are you going?" shouted the witch, perplexed.

"I'll be back soon!" Agnes hoped it was true. *Please let it not be a mistake,* she thought, over and over as she ran, like a mantra, *don't let it be too late.*

At first, she thought the pigeon was dead, and her heart lurched, but then she saw the gentle rising and falling of his chest and said a silent prayer of thanks. When she gently stroked his feathers, the pigeon opened a sleepy eye and, with a soft cry of relief, tried to struggle to his feet.

"No, my friend," Agnes whispered softly, "you are safe now." She lifted him gently into her pocket and he snuggled comfortably, enjoying the warmth of her body. Stepping back through the portal and into the witch's world, Agnes bypassed the village and called the woodland creatures to her. There was great rejoicing at their return and congratulations for the pigeon on his bravery.

Cradled in Agnes's arms, he tried to answer the questions that came from all sides, but soon he yawned widely, his head lolling to one side and his eyes drooping. At once, a larger bird, a heron, took him gently in her beak and flew high into a tree. She settled him into a nest and within seconds the pigeon was fast asleep and snoring gently.

Later, refreshed from his rest, the pigeon told his tale while Agnes and the woodland creatures listened, their faces turning grim as they learned of the approaching menace. There were dark murmurings from some and offers to help fight from others, but Agnes shook her head. She knew there was nothing they could do except keep themselves safe.

Anxious to warn the village, she said her farewells, and the woodland creatures scurried to make their preparations. But as they left, she called one of them to her and whispered hurried instructions into his ear. The squirrel, old now and his coat streaked with silver, had been a messenger for the village for countless years and now he nodded, making sure he understood the message before bounding away, still spritely despite his age, to the waterfall a few kilometres from the village.

Agnes knocked on the door of the village elder, and before long everyone was gathered at the traditional meeting place in the centre of the village. The air was filled with chatter and there was a faint tinge of excitement, all wondering what was so important. When they were quiet at last, Agnes told the pigeon's story.

*   *   *   *

"It won't be long now," Anarkus boasted. "Soon I will lead my armies against the mortals." He spun a tale where he was the architect of the entire scheme, while Portia and the others were mere bit part players. "Soon the mortals, Aeryn, the witches, goblins, and *particularly* those of the Sanctuary will either be dead or under my power!" He paused his rant, suddenly out of breath, and looked at her.

123

Amelia may not have had much education in recent years, but she knew the word megalomaniac and felt a shiver run down her spine. She'd known he was dangerous, of course, but perhaps she'd underestimated how dangerous. Forcing herself to remain calm, she smiled sweetly at him, a false look of admiration – that fooled him not at all – trying to hide her doubts, which had resurfaced.

"I have every faith in you," she said, before lowering her eyes demurely. But her mind was in turmoil; she'd never dreamed he was planning something so diabolical.

Do I want him to be so powerful? she wondered. *For everyone to be killed? After all, this is still my world, even if it has treated me badly.*

But Anarkus knew exactly what she was thinking. Master of manipulation that he was, his next words, along with the faintest twitch of his wand, again cast all doubt from her mind. "It is time for you to go among the mortals."

Again the excitement, already planning how she would use her powers, limited though they were. Amelia took out her wand and stroked its smooth surface fondly.

Anarkus watched her cynically, his face a careful mask of approval. *Silly fool,* he thought. *When I am master of all, you'd better hope I let you live.* Aloud he said, "Go, do what you will. When next you see me, it will be at the head of my army. I will send for you."

And then he was gone, and Amelia barely noticed, so intent was she on her wand. As for Anarkus, he was going to the land of the witch and wizard council, but not yet. First, he would wait a while and see what happened…

Chapter 22

In the years since the wedding of Daraproud and Alessandro, there had been peace and prosperity, which was fortunate because of the curse that had blighted Aeryn's world for many centuries. The curse had killed her father and decreed that no woman for the next thousand years would bear children unless the queen of the land did so. Shortly after, her mother, devasted at her husband's death had followed him and Aeryn had become queen.

Already a fearsome warrior, she preferred fighting to marriage and had never found a man able to live up to her standards of bravery and honour. Not, that is, until she met Morgan. But by that time, her army, once thousands strong, had been depleted as it died, either in battle or of old age, with nobody to replace it.

There had been hope that she and Morgan might marry and bear a child, thus lifting the curse, but it was not to be. Morgan's first duty was to the mortal race and their protection and, as leader of the Sanctuary, he had shamelessly used Aeryn's army, thus exhausting it further. Aeryn shared a similar duty to her people and, devastating as it had been, had banished Morgan from her realm.

For two hundred years they saw nothing of each other until Penelope found a forbidden spell and entered Aeryn's world, seeking aid against Kanzser and his demon hordes. Morgan, appalled at the risk she'd taken, had followed and confronted the warrior queen and, having found each other again, neither had been willing to deny their love a second time. With her aid, the demons were annihilated, Cissy became leader of the Sanctuary and Morgan returned with Aeryn to her world.

Soon after the battle, her sister Daraproud married Alessandro, the Sanctuary chef, and the talk among the villagers had turned quite naturally to their queen; would she and Morgan marry at last? Both were content and marriage didn't seem important, but they recognised the duty they owed their people, and, just a few months later, wedding bells again rang out across the land.

There was more rejoicing when the queen bore a daughter, Marguerite, and in the ensuing months, as if determined to make up for lost time, there was a spate of pregnancies, and now, a decade later, the sounds of children's laughter filled the town.

Despite the long hiatus of peace, Aeryn and Daraproud were not complacent and continued to spar regularly, keeping their skills honed and ready. They were doing so one day when Daraproud's sharp ears heard barking; she knew instantly it wasn't one of the castle dogs. When they both sensed the opening of the castle door, they dashed from the room to the top of the long staircase, swords ready.

*   *   *   *

The arguments had raged for days, and Agnes had had enough. "Oh, for goodness' sake!" she snapped. "We need to make up our minds!" She glared at her fellow witches and the noise subsided into a few isolated mutterings. "Need I remind you that an army more terrible than we've ever faced is on its way!"

"I agree." The village elder looked at her gratefully. She'd made several attempts to interrupt the arguments but had been shouted down each time. Not for the first time, she wished she could wield more authority.

"I remember when we were tricked by the wizard Cornelius into fighting with him against the Necromancer," an ancient witch said quietly. Even after so many centuries, there was raw emotion in the statement as she added, "Our race was decimated, almost wiped out. Tell me, Agnes, why should we join his war again and risk the same?"

Agnes, respecting the revered elder, kept her voice even. "I understand," she agreed, "but this is different. Portia is sending her army to all the dimensions, not just that of the mortals. If we don't fight, there is a real chance we will die anyway."

"I still think we should hide in the mountains," said another. "These creatures will not find us there." There were nods of agreement from most of those gathered, only the few who sided with Agnes remained silent.

"Alright then,"—Agnes would argue no longer—"you should make your preparations quickly. I will depart tonight with those who have pledged to accompany me."

There were murmurs of protest and, eventually, someone spoke up. "Those you will take with you are young, while those who are to remain are old. The way to the mountains is long and fraught with difficulty; will you leave us to struggle alone?"

Inside, Agnes screamed, *It is your own choice!* But she knew they were right. "Of course." She bowed her head to hide her frustration. "We will assist you in your quest and help guide you to safety." She knew that by the time they'd done so, it might already be too late to help save the mortal world.

Chapter 23

The squirrel soon reached the waterfall and passed through its crystal-clear water to where the portal lay. He stepped through and less than a second later was hurrying across the fields to the ancient inn. The Landlord spotted him before he'd covered half the distance and sighed. He and the squirrel were old friends and often got together for a chat over a few beers and a bowl of nuts, but somehow the

Landlord didn't think this was going to be a social visit. *I knew there was trouble coming,* he thought after the squirrel had delivered his news, not in the least surprised that Portia was at the centre of it.

Thanking his friend, he bade a hasty goodbye and watched him skip nimbly over the grass and disappear, wondering if they would ever meet again. Then he stepped back inside the inn and flumped heavily down into an old armchair, sending a small cloud of dust into the air.

The Landlord pondered deeply for a few moments, then he took pen and paper, scribbled a hurried note, and attached it to Oscar's collar.

"I need you to do something, Oscar, something very brave indeed." When he had finished, the dog barked its assent and the two of them walked through the back door of the inn and into 17th Century Wales. He was about to begin the spell when Oscar barked sharply.

"Yes, of course, you're right," the Landlord agreed. "The villagers will wonder what's happening; we must warn them." Oscar scampered up the long flight of steps to the path at the top, the Landlord following close behind, hoping his defences would hold if the creatures attacked while he was gone. An hour later, the elders of the village had been told of the menace that was coming. Then he outlined his plan and the spell he must perform.

"You should all be safe here," he reassured them, "the creatures will not easily breach my defences. But perhaps you should retreat to the caves?" The elders nodded and immediately began making preparations. The Landlord turned to Gruffydd, who'd been listening avidly. He felt a twinge of guilt, knowing how much the boy missed Catrin, knowing also that he should have made much more time for him than he had.

"Gruffydd,"—he smiled down at him—"perhaps you could go with Oscar? You'd be doing me a tremendous service."

Almost swelling with pride, Gruffydd nodded eagerly. "What shall I tell them?" he asked, eyes shining with excitement.

"You don't have to tell them anything, it's all in the note. Just keep Oscar safe, he must stay with you here when you return. And, Gruffydd,"—he faltered for a moment—"if I don't make it back…"

"I'll look after him," Gruffydd promised, but his eyes were no longer shining, "but you will come back, Landlord, won't you?"

Without answering, the Landlord crouched and embraced Oscar tightly, whispering into his ear. In turn, the little dog licked his face and made soft crying noises. Then, with tears running down his cheeks, the Landlord stood, knowing if he delayed longer he might never have the courage to part from his beloved companion. Raising his wand, he spoke to the sky, softly at first but quickly gaining momentum so that soon he was almost shouting.

"Keepers of the sky!" he cried, "Skuarapariximordani! Allow entry in our time of need! Imxploridai!"

Over and over he repeated the ancient words as one hour passed, then another and another. Panting with exertion now, sweat pouring from his body, the Landlord began to worry he'd got the spell wrong somehow. Another hour passed.

"Skuarapariximordani! Imxploridai!"

Suddenly his wand seemed to pierce the air and a blinding stream of white light shone through. He dragged his wand sideways, almost collapsing with the effort, and a long tear appeared, its edges flapping in the breeze.

"Quickly, Gruffydd," he gasped, and the boy ran to pull the edges wide, bathing the entire valley in a luminescent shroud. Oscar gave a bark of farewell and leaped through the gap, closely followed by Gruffydd, and the tear snapped shut.

Fighting back tears, the Landlord nodded briefly to the few villagers who'd remained, not trusting himself to speak, and ran quickly back to the inn.

Chapter 24

Anarkus had thought long about whether he should give Amelia the power to breach the portal and move in between her world and his. At last, he decided he would, realising it would be an excellent test of her loyalty. Watching her now from the shadows of the alley, as she leaped up the wall and through the window, he knew it was a test she would fail, and he smiled grimly.

As soon as she heard him leave, Amelia grabbed her coat and left the old mansion too. Soon she was in the alley, heading for the portal, then into modern-day London where she looked around, wondering what mischief she could cause.

She spent the next couple of hours on petty tricks and inconveniences, amused at the perplexed looks on people's faces, but she soon became bored. *Surely I can think of something better than this,* she thought, *something truly wicked?*

Just then, an open-topped tourist bus stopped across the road and, as Amelia idly glanced at it, she saw someone looking at her from the top level. It was a little girl with pretty blonde hair eating an ice-cream. *And she was wearing a red coat!* Within seconds, Amelia had crossed the road and jumped onto the bus. Passing the driver, he berated her for not paying, but she silenced him with a hostile glance and moments later was up the stairs and sitting opposite the girl.

Her mother was busy texting, oblivious to the young woman who stared at her daughter with such intensity. Amelia felt her anger rising at her neglect and a roaring, pounding sound filled her head. *You should take better care of her, you bitch,* she thought. *And now you're going to pay the price.* She took out her wand and hid it surreptitiously beside her leg as she considered a spell she could use. Then she smirked and gripped the wand more tightly; she knew the very one.

The little girl had nearly finished her ice-cream, much of which had dripped onto her knees, and was about to take a final mouthful when she stopped. Moving to the edge of the seat, she looked at Amelia and smiled, then offered it to her. It was such an act of simple kindness and so unexpected that Amelia hesitated, then took it. *Why did she do that?* she wondered. *People don't give things for nothing, they always want something in return.*

"Thank you," she said, and looked at the remains of the cone, its edges damp and chewed. Suddenly, the mother looked up and exclaimed loudly, then stood and hustled her daughter along the bus, down the steps, and onto the street. The little girl looked up and waved, but Amelia barely noticed. The pounding in her head had stopped, replaced with anger and puzzlement at her hesitation and failure to cause the harm she had so wanted. Feeling suddenly exposed, she imagined everyone staring at her and, dropping the cone to the floor, she left the bus at the next stop and barged her way through the crowds.

Amelia found herself drawn, as if by a magnet, to the nearest park. It was as if she needed to torture herself by witnessing the happiness of others when she was so deeply unhappy. Inside, people were taking selfies, picnicking, feeding the ducks on the lake, and a dozen other simple pleasures; Amelia regarded them all with distaste. *You don't know the danger you're all in*, she sneered to herself and, once again, took out her wand; this time she would not fail.

Don't do it. The voice in her head was so real she spun around, searching, but she recognised nobody. The voice, familiar now, spoke again, *Please Amelia, don't.*

"Get out of my mind," she muttered as Penelope's image filled her vision. "Get out!" she said, loud enough that some people turned to look. Amelia tried to summon a spell, any spell that would make them sorry they had noticed her, but she couldn't concentrate.

Don't do it. Penelope's voice was louder, insistent, unrelenting. *Don't, don't, don't.* But now Anarkus was in her head, forcing Penelope out. She could see him grinning sardonically and Amelia knew her weaknesses were on display for everyone to see, to laugh at. And he was talking, goading. *Go on, use your wand, kill the mortals.*

"Get out!" She was moaning with terror now, gripping her head tightly, squeezing, trying to make him leave. People, frightened, were gathering their things and moving away.

"It's alright," Amelia gasped. "I won't hurt you. Don't leave me alone with him. Please don't leave me!" Safely at a distance, a crowd gathered, whispering, pointing. She felt Penelope try to force her way back in, and heard her words, faint, *Don't give up, Amelia, you are good, there is hope.* But Anarkus was laughing, mocking her, and when next he spoke, she knew the truth of his words. *You are evil, there is no hope for you, little girl. Evil!*

And the crowd had grown, moving closer, grinning at her, mouths wide open. Their bodies were shrinking, hair changing colour, blonde like corn in summer. Then they were turning red, their clothes; red, the colour of blood.

Amelia closed her eyes tightly, willing them to go away. But when she opened them again, all she saw was a multitude, all mirror images of herself, the little girl in the red coat. They were calling, arms outstretched, tempting her to join them, their mouths getting bigger, filling their faces. And when she looked inside, she could see the demons, hungry, waiting, eager to come out and play. As Anarkus' laughter continued to bludgeon her mind, she sank to her knees, screaming, laying in the foetal position, hiding from the world, from the pain.

After what seemed like an age, the noise in Amelia's head subsided and she lifted her head, warily. The crowd was still there but thinner and, to her intense relief, normal. Someone had called an ambulance and Amelia saw two green-clad paramedics hurrying toward her; beyond them a police car was drawing up to the gates, blue lights flashing. She got quickly to her feet and fled.

*   *   *   *

The tear in the fabric of the sky closed and they found themselves on a narrow road that snaked through the mountains, which towered majestically on either side. In the distance were soaring towers of a magnificent castle, its stone walls blazing white in the sunshine. Gruffydd was nervous about the coming encounter and he walked in silence, Oscar trotting by his side, his footpads making soft slapping noises on the hard road.

Presently they reached the castle and crossed the drawbridge to a huge wooden door. Its two guards drew their swords at their approach but lowered them slightly, grinning when they saw the dog. They bent and welcomed him as he charged the last few meters and flung himself at them, licking their faces and barking loudly. He and the Landlord were regular visitors to Aeryn's world and both were well known and popular with all.

"Down, boy." They laughed, turning suspicious frowns upon Gruffydd. "Where is Cornelius?"

"C… Corne..?" he stammered. "Oh, you mean the Landlord." Sensing the change in mood, Oscar returned to Gruffydd and stood loyally by his side. "He's not here…"

"I can see that, boy," one of the guards answered, not unkindly, "but his absence signals trouble to me. Again, why are you here?"

"Yes," Gruffydd rallied, "there is trouble! The Landlord… Cornelius sent me here with Oscar to warn the queen!"

"Why didn't he come himself?"

"He… he stayed to fight the… the whatever it is."

The guards held a hurried conference, both agreeing the boy was harmless and that Oscar's presence vouched for him. "Come then." They pushed open the doors and Oscar ran inside, Gruffydd behind him.

*   *   *   *

Daraproud reached the bottom of the steps first, only because in her usual flamboyant style, she slid the whole way down the banister. She knew it annoyed her sister – it was part of the fun – and she smiled innocently as Aeryn regarded her sourly, mainly because it was a move she could never replicate herself, no matter how many times she tried. But for once, Daraproud chose not to tease, for she'd recognised their visitor.

"Oscar!" Daraproud lowered her sword, and the dog leaped into her outspread arms. Aeryn glared at the boy who hung back nervously. She vaguely thought she recognised him but wasn't sure.

"Your visit is unexpected and uninvited. Why are you here?"

Daraproud dug her sharply in the ribs; there had been a time when intrusion into the land was forbidden, but those days were past. Aeryn occasionally needed reminding of that. But Morgan had also recognised the barking and hurried into the hall. When he saw the boy, a worried frown creased his face.

"Gruffydd!" he said quietly. "What is it, what has happened?"

Chapter 25

A fortnight had passed, and Penelope had no idea if she'd ever see Amelia again, something she dreaded and longed for in equal measure. She'd lost interest in everything she enjoyed and was fractious and argumentative, spending most of her time in her bedroom, staring at the walls. She'd even taken time off work, something she'd never done before. She simply couldn't face sitting in the office all day trying to concentrate on a job she didn't like very much. And she knew that if Tom even looked at her, she'd probably kill him. Every time the doorbell rang, she raced to the window, only to be disappointed. *Might as well face it,* she thought, *she's not coming back.*

Charles found himself in the difficult position of wanting to comfort her while feeling secretly relieved that the girl was gone for good. He'd sensed something wrong in her that very first time, and he was certain money had disappeared from his wallet. But it wasn't that; Charles could tell the girl was badly damaged and very dangerous. Penelope was too trusting and despite her streetwise attitude, was anything but. He sighed unhappily, wishing the carefree days would return.

"There's no cheese," Penelope announced, making him jump.

"Okay…" he said carefully. They'd argued more in the past fortnight than they'd ever done, and he was getting tired of it.

"Well I haven't eaten it all!" she exclaimed, knowing she was being a bitch but unable to help it.

"So get some more!" he snapped, in a rare display of temper. He dug into his pocket and threw some coins on the table. "I really don't care, Penelope!" They stared at each other, neither knowing how to heal the breach that had come between them. Charles sighed and said more quietly, "I'm going out for a while, give you a chance to calm down."

"Dad," she said quietly as he pulled on his jacket. He turned and looked at her, his heart breaking at the anguish he saw there. "I… I'm…" Her voice trailed away and her shoulders slumped.

"I know, love," he said gently and kissed her cheek, surprised when she didn't turn away. "I'll be back soon."

When he'd gone, Penelope sat at the kitchen table and wept, great heaving sobs of self-pity. She hated herself right now, hated her weakness in missing Amelia so much, but most of all for the way she was treating Charles. Presently her tears ceased, and she felt a little better, resolving to forget about Amelia and get her life back on track. So engrossed was she in her thoughts that at first she didn't hear the faint knocking at the door and was only drawn from her reverie when it became more insistent.

Oh, for goodness' sake, Charles, she thought, thinking he'd probably forgotten his keys again. She smiled for the first time in what felt like ages and opened the door, ready to tease him and get a much-needed hug. Then she gaped, shocked at the sight that met her eyes.

*   *   *   *

After Kamontip's revelation, the twins took to the task of getting the goblin population to safety with enthusiasm. Myla, the mischievous one, surprised everyone with how seriously she carried out her directions and all forgave her when she became a tad bossy, which was often. As for Maisey, she teased her mercilessly but couldn't help feeling impressed at the change in her sister.

Each day they worked long into the night, and when an exhausted Maisey retired to bed at last, still Myla carried on, often until dawn. Their first task was for a small group to go ahead and prepare the hideout, which had been unused for many centuries, not since the Necromancer had threatened. It would be cold and dusty, they would need wood for fires, food and water, beds to lay on, and blankets for warmth.

After this group had set off for the mountains, volunteers were found to assist the parents of young goblins, both in getting them to the hideout and keeping them occupied once they were there. Goblins did not like to be enclosed and, for the children, boredom would be their greatest enemy.

Animals roamed free in the goblin world and were used neither for food nor as beasts of burden, so everything needed would have to be carried. Myla spoke to her childhood friend Pyx and requested he recruit some of the stronger goblins for the task.

There were a hundred other details to be considered and, even when these had been resolved, still they found others, until finally both Maisey and Myla were satisfied they could do no more. Myla slept for a whole day and night, and nobody tried to rouse her; this young goblin, not yet fully grown, had earned the respect of all.

Before the trek began, Kamontip addressed the gathered crowd gravely, informing them of the coming threat and giving words of comfort and hope. Afterward, she praised the two young goblins so effusively they blushed.

"We *will* win this war, won't we?" Maisey asked shyly, unable to hide her worry, and Kamontip hesitated.

"I have done everything in my power to ensure it is so," she said at last.

"But you have the Queen's Wand," objected Myla, "nothing is more powerful than that."

Kamontip sighed; this wasn't a discussion she'd wanted to have. "No, Myla, it is not so," she admitted. "The wand given to the leaders of the witch and wizard council has more power."

The twins were stunned into silence as they felt everything they'd ever been taught shift beneath them. "But," Maisey said at last, "how, why? I mean, how could that be?"

Kamontip shook her head impatiently. "The reasons go far back in time," she explained. "It was gifted to them by the goblins many millennia ago." Her tone suggested she still couldn't quite believe such stupidity.

"I wonder which idiot had *that* idea," remarked Myla, who as usual had no filter. But Kamontip smiled grimly, for she agreed.

"It was controversial then and still is now. I was against it, as were many, but we did not prevail." She gave the twins a piercing look. "I believe our land and our people to be safe," she said, hoping to reassure. "My preparations have been thorough, as have yours," she added, smiling. "But as for the other dimensions, the mortals in particular, I cannot say."

And with that, they had to be content. Mustering their courage, they said their goodbyes, and then the exodus into the mountains began at last.

Chapter 26

Amelia had no idea what direction she was headed, only that she needed to escape, and not until the park was far behind did she slow to a walk. At first, she felt only relief, particularly as there were fewer people around now, but the day was turning cold as evening approached and she wore only a thin tee-shirt. Then it started to rain, and the reality of her situation could no longer be ignored; she had nowhere to go. *Not back to the mansion, certainly.* She shuddered.

At first, the exertion kept her warm, but as the rain became heavy, she was soon soaked to the skin. Several hours later, cold and exhausted, pangs of hunger gnawing at her stomach, she wandered into the garden of a large suburban house, crawled beneath a thick hedge, and lay down.

It was uncomfortable and the ground was hard, but at least she had some protection from the rain. Wide awake, Amelia had time to think. *What happened in the park?* she wondered. *Surely none of that was real?* Her thoughts turned to the girl on the bus. *Why did I want to hurt her?* Suddenly she remembered her wand and delved into her pockets, but it was gone. She felt a tinge of relief and her mind became calmer.

For a long time, the noises of the night kept her awake; the hoot of an owl, a dog barking somewhere, animals scuffling in the hedge nearby, rats probably. But at last, she slipped into a fitful slumber.

She was awakened by the sounds of traffic and, after stretching her cramped limbs, crawled cautiously from the hedge. Her clothes were still damp, and she shivered, but at least it had stopped raining and the sun was shining. She was in a large garden, but the house was nearby and she would have to be careful not to be seen. She glanced around, making sure nobody was about, then walked quickly onto the driveway. But then she stopped and turned to look at it again.

Surely it can't be? She shivered again and this time it was nothing to do with the cold. *How?* A wave of superstitious awe passed through her but, thrusting it aside, she walked quickly to the door of the house and, after a moment's hesitation, knocked. There was no answer, although she could hear arguing from inside. Suddenly she heard heavy steps approaching the door and, scared, she crouched to one side, relieved she had done so when Penelope's father hurried out, got into his car, and drove off. Then, weak with hunger, she sat on the doorstep and knocked again, more insistently this time. She was about to knock for a third time when the door opened.

"Amelia!" Penelope gaped with astonishment at the dirty, bedraggled girl who sat there, forlorn and lost.

"I'm sorry," Amelia said, getting unsteadily to her feet, "for everything. For coming here. I don't know how I..." She stopped, knowing how mad it would sound if she explained how by pure chance, out of all the thousands of houses in London, her feet had brought her to this one.

"It doesn't matter." Tears pricked Penelope's eyes. "I'm sorry too."

"You've nothing to be sorry for—" Amelia started, but Penelope placed her fingers against her lips.

"It doesn't matter. Look, my dad's out, do you want to come inside?"

Amelia nodded and sat in the kitchen while Penelope made coffee.

Watching, unseen and unsuspected, Anarkus saw her enter the mortal girl's house and, more irked than angry, he walked away, already planning his next move.

Coffee made, they sat, both suddenly shy, each with a million questions but not knowing how to ask them.

"I've made a decision!"

Penelope felt her stomach clench. "A decision?" she asked hesitantly. "About what?"

Amelia reached for her hand. "It's nothing bad."

"Okay." Penelope nodded. "Go on."

"I think I want to tell you about me, but first I need to know if you like me." She realised how needy that sounded. "I mean, if you think maybe we have a future." This was all coming out wrong and the urge to leave was suddenly strong. Now she wasn't sure whether she hoped for a yes or no.

Penelope almost shouted, *Yes!* But she forced herself to stop and think. *Do I?* she wondered. *Really?* Amelia was volatile; their time together so far had hardly been straightforward. But she was exciting too, and so beautiful.

"Yes," she said at last, "I do, a lot." She felt butterflies in her stomach. "But we have to trust each other and stop keeping secrets, *both* of us."

Amelia fought her panic at the word trust. "It's why I want to tell you, I'm tired of the lies and deceit. I want to stop feeling so angry." Sensing her inner struggle, Penelope remained silent. "A lot of stuff has happened to me," she began, "since I was a child. It's why I'm like I am, bad-tempered and stuff, I mean."

"Go on," Penelope encouraged, curious now, "I'm listening." She leaned and kissed her cheek. "Take your time."

"That's just it, there isn't time!" Amelia suddenly remembered the approaching war. "Not now."

"Oh, for goodness' sake!" Penelope stood up, annoyed, but Amelia pulled her gently back down.

"I will tell you, I want to tell you," she urged, her blue eyes staring into Penelope's, "but something really bad is happening, you have to warn those friends of yours." She hesitated. "The one's inside the lamppost."

Penelope didn't deny it. She couldn't, considering what she'd just said about trust. Ten minutes later, she knew everything and was already in a whirl of near panic. She grabbed her coat and ran to the door, then turned and looked at Amelia, who was still shivering a little in her damp clothes. *I can't just leave her, where will she go?*

"Come on." She took her hand and ran upstairs to her bedroom. "You can wear some of my clothes for now, I'll wash yours later." Hurrying to the bathroom, she ran the water in the tub and threw in a couple of bath bombs. "Have a bath, it'll warm you up."

Amelia's eyes gleamed; she couldn't remember the last time she'd had a real bath, instead of just a tepid shower in the hospital or the hostel. She looked at Penelope gratefully. *She really is magnificent when she takes charge!*

"Oh," Penelope remembered, "Charles may be home soon, you'd best stay up here and keep quiet until I get back." For the first time, she saw how utterly exhausted Amelia was and forced herself to slow down. Tenderly, she brushed a stray lock of lank hair from her forehead and kissed her. "Bath, then get into bed," she ordered softly, "you need sleep."

Grateful, Amelia nodded and sat on the bed, then another swift hug and kiss, and Penelope was gone, the door slamming behind her. She ran the entire way to the lamppost, resting her head against its cold metal for a few moments, panting heavily. Then she took out her wand, said the words, and waited expectantly for the tiny door to open, as it always did. Except this time, it didn't. Puzzled, she repeated the words, and again, and half a dozen more times. She bent and tugged at the knob of the tiny door but it was stuck fast.

Anarkus grinned and raised his wand, pointing it at her back. Three words would incinerate her on the spot, but after uttering the second, he paused. *No,* he mused, *there's a better way.* He had thought of keeping Amelia as some kind of servant after the mortal race had been exterminated and the other worlds conquered, but the idea no longer appealed. *She will die in the utmost agony,* he decided, *but first I will watch as she kills the mortal girl.* Satisfied, he left Penelope to her struggles and made his way quickly to the portal that would take him to Portia and their army.

Penelope gave one last try with her wand, then, unaware of how her life had hung in the balance, she trudged home, hoping that Charles would return soon. He would know what to do – or so she hoped.

Chapter 27

Portia stood on the edge of the plateau and looked down upon her vast army. Beside her were Anarkus and the four other remaining wizards of the council. The air was filled with the hubbub of men eager to begin the fight; they had waited a long time and they were impatient and fractious. Here and there fights broke out, the outcome usually swift and bloody, and the sounds of cheers and boos punctuated the air.

If Portia was concerned about her army killing each other she didn't show it. Anyway, the fights were useful in counteracting the boredom. But now the time had come at last and she raised her arms for silence; it came almost instantly, none wanting to risk the ire of their powerful leader. Many who'd already done so had paid with their lives.

"Friends," she proclaimed, "I welcome you!" Her next words were drowned in an eruption of cheers and for a few moments she let it continue until her arms raised once more. "Friends, your time has come at last. *Our* time has come!"

"Friends?" whispered Anarkus, sardonically. "Laying it on a bit thick, aren't you?"

"Hush." She nudged him good-humouredly. "Look at the fools, they're lapping it up!" She turned back to her army. "Soon you will be conquerors and there will be much opportunity for killing!"

They roared their approval at that, and this time Portia let it continue until, after many minutes, it eventually subsided.

"And when the war is won, you will receive your reward, every last one of you!" As the cheers rang out again, Anarkus moved closer.

"What will their reward be, exactly?" he murmured, genuinely interested. "Will we keep them as some kind of private army?"

"You're joking, of course." She laughed scornfully. "Do you have any idea how expensive it is to keep and feed an army? No, once they have served their purpose, those who remain will be killed." She gave Anarkus a speculative look. "Perhaps you'd like that task, Anarkus?" He grinned; she knew him so well.

"And what about those four?" He gave an imperceptible nod to the other wizards. "What's the plan for them?"

Portia gave him a hard stare, wondering how much he suspected. "One does not waste talent," she lied. He nodded, not believing her for an instant.

Chapter 28

Inside the Sanctuary, Cissy was asleep in her prison. Today had been a good day and she'd recognised Molly; they'd even laughed about the old days when the girl had first come to the Sanctuary. But then the cloak of suspicion had descended once more, and she had become hostile. Molly had quickly waved a sleeping spell over her, and she'd collapsed onto the bed, suddenly exhausted.

When she slept, Lucy entered the room and, under Molly's watchful eye, she brushed her daughter's hair, fussed around her a little, then sat on the bed, holding her hand. After a few minutes, she kissed Cissy's forehead tenderly before whispering, *sweet dreams,* and leaving the room. It was a ritual she performed every night.

As always, Molly asked Lucy to join her in the lounge, but predictably she declined, preferring as usual to be alone in her room. Luke and Wallace had both gone to bed; it was already well into the early hours of the next morning.

"Always left on my own," she muttered grumpily. "It's bleedin' inconsiderate." Already bored, she turned on the TV and flumped down onto the sofa, suddenly tired. She'd dozed for perhaps an hour then awoke, feeling fuzzy-headed with fatigue. Too tired to face the stairs to her bedroom, she put her legs up on the sofa, put a cushion under her head, and slept.

Dawn was breaking in the mortal world when she sat bolt upright, her senses screaming *danger!* She leaped to her feet, ran to the bottom of the long, winding staircase, and screamed for Wallace and Luke, just as the door from the passage-between-the-worlds exploded. Through the dense cloud of dust, two figures emerged, treading through the rubble; they were followed by dozens of creatures, deformed, horrible beings who surrounded the witch at once.

"Molly!" Portia beamed. "How are you, it's been such a long time!" She turned to Anarkus. "This is Molly... Oh, but you've already met, I forgot!"

Anarkus frowned at the gibe but chose not to comment.

"So," Portia continued, "you can either surrender and return with me to face trial, or you can die now. What do you think?" The offer was made with such sweetness Molly thought she'd misheard.

"Don't be so bleedin' stupid," she retorted. "Face trial for what exactly?"

"Oh, I'm sure I'll think of something!" Portia's laugh tinkled unnaturally around the room just as Luke and Wallace arrived, swords raised. Immediately they were surrounded by more of the unlucky ones.

"Hi, you two," Molly tried for nonchalance. "Apparently I have to go stand trial."

"My dear Molly,"—Portia wagged her finger playfully—"I wouldn't dream of being so selfish." Her voice hardened. "Your friends will be coming too."

"What do you think, boys?" Molly ignored her. "Should we accept her kind offer?"

"You need to ask?" Wallace replied, his face impassive.

"Not really." Molly grinned, trying to sound confident, though she knew the odds of surviving were slim. "Luke?"

"Not a chance," he replied, trying to match her confident tone.

"Good lad." She nodded approvingly and tried to telepath the message that everything would be okay.

"Portiaaaa," Anarkus made his first contribution, sounding bored, "how long will this charade continue? Let's end this."

"I agree." She nodded and looked at Molly. "Will you come quietly?"

In answer, Molly turned as if to address Wallace and Luke, then swivelled and sent a lightning-fast bolt of wand fire at Portia.

It was deflected with ease. And then mayhem ensued.

PART TWO

Chapter 29

"I've come for the potion." Catrin had given no thought to how she would get inside the land of the dead and was astonished at her own temerity. *These are witches, for goodness' sake!* she thought. *Dead ones!* She wondered whether she'd be turned to stone or something for her boldness. But the witch had kind eyes, Catrin decided, though the one who stood close by, an expression of thunder on her face, did not.

Siwaraksa's eyes narrowed slightly, and then she smiled again. "You'd best come inside then."

Catrin found herself in a huge, cave-like room with high, cavernous ceilings and rough stone walls. It was dimly lit with torches and cool after the warmth outside, and she shivered slightly.

"Ah, yes, it is a little cold in here." Siwaraksa led her to the centre of the room where a large brazier was already set with logs. She muttered a few words and flames burst instantly from between them, illuminating the room and quickly filling it with heat. Gratefully, Catrin moved close to the fire. "Now, I will arrange refreshments for you shortly," said the old witch. "We have no need of such things here, but I'm sure we can rustle something up. Have you warmed a little?"

"Yes, thank you." Catrin nodded gratefully.

"Good. But first, you mentioned some kind of potion?"

"How does she know about it?" the other witch barked. "Have you considered she might be a spy?"

"Oh, don't be ridiculous," snapped Siwaraksa, "look at her. I've never seen anyone who looks less like a spy!"

"You can't know that. Our enemies—"

"We don't *have* any enemies, Racine, we're dead already! Now be quiet!" Catrin stared at her; this witch looked anything but dead, sparkling with personality as she did. *And there's a look of mischief in her eyes, but not in a bad way.* Catrin decided she liked Siwaraksa. "Now, my dear, you were saying?"

Catrin cast a nervous glance at Racine. "I was told there is a potion that can cure the evilest of ills."

"I see," said Siwaraksa, noncommittedly. "You were very brave to tread the path of the dead, even braver to succeed in getting to the end."

"I had help," Catrin admitted. "A witch, like you, guided me past the trees." She shuddered involuntarily. "She's waiting outside beyond the river."

"Yes, she has been seen; you were both very closely monitored throughout, but she cannot cross the bridge. And it is true, there is such a potion." She saw the look of relief on Catrin's face and laughed. "Yes, you've come to the right place and, as I said, neither you nor Rosalind were ever in any real danger."

"You know Rosalind?"

"Of course, my dear, Rosalind and I are great friends, or at least we were before I died. Is that how you learned of the potion, from Rosalind? Few have heard of it, you know."

"They should never have been allowed in!" The interruption was loud in the ambiance of the room.

"Racine, please," sighed the witch. "Why don't you organise a snack for our guest?"

"So I'm her servant now, am I?"

"Oh, for goodness' sake," Siwaraksa muttered and rolled her eyes at Catrin, who smothered a smile. "But Racine is right about one thing," the witch continued. "How did you enter the land of the dead? It is not something we encourage. Rosalind is a powerful witch, but not so much she could open the portal, I don't think."

"No, it wasn't her," Catrin admitted, "it was a friend of mine."

"A powerful friend indeed. And who is he?"

"Who said it was a *he?*"

Siwaraksa's eyes twinkled. "Just a guess, dear; of course, it might be a she." Catrin had the strong impression she knew exactly who'd helped her.

"He's called the Landlord. That's not his real name of course, just what everyone calls him."

"And his real name…?"

"He's called Cornelius, and he—"

There was a hiss from Racine, and she stepped forward threateningly, glaring at Catrin. "You'd do well not to mention that name here."

Refusing to show her fear, Catrin stood her ground. "I was asked a question and I answered it. Do you have a problem with that?"

Siwaraksa clapped delightedly. "You can't deny it, Racine, she's quite right!" She looked at Catrin with respect. "You have courage."

Not really, Catrin thought, *that old witch scares me.* But she nodded, wondering why Racine had reacted like that. How could anyone not like the Landlord?

"Their rift goes back many centuries," said Siwaraksa, reading her thoughts. "But I'm surprised Cornelius sent you to get the potion in his stead. It is most unlike him to lack the courage to come himself. Who does he want it for?"

"Oh, it's not him who wants it, it's me; I need it to cure my friend Cissy. And he did offer to get it for me." She stopped, suddenly uncertain. "It will cure her, won't it?"

"Undoubtedly, *if* you can reach it." From behind, Racine snorted, derisively. Siwaraksa nodded. "Racine makes a valid point with her snorting." She smirked. "The path to the potion isn't an impossible one, but neither do we make it easy. Not everyone can succeed; it takes courage and resourcefulness."

Catrin nodded. "So when can I start?"

"Immediately, I should think. Perhaps I should give you a few pointers first."

"It is forbidden!" snarled Racine. "You cannot help her; it is against the law!"

"Ah, yes, I'd quite forgotten." Siwaraksa winked at Catrin. "No doubt I'd be arrested and cast into a dungeon. Although quite who would arrest me is unclear and, anyway, there aren't any dungeons here."

"It is not a matter for mirth!"

"Nothing ever is for you, Racine," she muttered softly, then louder, "Alright, alright!" She looked coldly at the witch. "No pointers, just a little advice, perhaps."

Racine stormed from the room, complaining loudly.

Chapter 30

Catrin heaved a sigh of relief when she'd gone. "What is it with her?" she asked. "Why is she so angry?"

"I suspect Racine was born angry," she said, but she didn't elaborate. "And I've no doubt that even now she is setting traps to ensure you fail in your quest. I will do what I can to find them all, but you should be always on your guard. Racine will not care if harm befalls you." *In fact, she may be counting on it.* For the thousandth time, she wondered what had made the witch so embittered and twisted; she suspected it had always been so.

"Thank you." Catrin felt nerves fluttering in her stomach at the thought of the traps Racine might even now be creating. "You seem keen for me to succeed."

"Oh, I'm completely impartial,"—Siwaraksa smiled—"but what was done to the leader of the Sanctuary was wrong. Let's just say I wish you every success." *I suspect the survival of the mortals depends on it.*

"What's upset her now?" a voice interrupted and Catrin turned to see a woman rapidly approaching them. "Racine I mean."

"Mitra!" A smile broke over Siwaraksa's face. "You're just in time to meet Catrin."

"Ah! The girl with the audacity to invade our world!"

Catrin stared, momentarily lost for words; Mitra was the most beautiful woman she'd ever seen. Where Siwaraksa's eyes twinkled with merriment, Mitra's simply danced with kindness and humour. And with her perfect features and lovely long hair that shimmered to her waist, Catrin was entranced.

Aware of the lengthening silence, she stammered, "Yes, I guess so."

"Well, you are very welcome." Mitra hugged her. "And hopefully you will succeed in getting the potion for Cissy. I've met that girl and I like her. She certainly didn't deserve the fate that has befallen her."

"I was saying the same, Mitra. Anyway, I'm sure Catrin will manage somehow."

"And I'm sure you've been giving her a few clues." Mitra laughed.

"Ah, that is the cause of Racine's anger. Anyway, not too many, just a little advice. There are rules, after all."

Mitra laughed. "And when did rules ever concern you!"

"I know," Siwaraksa acknowledged, "but we do need to be careful. Finding the potion is meant to be a trial. If we make it too easy for Catrin, it will not be as effective in curing Cissy."

"That's true." Mitra became serious. "Just be careful of Racine." She squeezed the girl's arm. "I saw her on one of the narrow ledges, prodding at the stone with her wand. When I asked her what she was doing, she swore at me and stormed off!"

"See?" Siwaraksa said gravely. "Measure every single step, Catrin, for each one may be treacherous." She noticed the worried frown on Catrin's face and turned to Mitra. "Catrin is a friend to Cornelius," she said gently.

"Really?" For the first time, Mitra appeared flustered. "How is he?" she asked eagerly. "Is he looking after himself properly?"

"I think so." Catrin wondered why Mitra was suddenly so animated. "Well, he's Cornelius, he kind of does his own thing."

"Yes, he does!" Mitra grinned, then turned away, momentarily lost in her memories. Presently she said, "I was just talking to Rosalind, beyond the bridge. Can't we invite her in to wait?"

Siwaraksa laughed. "I fear Racine would develop apoplexy if we did so. Don't worry, I've arranged for the weather to be mild tonight; she will be fine."

Mitra nodded. "Well, my dear,"—she smiled at Catrin—"are you ready to begin?"

"Yes, of course." She smiled back, trying to hide her nerves now that the time had come. "Where do I go?"

"Come." The two witches led her to the far corner of the room, which was even larger than Catrin had realised, where three huge banners hung from ceiling to floor.

"Each of these conceals the entrance to a passage," said Siwaraksa. "You must choose wisely; black, white, or purple. Your choice may well determine the success or failure of your mission." She ignored Mitra's sidelong glance of surprise.

Catrin scrutinised the banners uncertainly, having no idea which one to choose. *Is it to do with the colour?* she wondered. *Do I just choose the one I like best?* She touched each one; the material was smooth and cool, but it offered no clues. *Does black mean it's bad; white good?* she wondered. *Or, purple is my favourite colour, perhaps I go that way.*

She glanced at the two witches, but their faces gave no clues, although she swore there was a hint of mirth in Mitra's eyes. Finally, she made up her mind. "That way." She pointed at the purple banner. "I will go that way."

"Then we wish you good luck." Siwaraksa smiled and both witches hugged her, then Catrin moved the purple banner aside and stepped beyond.

Once she had disappeared, Mitra nudged her companion. "What was all that about, the thing with the banners?"

Siwaraksa laughed, a little sheepishly. "Well, I thought we should put on a bit of a show," she admitted. "Now, let's go, we need to find as many of Racine's traps as possible."

Chapter 31

The passage was dim but light enough to see and Catrin stepped cautiously forward, Siwaraksa's whispered words still resounding through her mind. *Remember, suspect treachery always; Racine's cunning knows no bounds. She wants you to fail!*

She'd walked for more than an hour without incident and her steps became more confident. Then she came to a fork in the passage. *I guess this is the first test,* she thought, pondering which way to go. After ten minutes of deliberation, she was no closer to deciding and resorted to the childhood rhyme she and the other children of her village had always used.

Dip, dip, dip, she pointed to each passage in turn, in rhythm with the words, *my blue ship. Sailing on the water like a...* It was then that she noticed a small arrow, scratched into the wall of the right-hand passage. *Was that there a minute ago?* She didn't think it had been. "Oh well,"—she shrugged—"it's either a trap or it isn't."

As she crept forward, there seemed to be nothing dangerous and she let out her breath, not realising she'd been holding it. Soon she came to a door that opened inwards and was met with a gaping hole that seemed to draw her into its inky, black maw. She jumped back quickly, with a small scream, and sank to her knees, gasping and not daring to look again into the dark, rectangular blackness. *I'll go back and try the other passage,* she thought, but just then a torch beyond the door flared into life and she made out a long flight of rough, uneven steps leading down.

Okay then. She took a first tentative step down, then another, wary of missing steps and deep holes. They seemed to go on forever but every now and then another torch lit her way and at last she was confronted by another door. She opened it and, finding no gaping hole to meet her this time, stepped through, only to find herself back in the same huge room she'd first entered with Siwaraksa.

"Really?" she shouted angrily. "That's just ridiculous." The words echoed around the room. "Is that the best you can do?" She half expected Racine to appear and waited with bated breath, relieved when she didn't. *You won't get rid of me that easily,* she thought, new determination rising within. *This time I'll try the white one.*

She swept aside the banner and headed into a passage that stretched into the distance, much like the first one. In fact, it looked the same and she wasn't so surprised when she once again came to the fork. The arrow had switched to the left-hand passage and she decided to call Racine's bluff, if indeed this was the witch's doing, and take the same right-hand fork. Still walking cautiously, she expected to come face to face with another creepy door, but instead became gradually aware of a roaring sound that got louder as she went on. *Water,* she surmised, *it's running water.* Then the passage opened out into a large cave, and a deafening cacophony of noise.

Its ceiling was somewhere far above and shrouded in shadow, but an unseen light source, which looked suspiciously like daylight, although goodness knew how, allowed her to shuffle gingerly to the edge of the path and look down. What looked like hundreds of meters below, she found the source of the noise. It was a wide, raging river, so turbulent it foamed into herds of small, white horses that jostled each other as if joined in some strange, magical dance.

As vertigo threatened, she stepped quickly back onto the comforting solidity of the path, grateful it was wide enough to walk upon safely. Suddenly, the whole cave was lit with a soft, golden glow, which quickly became blinding in its intensity. Catrin shielded her eyes and, as if sensing her discomfort, the light dimmed a little and she could see it came from a wand, held by an unfeasibly tall and extremely thin figure. He stood at the edge of the wide chasm that separated them.

"They told me you'd be coming along," he grumbled, in a surprisingly high-pitched voice. "I don't know why I can't be left in peace."

Wrong-footed, Catrin didn't quite know what to say, and she settled for, "Hello, I'm Catrin."

"Doesn't matter who you are," he said curtly, "you're not coming past." He folded his arms and stood facing her, as if to reinforce the point.

"You could at least tell me your name," she snapped, annoyed at his rudeness, and the man bowed deeply.

"Forgive me," he said in a slightly less high-pitched voice, "I'm not used to… people these days. I am called Liias, but you're still—"

"Not coming past," Catrin interrupted, "yeah, I heard you the first time." But now she had a dilemma; how was she going to persuade him? "So, what do I do now?" she asked at last, but the man shrugged.

"You can wait there," he said, "for all eternity, or you could go back. And when you do, tell Siwaraksa I do not appreciate being disturbed."

"No!" she exclaimed, louder than she'd intended. "I've already had to return once; I chose the wrong banner to pass through."

Liias grinned. "Oh, Siwaraksa only does that to be dramatic," he confided. "Doesn't matter which banner you choose; they all lead the same way, to the fork in the passage." Catrin glared at him, cursing her own stupidity.

"Bye then!" And with that, he turned and stomped away into the gloom.

"Wait!" He turned and raised a questioning eyebrow. "I'm not going anywhere."

Infuriatingly, he shrugged again. "Eternity it is then."

"Couldn't you just…" She thought desperately for an excuse to keep him there. "I… I'm frightened." She gestured at the water below. "This path is very narrow." She winced at the lie; the path was at least two meters wide and she was perfectly safe.

"So go back, nobody's stopping you." Catrin cursed and thought again. She remembered how, as a child, she'd been able to twist her grandfather around her little finger. She'd simply think of the time when her favourite puppy had gone missing and tears were sure to follow. Older now, she realised Ffranc had always known he was being manipulated but had let her have her own way.

She almost smiled at the memory but kept her expression neutral. "I c… can't." She was pleased with the catch in her throat and thought of the puppy. Sure enough, tears came instantly to her eyes.

"Well, it looks like you're stuck then." But he sounded less certain, and, sensing he was wavering, Catrin felt a surge of triumph.

"It looks wider where you are," she said. "Couldn't I…?" She let the question hang.

"For someone supposedly brave enough to try for the potion," he grumbled, "you're rather timid."

So he knows why I'm here then. Catrin didn't reply, letting the silence draw out until he sighed.

"Alright, but this is as far as you come."

We'll see about that. She smiled sweetly at him. "You're very, *very* kind," she gushed. "I'm so grateful." For a moment she wondered if she had overdone it, but then he raised his wand, and a narrow bridge formed across the chasm.

And it *was* narrow; she looked at it doubtfully.

"Trust me,"—he'd seen her hesitation—"I won't let you fall."

And curiously, Catrin did trust him. Behind his grumbles and frowns, she sensed no threat from this wizard. Before he could change his mind, she had skipped across, smiling broadly, a smile so infectious that for a moment, Liias forgot to be grumpy, and smiled back. He led her further into the cave, where the sounds of the river became muted and they could talk comfortably.

"Coffee?"

Catrin's mouth watered; coffee was something she only ever drank on the rare occasions she visited the Sanctuary. While Liias conjured up a coffee pot and cups from nowhere, he chatted idly.

"So, tell me who you want the potion for. Not that you'll reach it," he reminded her.

"For my friend Cissy, the leader of the Sanctuary."

He looked at her in surprise. "Morgan isn't the leader still?"

"No, he lives with Aeryn now, you know, the warrior queen?"

"My, my,"—he shook his head, bemused—"things have certainly changed since I was a member of the council."

"You were?" It was Catrin's turn to be surprised. "How come you left?"

"I didn't leave," he said drily, "I died."

There seemed to be nothing to say after that, and there was silence. Presently, she dozed. When she awoke, Liias had gone, but she saw he'd lit a small fire. She was touched by his thoughtfulness and wondered if he would return. She stood and wandered up the passage, hoping she could sneak past him, only to be met with a solid stone wall. Frustrated, she went back and amused herself by staring down over the chasm at the water below.

"I thought you were frightened."

Catrin jumped, startled.

"I'm getting over it," she remarked, embarrassed. Liias smiled but said nothing. "I'm hungry." Suddenly it felt like ages since she'd eaten and her stomach was protesting.

"You could just return. I'm sure Siwaraksa will feed you. I don't keep any food here. The dead don't tend to need it."

"I can't. And why are you so anxious to stop me from getting the potion anyway?"

"Well, because… because." He paused, unable to think of a reason that would satisfy her. "Because it's the rules, I suppose." Catrin snorted derisively and he flushed. "Tell me more about your friend," he said, changing the subject. "What happened to her?"

She told him the story of the attack on the Sanctuary, when Cissy had been wounded and made insane. He was only half listening, still wondering how he could persuade her to go back and leave him in peace. But suddenly a word penetrated and he stared at her.

"What was that name again?"

"Er… Molly?"

"No,"—he gestured impatiently—"I know Molly, we are old friends. The other one, the wizard."

"Oh, it was Anarkus."

It was a long time since Liias had heard that name, or thought of him, but now the memories of that day came flooding back; the day he'd been murdered.

Sensing he was troubled, Catrin asked hesitantly, "Do you know him?"

Liias nodded but made no reply, still lost in the awfulness of that day. "I suppose Portia took over as leader?" he asked finally.

Catrin didn't concern herself about things that happened way beyond the scope of her village, but she'd heard of Portia; her grandfather had sometimes remarked how he didn't trust her much. She nodded.

"I voted against her inclusion on the council, you know, but I was overruled." He shook his head sorrowfully. "I never quite trusted her. I wonder how the council has fared in the centuries since I…"

The silence stretched on and they sat side by side next to the fire, grateful for its warmth, for a breeze had sprung from some unknown source and it was getting colder.

"Your friend," he asked, "will she die without the potion?"

Catrin sensed he was wavering, but she told the truth. "I don't think so," she admitted, "rather she will remain insane, probably forever." She felt tears, real this time, spring unbidden into her eyes. "She'll remain a prisoner, locked away for the rest of her life." Again there was a long silence.

"It wasn't right, what Anarkus did to her." The way he spat the name made her wonder. Abruptly, he got to his feet. "Come," he ordered, marching toward the same blank wall she'd found earlier. Without his seeming to do anything, a door appeared before them. "Keep to the right," he advised, "and beware of treacherous paths."

Bewildered at his change of heart, Catrin tried to thank him but he waved her to silence. "Good luck to your friend," he said quietly. "Now go." He pushed her gently through and by the time she could turn, the door had closed.

Chapter 32

The passage she found herself in was low-roofed, sometimes uncomfortably so, and she had to stoop, or even crawl. It forked several times but, taking Liias's advice, she took the right-hand each time until she came to yet another cavernous space. In the centre was a square-shaped iron stairway, rather like those fire escapes mortals have on old buildings. It wound upward, far into the gloom of the cavern.

She counted thirteen steps in each flight, a number considered unlucky by some in her village, although Catrin had no time for such nonsense. At the top, faint in the distance, she could see a closed door.

But now she had a dilemma, for at the far side of the cavern she could see an open doorway, lit with a soft, welcoming glow. *Which way should she choose?* Using the logic that one door was open and the other wasn't, she chose to ignore the steps for now. *Or was that what she was supposed to think, drawing her into a trap?* She quickly dismissed the thought; there was only one way to find out.

This time there were no narrow ledges, no roiling river, just a flat expanse of stone that could be walked upon easily. Yet it seemed too easy and Catrin was mindful of the warnings to be on her guard. *Should I have chosen the steps instead?* She took a tentative step forward, then another until, relieved, she saw the door was close.

Unable to resist running the last few meters, Catrin was about to reach the welcoming light when the door slammed in her face. She whirled round frantically. It had been a trap after all, and she was about to run back across the expanse of stone when it simply melted before her eyes. Confronting her was a lake of molten stone and, teetering on the edge, she only just managed to regain her balance. The heat was tremendous and she was instantly drenched with sweat, her face feeling like it would melt.

She looked down and saw the thin strip of stone on which she stood, all that separated her from certain death. And it was becoming noticeably narrower with each second. *It's just a test,* she told herself over and over, *it's not real, it's just a test.* But it felt real and the ledge was definitely getting narrower. She looked behind in the vain hope that the door had somehow opened again, but of course it had not.

"Help!" she screamed, unable to comprehend it could all end like this. "Help!" The heat sapped her energy and dried her throat. When she tried to shout again, it came out as a weak croak. But the first two cries had been enough.

Siwaraksa and Mitra had searched and found many of the snares Racine had set, but neither dreamed she would do something to put the girl's life in danger. It was Mitra who first heard the screams and she shouted for Siwaraksa. Following the sound, they burst onto a small balcony high up near the ceiling of the cavern, appalled at what they saw.

"Quickly!" gasped Mitra, and together they directed their wands upward. There were several loud claps of thunder and a torrential downpour began. As the rain hit the molten rock, there was a deafening hissing sound and the cavern filled with steam, so thick that neither witch could tell whether they'd managed to save the girl or not.

Mitra had never seen her friend so angry. Even when the steam cleared and they saw Catrin sitting, distraught but safe, Siwaraksa had no time for relief, only a cold, implacable rage. "Come on," she said quietly, "let's find Racine."

Catrin sat for a long time, shaking uncontrollably, not understanding what had just happened or how she had survived. She could only imagine it was a vile trick Racine had played, and that she'd not intended to actually kill her. When she had recovered enough to stand, she looked across the floor of the cavern. Whereas before it had been smooth stone, now it was a sculpture of ripples and waves, trapped by the freezing cold rain that had suddenly appeared. With trepidation, she again set off walking, but there were no more dramas and she quickly reached the other side where, suddenly weak and ravenously hungry, she lay on the ground and closed her eyes, feeling thoroughly miserable.

She didn't sleep, but after a while she felt better and sat up, still hungry, and as if to torture her further, she was sure she could smell food. Despite knowing it was an illusion, she looked around hopefully, and to her surprise saw a large bowl of soup, bread, and a jug of water. Next to it was a note, and she smiled when she read it: *my special homemade recipe, enjoy! Good luck, L.*

The meal cheered her up and she felt ready to tackle the staircase, wondering what surprises that would bring. She climbed the first flight slowly, and the second, then gaining confidence, ran up the next few. Looking over the railing, she saw she was already quite far up, but still with a long way to go. When she turned the next corner, she had a shock.

What? She was back at the foot of the stairs, right back where she'd started. She tried again and again, five times in total. Sometimes she got further, once so far she almost thought she'd made it, other times not as far.

This is ridiculous! she thought, and slammed the palm of her hand against the underside of the steps in frustration. To her amazement, it stuck fast, requiring a firm tug to free it. She tried again, this time with both hands, and the same thing happened. Experimentally, she swung one leg up, then the other until she hung suspended, like a spider on a ceiling.

I wonder, she thought, *is this how…?* It was slow work at first, and tiring as she moved slowly up the first flight, and it required some dexterity to wriggle her way onto the next. But she soon got into a rhythm and an hour later, with many stops to rest, she found herself near the top.

This had better not go wrong now, she thought, *or I'll scream. And fall a long way,* she added, trying not to look down. *But what about the door?* No sooner had she thought it than a mirror image of the door above the steps appeared behind her. Carefully freeing one hand, she reached down and twisted the knob. The door swung open, and it took only a little agile dexterity before she was standing at last in the room beyond, panting heavily.

The room was dark and Catrin moved forward hesitantly. Suddenly, a dim light appeared in one corner and she could vaguely make out the shape of someone sitting, waiting.

Chapter 33

"I see you got this far," a voice came from the gloom, mocking her. "I suppose I should congratulate you."

"I was nearly killed back there!" Catrin shouted, shuddering at how close she had been to falling into the molten lake.

"Yesss," Racine drew out the word, "so unlucky. I'll try harder next time!" She cackled madly, pleased at her own joke.

"Why don't you like me?"

"Well now,"—Racine appeared nonplussed by the question—"I don't know. Except that I've never really liked anyone."

"You won't stop me, you know," Catrin replied defiantly. "And anyway, Siwaraksa and Mitra won't be pleased with what you're doing. They'll stop you if you try anything else."

"They have to find me first." She laughed. "And so far they're doing a terrible job. So easy to evade; they're so noisy!"

"I don't know why they don't rid themselves of you," Catrin snapped back. "You're so… so… evil!"

Racine laughed. "I certainly do my best to be. I'm having more fun with you than I've had in years. As for getting rid of me, Siwaraksa won't do it, she's too noble." She made the last word sound like a curse.

"Do they know you dislike them so much?"

"Dislike? Oh, I don't dislike them, I hate them! But no, Siwaraksa thinks everyone loves her, which they probably do. As for Mitra, so cute and pretty, so in love with that wizard you call Landlord. It's pathetic!"

Mitra in love with Cornelius? Catrin thought. *How can that be?*

But before she could respond, another voice spoke quietly. "I never suspected you hated us so much." That wasn't strictly true; Mitra had always known.

"Yes, Mitra, it comes as quite a shock, doesn't it?" It was said with heavy sarcasm, and as Siwaraksa entered the light, Catrin saw her eyes were chips of granite.

"Well now," Racine boomed heartily, "welcome to the party. Your little friend and I were just discussing how well she's been doing." But behind the bravado, Racine sounded uncertain.

"You're coming with us." Siwaraksa's tone was implacable, brooking no argument. Racine knew it but still tried for the last word.

"I surrender!" She cackled. "Do with me as you will." She turned to Catrin and sneered. "Just watch out for all the other traps I've laid." As she was escorted from the room, her arm in Siwaraksa's painful grip, Mitra followed, but not before she gave Catrin a quick hug and a hurried whisper.

"Go through that door there." She pointed. "Be careful, and good luck." Before she could respond, they were gone, and Catrin stared after them, bewildered. Then, suddenly exhausted, she sat in the chair recently vacated by Racine and slept for the next few hours.

Still held by Siwaraksa's pincer-like grip, Racine was thrust into her room, none too gently, and the door slammed shut and locked. There, despite her curses and cries to be let out, she spent the night, keeping up a constant stream of insults and threats, so loud that Siwaraksa and Mitra had to use earplugs to drown out the sound.

Consequently, they had a good night's sleep. Racine did not, and when they returned the next day, deliberately waiting until the evening, she was furious. "You can't do this," she snarled, "it's against all precedent for a witch to imprison another!"

Mitra stared at her, incredulous. "Precedent? You dare to talk about *precedent?*" The memory of her incarceration at Racine's hand, though many centuries ago, was still fresh. She still felt sick whenever she thought of how close she and Cornelius had been to death.

"That was different!" snapped Racine. "You had no right to bring that wizard into our midst!"

"Enough," said Siwaraksa quietly, "you are not being imprisoned, but we will be keeping a close eye on you from now on. Now, where are your other traps, Racine?"

"What traps?" Her face was a picture of innocence.

"Don't play your games with me—"

"Oh relax, Siwaraksa," Racine interrupted, rolling her eyes, "there are no other traps, I didn't have time."

If the two witches hadn't known her so well, they would have sworn Racine was telling the truth, so convincing was she. As it was, they knew she was lying. They spent the rest of that evening and well into the night cajoling, threatening, and pleading, but Racine refused to speak. At last, frustrated, they gave up.

The next morning, they made one last attempt, but Racine was either asleep or, more probably, pretending to be.

"What do we do now?" asked Mitra as they left her room. "She's too slippery to be trusted."

"I know," Siwaraksa muttered, thinking. "The best thing is if I watch her, while you follow Catrin and keep her safe."

"It's not much of a plan," Mitra complained, and her friend frowned slightly, knowing it was true.

"Well, if you've a better one, let's hear—"

It was then they heard the scream.

Chapter 34

Catrin's dreams were filled with visions of her climbing an endless staircase, chased by an old hag who cackled with glee as she drew ever closer. Of reaching the safety of the clouds, just as the old hag's fingers were about to grasp hold, only for the clouds to transform into a downpour of hot tears that burned her skin and splashed to the ground, setting it aflame.

Her tears were still falling when she awoke feeling stiff and cold. She looked around, fearfully before remembering that Racine was no longer there. She stood and stretched her aching limbs, then opened the door indicated by Mitra. She stepped through, expecting yet another dreary stone passage. Instead, she was met with something so unexpected, so out of place, she could only stare in wonder.

It was a garden, beautiful, astoundingly so. She was in a huge, diamond-shaped arena, roofed with glass and filled with a vast array of trees, shrubs, plants, and flowers that filled every centimetre of the room with colour and doused the air with a sweet, heady aroma. Through its ceiling, the sun shone hotly, causing beads of sweat to form on Catrin's forehead, and billions of dust motes danced in the shimmering air above her head.

But her amazement didn't end there as, for the first time, she saw other people in the land of shades. *Dead people,* she reminded herself, all of them engaged in some task or other, each lovingly tending this oasis of paradise.

She wandered slowly through the garden's narrow paths, brushing her fingertips against a flower here, a leaf there, gradually aware of the musical sounds of water trickling somewhere close by. Some of the flowers and trees she recognised – the land of her village was a lush, vibrant place – but many she did not, and she wondered where they had come from. Rounding a bend, she came across a witch standing on a stool with her head burrowed inside a large bush, pruning scissors in her hand.

"Hello," she said, and the witch jumped and turned.

"Ah, you must be the girl who seeks the potion." She was pretty and very young, and Catrin wondered what had caused her life to be so short. "Welcome to our garden." She smiled. "Do you like it?"

"Yes," Catrin said, smiling back, liking the witch instantly, "it's…"

"Unexpected?" The witch laughed.

"Well, yes! It's certainly that. Such life in a place that's so…"

"So dead," the witch finished. "We can thank Mitra for that, this was her dream. It used to be a stark, barren place, but now there are flowers and plants from all the dimensions and it is a sanctuary of calm for any who wish to use it." She jumped from the stool and stood aside as an older wizard passed by and nodded politely to them both. "My name is Eloise,"—she gave a slight bow—"and you are Catrin, I believe?"

Introductions finished, Catrin had many questions, bombarding Eloise until she held up her hands in mock surrender. Taking Catrin's hand, she led her further into the garden until they came to a clearing where many more people were gathered. All were wizards or witches; seemingly that was the case for the whole of the land of shades. Some looked no older than Catrin herself, although, of course, they were, while others had ancient, lined faces, testament to a life of many thousands of years.

They were effusive in their welcome and for the first time since entering the land of shades, Catrin felt her cares fall away and she was able to relax. She ate, drank, and chatted, answering their questions and asking many of her own. But the sun slid across and then beyond the glass roof and evening shadows began to form. People started to drift away, and Eloise stirred and stood.

"It is time for us to end our labours for the day,"—she smiled sadly—"and for you to continue your journey." Together they walked through the garden until the trees and flowers grew sparse and then stopped. "This garden ends and another begins." She hesitated. "The plants here are different, not so benign." She stopped, unsure how much she should say. "It is a place of peril," she whispered at last.

"Thank you." Catrin hugged her. "I'll be fine from here." But secretly she felt terribly lonely and wished Eloise was coming with her. She strode forward with a show of confidence she didn't feel and, with a brief wave, disappeared out of sight into a dark, grey world. Here, there was no colour, only grey, and the plants, of which there was an abundance, seemed to watch her menacingly as she passed.

What a contrast, she thought, as a tall plant with wicked, ugly thorns leaned toward her, and she gave it a wide berth. *I don't think these plants welcome strangers.* As if to confirm her suspicions, a vine as thick as her arm shot out from the undergrowth, grabbed her ankle, and sent her crashing to the ground. She jumped quickly back to her feet, but the vine was already slithering away.

So that's how it's going to be, is it? she thought as she continued warily along the path. *Well, do your worst!* As if accepting the challenge, there were loud hissing sounds from within the undergrowth and the atmosphere around her became heavy with malevolence. Suddenly her way was blocked by dense, nettle-like plants that crowded the path in front. She had no choice but to try and get through, but as she did so, as carefully as she could, she felt their painful stings jabbing at her, piercing her clothing and leaving large, painful welts across much of her body.

Sobbing with the pain, she forced her way forward as quickly as she could but, whether by chance or design, the ground was slimy and slick, and she slipped. At once the nettles crowded closer, jabbing, prodding, poking, and the hissing became louder, mocking her. For long moments she remained still, crouched down with her hands wrapped around her head, trying to protect her face and eyes. She tried to shuffle forward on her knees, unable for the moment to stand, and as she did so her hand fell upon a short, thick piece of broken branch. She grasped it, gathered her courage, then reared to her feet.

"I…"—she swung the branch in a wide arc through the nettles, scattering their poison-tipped leaves everywhere—"will not…"—she swung the other way, destroying more of the malicious plants—"let you…"—now they were disappearing into the undergrowth and the path was clear—"stop me!" Panting with exertion, she rested a few moments but, knowing the next attack would not be long in coming, she continued walking, even more quickly now, her weapon held defiantly in front.

Catrin had been right, and the next peril was soon upon her in the shape of a copse of trees, poor stunted things with long, spindly branches that clawed at her as she passed. But in comparison to the nettles, these were easy to fend off and a few well-timed blows soon discouraged them. Until, that is, they were joined by a multitude of tall flowers, much like sunflowers except their heads had eyes and mouths with sharp, jagged teeth. Immediately they began snapping at her, the noise of their teeth clacking together very loud. The trees took courage and renewed their attack and to her dismay she could see the nettles regrouping, ready to pounce.

Dismay turned suddenly to rage and Catrin, no longer frightened, just thoroughly, utterly sick of the whole thing, went on the offensive. Whirling, she decapitated the first sunflower, then another and another, then when they retreated, went after the trees, who simply gave up the fight and melted away into the gloom. Warily now, her attackers kept a distance and when she feinted to attack, reared back hurriedly. Then one of the flowers, much taller than the rest and perhaps their leader, darted forward, its wicked teeth centimetres from biting off her nose had she not reacted quickly. Encouraged, the nettles swarmed around her, stinging viciously, but she hardly felt them, such was her anger. Like a dancer, she stepped back to give herself room and decapitated the flower, along with a good number of nettles.

And that was it, she'd done enough. Her attackers gave up the fight and simply melted away, hoping perhaps for easier prey another day. Elated, adrenaline surging through her veins,

Catrin gave a loud whoop of joy. "Bet you regret doing that!" she screamed triumphantly. "Not as easy as you thought, was it?"

It was a mistake. Perhaps if she'd kept quiet, this sinister garden would have accepted its defeat. The first creeper came slithering quickly toward her, then a second. Five, ten, a hundred; in no time it was a multitude and Catrin turned and ran. Fast as she was, the vines were faster and gaining rapidly; being caught, she suspected, was not an option. She didn't know if their intent was to harm, even kill her, or merely to frighten, and she didn't fancy finding out. But they were gaining rapidly now, approaching from each side and, when she saw more of them ahead, her heart sank and she slowed to a walk.

Trapped in a circle of wriggling, writhing creepers that were moving slowly closer, Catrin waited, tensed and ready. They hadn't attacked yet, toying with her, making sure she knew the fate that awaited, savouring their victory, enjoying her fear even more. Catrin knew she was in big trouble yet still she held her weapon, ready to fight, determined not to accept defeat easily. At last, telepathically, the creepers reared up in unison, rearing back like cobras ready to strike.

"Get on with it," Catrin muttered, just as a bright pinpoint of light pierced the room and she heard words, loud and in a language she didn't understand. Shrinking back in terror, her adversaries forgot about her and fled, leaving the ground around her clear and uncluttered.

Chapter 35

"Eloise!" Catrin gasped as the welcome sight of the witch approached. "How did you know I needed help?"

The young witch smiled at the understatement. "I've been watching your progress. You showed great courage, my dear." But she frowned at the ugly wounds on Catrin's face and arms. "You are hurt, come with me."

Suddenly, shock overcame Catrin, and to her shame she found herself shaking and quite unable to move. Eloise took her in her arms and held her gently, kissing her forehead.

"It will pass," she soothed, "hush, my dear, you have undergone a great ordeal. Relax now and come with me." Whether it was the soothing words or the calming spell that Eloise muttered softly, soon Catrin felt better and allowed the witch to lead her, at last, from that dreary, horrible place.

"Would those things really have killed me?"

Eloise pondered the question. "They're certainly not designed to kill," she said, "merely to frighten and sting a little. But,"—she looked at Catrin's ravaged face—"the ferocity of their attack, the wounds they inflicted…"

"Yes?" Catrin asked, wondering.

"I detect Racine's interference in this." She was reluctant to frighten the girl further. "But I find it hard to believe even she would wish you dead."

Catrin wasn't so sure about that and there was silence between them. Soon they entered a small cavern, its walls richly decorated with colour, a small pool of water at its centre. "Bathe here," Eloise said gently, "the water will heal your hurts." Then, seeing Catrin's look of doubt and sensing she was shy, added, "I will leave you for now."

When she had gone, Catrin removed her clothes and stepped into the pool. It was cool, but not unbearably so, and oh! The sensation! Immediately she felt the stinging of her wounds ease and, to her amazement, watched them slowly fade and disappear. She allowed herself to submerge, immersing herself fully, and when she returned to the surface, spluttering, she felt exhilarated and energised.

When she finally left the pool, she saw a table, lit by a lamp, and on it a towel and her clothes, which had somehow been freshly laundered. She wrapped the towel around her, luxuriating in its warmth and softness, then, feeling suddenly ravenous, she dressed quickly. She'd just finished when Eloise reappeared and led her to a small room with a table set with food and drink.

"Will you get into trouble for helping me?" Catrin asked, taking a bite from a large, juicy peach, something she'd never eaten before. "I'm supposed to manage the quest without help."

Eloise shrugged dismissively. "I shouldn't think so, we all want you to succeed and help your friend. Well," she admitted, "all except Racine." The dislike in her voice was obvious.

"What is it with her? Why does she want me to fail?"

"Ah, now there's a question." Eloise sighed heavily. "Jealousy? A hatred of seeing anyone do good for another? Who knows?"

"But has she always been like that? Was there a time when she was good?"

"Catrin, you ask difficult questions. Honestly, I don't know. All I do know is that she hates Mitra and has done so ever since she, Mitra I mean, escaped her village with Cornelius, despite Racine's best efforts to have them both executed."

"Now that's a story I'd love to hear," said Catrin eagerly, but Eloise shook her head.

"It is a long story; their love goes back many thousands of years. Perhaps you should ask Cornelius about it when next you see him. But I warn you, it is not always a happy one."

"Oh, to have a love such as that." Catrin sighed dreamily, thinking of Gruffydd and suddenly missing him terribly. "I suppose their love ended when Mitra died." Catrin badly wanted to ask how she had died, and Eloise too, for that matter, but knew she could not. Eyeing another peach, she said, "Although Racine did say Mitra was still in love with the Landlord. Sorry, Cornelius, I mean."

"Help yourself." Eloise smiled. "Delicious, aren't they?" Catrin nodded with delight as she bit into the soft, juicy flesh. "Yes, they love each other still. Mitra's death didn't stop it; made it even stronger, perhaps. Apparently – this is all before I was born, you understand – they were inseparable, so attuned it was as if they were one person. But then the blood moon was made…" She stopped, worried she was saying too much.

"Go on," Catrin prompted, but again Eloise shook her head.

"As I said, you should ask Cornelius or Mitra; it is their story to tell, not mine."

"I will." She nodded, wiping juice from her chin. Suddenly her earlier rush of energy dissipated and she yawned widely.

Eloise stood. "Come, it's been a busy day for you. Time you were in bed."

Chapter 36

Catrin had never lain in so soft a bed before; the one she had at home had only a thin mattress and a rough woollen blanket for warmth. But despite its unfamiliarity, she slept soundly, only awakening the next morning at the sound of someone entering her room. It was Eloise carrying a breakfast tray. They chatted while she ate and then, all too soon, it was time for her to continue her journey.

Catrin found herself once more in the grey gloom of another passage. And to make it worse, the ceiling soon lowered again, forcing her to crawl on her knees until they were bruised and sore. Presently she came to another fork with an arrow telling her to go left.

"Oh, just stop it!" she yelled in annoyance. "I know I have to go to the right!" She kept going, ignoring her aching back and the pains shooting through her knees, wondering how much longer her ordeal would last, wishing she'd thought to ask Eloise. She didn't know it, but she was getting very close to the potion now.

After an hour, which to Catrin felt like ten, her movements were automatic and her mind numb with pain and boredom. One hand after another she crawled, one knee forward then the next until suddenly her hand, instead of touching the ground, met with fresh air and she almost tumbled into a wide, yawning chasm. Heart hammering at her narrow escape, she sat against the wall of the passage, gasping. When her heart slowed, she peered into the gloom of yet another huge cavern, but this one was different – it had no floor.

Or rather, it did have a floor, but it looked to be several hundred meters below where she sat. The only way into the cavern was by a narrow ledge that encircled the wall to an even narrower stone path that crossed the centre and led to a door at the other side.

You have got to be kidding, she thought, trying not to look down. *I can't, I just can't.* But what alternative did she have? Go back? Admit she had failed? Condemn Cissy to a life of imprisonment and madness? Cursing to herself repeatedly, which made her feel a little better, she edged out on her hands and knees onto the ledge. *Safer if I crawl,* she thought, but soon found that to be impossible; the ledge was too narrow. Gingerly, she put her weight onto one foot and pushed herself carefully up until she stood, her back hugging the stone wall behind her.

With eyes tightly shut, peeping only occasionally, she inched along the ledge, sliding each foot only a few centimetres at a time, until finally she stood at the narrow bridge that dissected the cavern. Not allowing herself to hesitate, she stepped forward and found it wasn't so bad, so long as she didn't look down. The ledge was perhaps a half meter wide, more than enough if she took her time and went carefully. Sure enough, all went well until she neared the halfway point, relieved that the door was now not far away. But then she saw something that both horrified her and made her go hot with rage.

Catrin stared at the break in the bridge, suspecting this was another of Racine's snares, then laughed derisively. She knew she could clear the gap easily, but still, it was a long way down if she failed, and she hesitated for a long time. She had jumped streams wider than this as a youngster, playing with the other village children. She'd always been able to run faster, climb higher, and jump further than any of the boys, but this was different. It was an awfully long way down.

Stop it, she told the doubts in her mind, *go away.* But they were persistent and remained firmly lodged. She forced a memory into her mind of her and Gruffydd, both younger, daring each other to leap the stream that ran near the foot of their village. It was wide but Catrin had been certain she could clear it and so she did, just. Unfortunately, Gruffydd didn't and had got a soaking that day; she cursed herself for choosing that particular memory.

You're being ridiculous, she scolded herself, *get on with it.* She took a few steps backward, ran, and jumped, sailing easily across the gap. *Made it,* she thought triumphantly as her feet descended swiftly toward the safety of the other side. But suddenly the edges of the gap began to crumble away. It widened with astonishing speed and Catrin was running through the air, legs pedalling frantically as the chasm below sucked at her feet.

She almost got there as she thrust her body forward, hands grasping desperately for the edge. Her fingers clawed through the air, gripping the crumbling stone, and for a wild moment she thought she'd done it, but then it broke away in her fingers and she fell. It was indeed a long way down and her screams rang out with piercing terror for almost a minute until they stopped abruptly as her body hit the ground and she lay lifeless, twisted and broken.

Chapter 37

Siwaraksa and Mitra looked at each other for long seconds, then ran toward the scream, cursing Racine and already fearful of what they would find. Racine followed, grinning; she already knew. She caught up and found the two witches staring, horrified, at Catrin's mangled body.

If Siwaraksa had been angry before, now she was incandescent with rage. "Why Racine? she screamed, on the edge of losing control. "Why!"

"Well, you seemed to enjoy her company so much I thought you might enjoy her being here *permanently!*"

Racine saw the expression on Siwaraksa's face and took a step backward, knowing she'd gone too far and that her existence hung in the balance. What she saw was no longer anger or rage. It was the look of someone who had come to the extremity of their patience and she watched helplessly as Siwaraksa raised her wand.

"No." Mitra spoke very calmly as she stepped between the two witches, shielding Racine.

"What are you doing?" Siwaraksa growled, her voice low and dangerous. "Get out of the way."

"There's no time, not if we are to save the girl."

Siwaraksa's mind cleared and she nodded. "Liias!" Her shout echoed around the land of the dead and, within a minute, the old wizard had appeared. He looked equally horrified at the dreadful scene that confronted him. "Quickly! We need your help!"

"There's no time to move her," he said brusquely, "we must tend to her here." He looked at the anguish on Siwaraksa's face. "She may already be beyond all help."

"No," she said, "she hasn't been dead long; we can do it."

"Help her how, exactly?" Racine risked speaking again. "If she's dead, she's dead."

Mitra turned and faced her, the fury in her face quite out of character. "We will revive her," she snarled, "and you'd better hope we succeed!"

"You can't!" Racine would have been wise to keep quiet. "It's against the law!" The others didn't bother to reply; they were already gathered around Catrin, Siwaraksa at her head, the other two on each side. "I'll report you to the witch and wizard council!"

It was an empty threat and she knew it; the council didn't intervene here; they wouldn't dare. But Siwaraksa, already close to the edge of reason, was incensed. "Be… quiet!" she roared, and with a flick of her wand, she swept Racine high into the air, at the same time forming a huge web, like a spider's, across the gap in the bridge above. Racine crashed into it and hung there, helpless, raining curses down upon them, but quite unable to escape.

"Now," she said, "are we all ready?" They each nodded, just as Eloise appeared and stood, transfixed.

"Eloise!" shouted Siwaraksa. "Hurry, don't just stand there!" The young witch darted forward and placed herself at Catrin's feet. "Good, it will be easier with four of us." Siwaraksa smiled, satisfied. "Now, lift her." The four of them concentrated their wands and slowly Catrin raised a little, her long hair falling and its tips sweeping the ground.

"Do you remember the words?" Mitra fervently hoped she did. Siwaraksa was a famed healer, the best ever, but without the words…

"I can if you let me concentrate," she replied acidly; she too was hoping she could remember and felt a small flutter of panic.

The words were ancient and it was a long time, many thousands of years, since she'd last uttered them. There wasn't much call for them – it was indeed against the law to raise the dead. She needn't have worried; when she delved deep into her memories there they were, clear and fresh.

Taking a deep breath, she spoke them. Nothing happened. She hadn't got the intonation quite right. She tried again, but still nothing. She forced herself to relax. On the third attempt, her spirits rose as she saw a faint glow envelop Catrin's body. She nodded to the others to increase their power and the glow strengthened. It was a delicate balance, too much power and they would incinerate her, too little and they would fail. But Siwaraksa controlled the strength of the spell with minute care so that when Eloise became overexcited and allowed the power of her wand to surge, she doused it slightly and all was well.

Catrin was now completely consumed by the glow, which had changed from a pale yellow to a rich gold. Inside it, although the girl could no longer be seen, they could all sense her broken limbs reforming into their natural state, her damaged organs mending, her skin being cleansed of bruising. The time was fast approaching when Siwaraksa would enact the final portion of the spell, the one that would instil life once more, and she found herself sweating profusely with the strain and responsibility. For these words were a gift given to few and they could be uttered only once; get them wrong and Catrin would remain a corpse, healed and beautiful again, but still a corpse.

Concentrate now, you silly old woman, she told herself as she nodded for the power to be decreased. The golden glow returned to yellow, became fainter, then vanished and Catrin was lowered once again to the ground. Faintly they could still hear Racine's screams and insults, but Siwaraksa would not allow her concentration to be interrupted and it was Mitra who flicked her wand, silencing her. Then Siwaraksa said the final words of the spell. Almost immediately she smiled, knowing she'd got them just right, but still, there was a tense wait until, at last, Catrin's chest heaved upward as she sucked in a long, slow breath.

"I never doubted you for an instant." Mitra nudged her friend and Siwaraksa laughed a little shakily. Liias was already wandering away, back to his solitary existence, and responded with a raised hand to their shouts of thanks. Eloise meanwhile was knelt by the girl, stroking her forehead and smiling through her tears when Catrin's eyelids fluttered open.

Chapter 38

"**D**o you want to continue your quest, my dear?'
Siwaraksa asked. "Nobody would blame you if
you wanted to stop."

It was three days later and Catrin had spent most of it in
bed while Eloise looked after her. Siwaraksa and Mitra had
visited often, and even Liias had come. But the best surprise

was Rosalind, who'd been brought inside and given a place to sleep.

"You've done more than anyone could have asked," Rosalind said now, taking her hand. "We can go home if you want to."

"Of course I want to carry on," exclaimed Catrin, suddenly afraid Siwaraksa wouldn't let her, but the witch nodded.

"Very well," she agreed. "Tomorrow I will show you your path."

But when morning came, Catrin wondered if she was the subject of a monstrous joke. She was stood once more at the edge of the bridge that cut across the cavern and she gave the witch a horrified look.

"I'm sorry," Siwaraksa said, "but the quest dictates that you must cross it. Do not worry, it has been repaired and Racine has been unable to tamper with it. There will be no more tricks from her."

"Are you certain?" Catrin shivered, not entirely from the cool air.

She nodded. "It is but a short way to the potion, but this is the only path."

Seeing it was pointless to argue, Catrin said nothing. Instead, she took a deep breath and, putting her trust entirely in the witch, ran across the bridge, reaching the other side in no time at all. She turned and waved, grinning, then was gone.

Yet another passage, but this one was short and steep. At the top was a door, which she opened and stepped through.

The room was small and bare, with nothing but a table, upon which was set a small glass vial containing a clear liquid, and an ornate silver dagger.

Her insides surged with excitement; she had completed the quest! *I'm coming, Cissy*, she thought. *Just hold on, I'm coming.* Ignoring the dagger, she picked up the vial, hardly able to believe she was holding it at last. She turned to the door, but it slammed shut and no amount of tugging and twisting the doorknob would open it.

"What now?" she groaned. "What more do you want from me!" Catrin placed the vial back onto the table and picked up the knife, with a vague idea of trying to prise the door open somehow. But when she inserted it into the edge, near the catch, it emitted a bright shower of sparks, and she withdrew it hurriedly. Still holding the knife, she picked up the vial and peered into it. *What is your secret?* she wondered, just as the door swung open again.

So the answer to the riddle was clear; she had to take both items, but she was puzzled – why would she need the knife as well? Not stopping to ponder, she hurried from the room before the door could change its mind and was met with two stairways she was certain hadn't been there before. The one on the right led upward, the one on the left down. Seeing as she was so high up, the left one was the obvious choice. She chose the right.

The stairway wound up and up interminably until Catrin was out of breath and her legs ached. She was quickly becoming convinced she'd chosen the wrong way. *Just a few steps more and I'll turn back,* she promised herself, then when she'd done that, *just a few steps more.* But eventually, with no end in sight, she turned, ready to go back down, just as a door materialised beside her. She went through and found herself in the entranceway to the land of shades, Siwaraksa and Mitra grinning broadly.

"You did it!" Mitra cried, as both witches hugged her tightly.

"I know!" Catrin grinned back. "But those steps were horrible, so steep and long!"

"Ah," said Siwaraksa, becoming serious, "it is fortunate you chose them. The other one is infinite and allows no escape. If you'd chosen that way you'd have been lost forever."

Catrin gaped at her, shivering with fright at her narrow escape, until Mitra tutted and waved a finger at her friend. "You do tell such whopping lies!" She shook her head in despair and smiled at Catrin. "Nothing like that would have happened; the other staircase leads here too."

"Thank goodness for that." Catrin sighed with relief, then remembered the knife. "But what about this? I had to bring it too."

There was a long pause until Siwaraksa spoke at last. Catrin thought she sounded a little sheepish. "It is called the Knife of Rai."

"Okay, but why did I have to bring it too?"

Another pause. "Because they go together; they are inseparable, in fact."

"But why!"

Now Siwaraksa looked more than a little embarrassed. "We might, erm… not have been *entirely* accurate in describing the potion as a cure," she admitted.

"What?" exclaimed Catrin. "So what is it? Don't you dare tell me I've done all this for nothing! And what does the knife have to do with anything?"

"Oh, the knife is just a knife, although it is old and very beautiful." She smiled slightly and was lost in her memories for a moment until Mitra cleared her throat and brought her back to the present. "Yes, the Knife of Rai. It belonged to—"

Mitra nudged her. "Stop prevaricating."

Siwaraksa had completely lost her usually calm and cool exterior; Catrin could swear she was blushing. "It is the potion that holds the magic; it's just not a cure, not exactly."

Catrin strove for patience, and Mitra noticed. "You're talking in riddles, Siwaraksa," she admonished her friend, "and Catrin doesn't understand. In simple terms, please."

"I know, I know,"—the old witch was troubled—"but it's not easy to say out loud."

Mitra rolled her eyes. She was the kindest witch you could ever meet, but she wasn't one for pussyfooting around. "What my friend is trying to say," she told Catrin, "is that you must give Cissy the potion, then stab her with the knife."

Catrin stared at her, wondering if she'd heard it right. She smiled nervously, hoping she hadn't.

Siwaraksa shot Mitra a glare and hastened to explain. "The sliver from Anarkus' wand entered her head at the side. Is that correct?" Catrin nodded. "Then that is where the knife must enter. The potion, which you will have already given, will protect her and allow the poison to escape."

Catrin was appalled. "I don't think I can do it," she said at last. "What if I kill her?"

Mitra took her hand and squeezed it kindly. "The potion will protect her; you must put your trust in it."

"But someone else could do it, Molly or Luke, perhaps."

"No!" Siwaraksa spoke more sharply than she'd intended. "No, Catrin," she said again, softly now. "You are the one who removed the potion from its rightful place, you are its keeper."

"If you give it to someone else," Mitra continued, "it will not reveal its magic. It must be you."

Just then, Rosalind appeared. "You will have your friends with you." She comforted the astounded and frightened girl. "We will support you, though it is true; it is you who must wield the knife."

Catrin smiled gratefully at Rosalind and nodded. "So what happens now?"

"Now?" she replied. "Now we leave."

Minutes later, they had crossed the bridge once more and were walking to the forest and, eventually, the Landlord's portal.

PART THREE
DAY ONE

Chapter 39

The ancient inn felt strange and lonely without Oscar, and the Landlord questioned his decision to send the little dog into danger, although he knew Aeryn and Morgan would keep him safe, and Grufydd too, of course. *Perhaps I should have warned Morgan sooner*, he mused. *He's out of practice and no doubt has his head in the clouds.* For the umpteenth time, he looked across the fields to the spot where

Catrin and Rosalind had entered the portal, wondering when they would return. He didn't think it would be long now.

He'd felt too tense earlier that morning to eat breakfast and now it was lunchtime, he felt the same. *And what about the Sanctuary?* he thought, also for the umpteenth time. *Will Molly have sensed trouble is coming?* Making up his mind, he decided she might not and stepped quickly through the barrier to the other portal that would take him to the witch's land and from there to the corridor of dimensions. But no sooner was it opened than he wavered and turned away, allowing it to close again.

Unused to this uncharacteristic indecision, he moped around the inn for a while in frustration. *Should I enter the land of shades?* he dithered. *I could meet them before they step into danger.* But the thought had no sooner entered his mind when he saw movement far away across the fields. First one, then another hideously deformed creature was running toward him. Soon there were dozens, hundreds, thousands.

Astounded at the sheer number of them, and how quickly they had appeared, the Landlord was slow to retreat behind the barrier, and within seconds the first of the unlucky ones were throwing themselves against his defences. Not only were the creatures repulsed, but each one died instantly as it touched the invisible barrier.

Horrified at the number of bodies piling up in front of him, he could only watch helplessly. But the old familiar guilt whenever he took a life resurfaced, and he felt a surge of anger at whoever had caused this. *Who is controlling them?* he wondered. *Not Portia, she'll go to the mortal world.* He was answered immediately by the appearance, still in the distance, of a taller figure, bellowing orders and seeing his creatures dying before him, holding them back so that for a moment it seemed there was an impasse.

The tall figure marched through his army and approached the barrier, before stopping and grinning widely at the Landlord, who recognised him instantly. "It can't be," he breathed. "Suluhura?"

"Cornelius!" Suluhura laughed mockingly. "So good to see you again! How long has it been?" He pretended to think, then snapped his fingers. "Of course! It was when you rescued that idiot, Logan; when you broke the law."

"Really?" the Landlord replied dismissively. "I'd forgotten you were there."

Suluhura's face flushed with anger. "Ha! You mock me now, Cornelius, but let us see who is laughing when my army breaches your pathetic defence and you lay helpless at my feet!" He raised his wand and sent a stream of wand fire toward him.

The Landlord watched impassively as the bolts of power bounced off the barrier. When Suluhura was forced to rest, he smiled sardonically. But the attack was soon resumed with even greater ferocity and all at once a crack appeared, then another and another. There were screams of triumph from the unlucky ones and Suluhura's laughter rang out triumphantly.

If the Landlord was surprised that his defences were crumbling so quickly, he didn't show it. Despite his taunting, he knew Suluhura was a powerful wizard, but as he prepared to step through the barrier and face him, he was still confident of victory, despite the overwhelming odds. But then he took a habitual glance across the fields and, to his horror, his worst fears were realised as the door of the portal appeared and Rosalind stepped out, closely followed by Catrin. Instantly the portal disappeared behind them and they were trapped, as hordes of unlucky ones turned to observe them, surprise and delight spreading across their faces. Then they attacked.

Chapter 40

"C'mon, Cissy!" Molly grabbed her arm and dragged her through the door. As soon as she'd fired at Portia and Anarkus, she'd turned and ran up the wide, main staircase. Luke and Wallace had stayed, their swords flashing in the lamplight until Molly had screamed for them to *get up the bleedin' stairs!* Following, Wallace fended off more of the enemy while Luke raced along the corridor to fetch Lucy.

Bewildered, Cissy looked around, too stunned to resist – this was the first time she'd left her prison in ten years. As they left the room, Molly sent a vicious stream of wand fire that decimated those unlucky ones running up the stairs. As they fell, they impeded the progress of those following. She ducked, holding Cissy close as, from the bottom of the stairs, Portia retaliated. Then, as they all gathered together, she enveloped them in a glamour and hustled them away.

Confused, the unlucky ones milled around, wondering where they'd gone, but Portia and Anarkus could still see them. Only by some miracle did their bolts of power miss, instead destroying the old wooden banister that overlooked the entrance hall and leaving large holes in the wall.

As they entered the training room, Molly remembered something. "Get out through the portal!" she yelled. "There's something I have to do!" She continued down the corridor until it rounded a corner, then waited, trying to still the sounds of her panting, just as Anarkus appeared, closely followed by Portia, and they ran into the training room. When the corridor was clear, Molly ran back the way they'd come, praying nobody would see her as she passed the open door, back down the short stairway and into Morgan's old study.

"Get after them!" Portia roared, as Wallace hustled the others up the narrow stairway of the portal and out into the mortal world. "Anarkus, stop them!" The wizard nodded and he joined the horde of unlucky ones as they barged into each other, trying to get through the narrow portal. Portia turned, uncaring of whether Anarkus was successful or not; she had another task to perform.

Meanwhile, Molly was rifling through the drawers of Morgan's desk, which hadn't been touched since he left.

"I know it's here somewhere," she muttered. "Where did you bleedin' put it, Morgan?" She pulled out another drawer and it crashed to the floor, making her wince at the noise and look fearfully at the doorway. "Morgan!" she growled, sweating profusely now, knowing she had only seconds more to find it. "Did you have to hide it so well? I'm in a tight spot here, you inconsiderate bleedin'…"

At that moment, she found it, lying in full view in the next drawer she tried. Snatching it triumphantly, she shoved it into her pocket and ran out of the room to the top of the main staircase, just as Portia rounded the corner. Bewildered, Portia was slow to react and Molly had reached the bottom by the time she sent a lethal bolt of power. Molly ducked and it hit the wall close to her head. Then she was in the lounge, through the door and racing down the passage-between-the-worlds – *racing* being a relative term in Molly's case, but certainly faster than she'd run in a long time. Soon she entered the circular room and was out, through the lamppost, into the mortal world.

To her surprise, there were only a few unlucky ones there and she realised the narrowness of the portal had slowed them down. She dispatched them with ease and, thankful there was no sign of Anarkus as yet, she spotted the others hiding around a corner, and ran to join them.

Chapter 41

As always, the Landlord was racked with guilt at the deaths he caused, and with anger at Portia, who had made it necessary. His wand flew at a dizzying speed as the unlucky ones fell all around him and so far none were able to get close. As each of the enemy succumbed to his power, he gave a silent, sad apology.

Their wizard leader Suluhura, despite his earlier confidence, kept a safe distance, astounded at the power of his foe, and already planning his escape if things continued to go against him. *Still,* he thought, *he can't keep this up for long, then I will be the one to step in and administer the coup-de-grace.*

But the Landlord wasn't tiring just yet; magic and energy coursed through every fibre of his being as he danced and swirled, edging as quickly as possible toward the spot where, moments ago, the portal into the land of the dead had closed, leaving Rosalind and Catrin surrounded by a snarling, slavering multitude.

I'm not going to make it in time, he thought desperately, as from the corner of his eye he saw Rosalind struggling to keep Catrin safe. He let out a great roar of anger at the thought of anyone trying to harm them, and the fire from his wand intensified even further. The unlucky ones broke in terror and ran.

"Landlord!" cried Catrin, and she flung herself into his arms. "I got the potion!"

"Well done!" He grinned. "I never doubted it for a moment!"

"Maybe save the congratulations for later?" said Rosalind, ever practical. "And get out of this mess first?"

"Yeah, about that," he replied, pointing. Fifty meters away, the unlucky ones had regrouped, spurred on by dire threats from Suluhura, and were already making their way quickly, if a little more cautiously, toward them.

"Oh, this is so tedious!" exclaimed Rosalind, in perhaps the greatest understatement ever. She sent a fizzing bolt of power that obliterated the nearest group, now only a dozen or so meters away. Then the battle was on again, the Landlord and Rosalind standing back-to-back, with Catrin sandwiched in between. It was easier now with the two of them fighting but, despite the ever-growing carpet of dead around them, they could see no diminishing in the endless supply of Portia's victims.

The Landlord knew they had to get Catrin to safety, and quickly, but when he saw the seething profusion of adversaries that stood between them and the sanctuary of the barrier, even his heart quailed. And then the decision was taken from him as the air was rent with the deafening screaming of a whistle. It was an old steam train, resplendent in the sunshine that shone from its gleaming chrome and beautifully painted body, and it seemed to appear from nowhere.

How has he done that without a railway line? the Landlord thought irrelevantly as the enormous cowcatcher on the front mowed through scores of unlucky ones who were too slow in jumping aside. The train slowed and the Conductor's head popped out from the platform of the engine.

"Having a spot of trouble?" he said casually in his deep Southern American drawl. "Looks like y'all could do with some help."

"Yeah," the Landlord agreed, equally casually, "it is getting a little hot out here." He shoved Rosalind and Catrin toward the door that had swung open in the first of the three carriages. "Quickly, get in!" he urged, and they clambered inside as the huge wheels started to turn and the train shunted forward.

"Come on, Cornelius!" yelled Rosalind, frantic that he would miss the train. "Hurry!"

"No!" he shouted back, "I must protect the barrier, I can't risk them breaking through and invading Catrin's village." Seeing the look of horror on the girl's face, he smiled and winked. "Oh, don't worry, they won't!"

"But—" Rosalind wanted to argue, but he shook his head firmly.

"You must go, now! Warn the Sanctuary!" With that, he turned, just in time to destroy the next wave of unlucky ones who had gathered their resolve enough to attack once more. Soon the train was hurtling into the distance, then it vanished, just as abruptly as it had appeared.

"Ridiculous," he muttered, nonchalantly scything off the head of one who managed to get too close. "Whoever heard of a train without tracks?"

Chapter 42

In the days since Oscar and Gruffydd's warning, there had been frantic activity. A call to arms had been sent to their traditional enemy, the Viangg tribe, but though a long period of uneasy peace had existed between the two, none expected a reply.

Many of the town's older inhabitants had been evacuated across the border; there were villages friendly to the queen who would give shelter. With them went the younger children, including Marguerite, and some of the women, though many would stay and help defend the castle.

It was approaching noon when the first of the enemy were sighted by the lookouts. The great horn was sounded and the last of the town's remaining citizens hurried into the castle. The great iron portcullis was raised and out rode Aeryn, Daraproud, and Morgan, followed closely by Dominic who led their tiny army. Many citizens, in anticipation of such an attack, had been trained in archery, and they now lined the battlements, arrows nocked and ready. If the castle defences were breached, many stood ready in the great courtyard, armed with ancient old pikes, spears, rusty swords, shovels, scythes, and anything else they could lay their hands on.

By the time they'd ridden a hundred meters from the castle, thousands of figures, human in appearance but horribly deformed, were nearly upon them. Soon the small force was surrounded and fighting desperately. From their horses, they had an advantage, and the swords of Aeryn and Daraproud, broad and wickedly sharp, cut and sliced and thrust, dismembering limbs and decapitating heads. Nearby, Dominic had formed his army into an impenetrable circle with only just enough room between each horse for the soldiers to use their swords. From the castle, the strongest archers rained a steady torrent of silent death upon the enemy.

As for Morgan, he had never been comfortable in a saddle and when the fighting began, he slid from the back of Aeryn's horse, preferring to fight on foot. Now he sent huge arcs of power, killing a dozen, two dozen at a time. The battle went on for an hour, two hours, three, and so far they'd suffered no losses, while the enemy dead lay in their thousands, strewn far and wide. In the distance they could see somebody, much taller than the rest; presumably their leader. So far he had kept on the periphery, preferring to let his soldiers die, rather than risk his own skin.

But now he was approaching, striding quickly past the unlucky ones. When he was perhaps twenty meters away, a stream of wand power leaped from his wand, destroying ten or more of Dominic's already meagre army. Morgan recognised him at once but his brain struggled to compute what he was seeing. *One of Portia's wizards,* he realised, his mind shying from the implications. *Surely she can't be responsible for this?* The note from Cornelius had been hurried, and he hadn't specified. Gathering his wits, he ran forward.

"Leave him to me!" he yelled and sent a flashing stream of power that staggered the wizard but didn't knock him down. Instead, he recovered his balance and turned to face his foe. They met with a clash of wand fire and the unlucky ones scattered, hastily giving them room.

The wizard was tall and heavily muscled; in a contest of strength, he would have defeated Morgan with ease. But this was a test of magic and in this, few could equal him. Soon he had forced the wizard backward, relentlessly battering him with bolt after bolt of searing hot fire. When he was on his knees, Morgan raised his wand high, preparing to deliver the killing blow.

Chapter 43

"You made it!" Molly hugged Wallace and Luke in an uncharacteristic display of emotion. "You bleedin' made it!" She grinned at Lucy and turned to Cissy, arms outstretched, then stopped. "Cissy?" she said uncertainly, just as the young woman snarled, her eyes glazing over, the confusion gone, replaced by hatred. Quickly, Molly flicked her wand and Cissy slumped, falling as Wallace caught her and lifted her into his arms.

Lucy cried out at the sight of her unconscious daughter and Wallace shushed her urgently. "What's the plan?" He looked round the corner to where more unlucky ones were amassing. Then Anarkus appeared. "Anarkus!" he hissed. "We need a plan, now!"

"Why is it always bleedin' up to me?" Molly complained, then grinned. "I guess we run."

They ran for perhaps a kilometre or so before Molly stopped, red-faced and wheezing; she'd had more exercise today than she'd had in the last decade. "I think we've lost them for now," she gasped, "and I've been thinking." She turned to Lucy. "You need to go home, now before those creatures get organised."

A determined look came over Lucy's face and she opened her mouth to object, but Molly stopped her.

"No, Lucy." She took her hand and squeezed. "We will keep Cissy safe,"—she hoped fervently it was true—"but you must go back to Charles and Penelope, warn them, lock your doors, keep quiet, and don't turn on the lights." Lucy still looked mutinous and she added, "Go, now!"

Knowing it was useless to try and argue, Lucy nodded and, with a last kiss of her daughter's cheek, she was gone.

"Right," Molly said quietly, "that's one problem sorted. Let's go."

"Where to exactly?" Luke asked and received a glare in return.

"I'm still thinking."

"You'd better think quickly." He knew he was skating on thin ice, but his sharp ears had picked up the shouts of the enemy, and they weren't far away.

She stopped and folded her arms. "Alright, smart arse, where do *you* think we should go?"

"Well, I was thinking—"

"Quickly," she interrupted sarcastically.

"That we could go to that friend of yours. I've forgotten her name, but the one in the other dimension. Surely we'd be safe there?"

Molly bit back the stream of sarcastic comments she had lined up and looked at him. Then she hugged him and left a rather wet kiss on his cheek. "Luke, you are a bleedin' genius!" She thought for a moment as he surreptitiously wiped the spit from his face, then led them along a street, in a different direction.

Presently, with the sound of Portia's army getting closer, they entered the alley. A minute later they were through the portal and into the dimension beyond. Ten minutes after that, they entered the secret passage and knocked on Marica's door.

Chapter 44

As the last of her army passed through the portal into the mortal world, led by Anarkus, Portia looked at her surroundings. It was many centuries since she'd last been here, in the days when she'd been considered an ally of the Sanctuary. That was before her boredom and dissatisfaction had set in.

Life is much more exciting now, she thought happily, wondering if Anarkus had caught the old witch, Molly, yet. If so, she hoped he hadn't killed her. *I'll have fun torturing that one.* She wandered from room to room, broken glass and bits of fallen masonry crunching beneath her feet, ruminating on the prospect of killing each of her enemies using the most painful methods she could devise.

Her attack had been perfectly timed to catch Molly unawares, yet she was thankful Morgan was no longer the Sanctuary's leader. She shivered slightly, knowing the outcome might have been very different if he'd been there. Of Cissy she had very little opinion except that apparently she had gained some sort of power recently, and everybody thought she was marvellous. Portia's lip curled scornfully; she'd seen the girl, a gaunt, ruined-looking creature being hustled away to safety, and hadn't been impressed.

That one couldn't possibly be any threat. What were they thinking making her leader? She smiled a thin, rictus smile and thought of the fun she'd have finding this so-called leader and torturing her too. As she relished the scene in her imagination, her eyes shone like deep whirlpools of cruelty.

Pulling herself from her daydream, Portia knew that the mere destruction of the Sanctuary was not enough. The sheer power of the magic here was staggering, and it had to go. If anybody survived her war and managed to return here, leaving magic lying around was asking for trouble. Not that she intended to let anyone survive, but still…

Portia had spent many long years in devising the spell, working with the utmost care, checking and rechecking in preparation for this day. Every word, every syllable must be perfect, the tones and inflections pitched flawlessly. She knew that absolute synergy between the words and her wand was vital, every movement timed exquisitely. The consequences if she misjudged something even slightly didn't bear thinking about but think about it she must. Spoil even a minuscule element of the spell and the Sanctuary's magic would consume her.

Portia owned the most formidable wand in existence, more dominant even than the Queen's Wand. But the Sanctuary was wily and cunning; it would take all her skill and more than a little luck to subdue then destroy it. Standing with her arms lowered, wand held loosely, she closed her eyes and retreated into her mind as she communicated with every nerve fibre in her body, until soon she had reached an elevated state of readiness. Then she began.

She had chosen an ancient language, invented long ago when the witches and wizards had yet to leave their old home before its sun had begun to fail. By doing so she hoped to confuse the Sanctuary, but in this, she was disappointed, although not surprised. It reacted instantly, recognising the first attempts at assault, and Portia found herself flung backward into the wall behind with incredible force, leaving her momentarily stupefied.

She allowed a moment for the darkness in her head to clear, then once again reached within, calming every atom in her body, resisting the temptation to retaliate with violence. Slowly rising to her feet, she spoke again, lower this time, inaudible to any human or animal. Now the Sanctuary could only listen, unable to respond as the words meandered into its psyche with compelling irresistibility.

Suddenly, Portia sensed its vulnerability and felt a surge of excitement that she quickly dampened. *Surely it can't be this easy?* she thought, and of course, it wasn't. Taking advantage of her distraction, the shades of every leader of the Sanctuary since its creation materialised before her, screaming their defiance. All at once she felt a frisson of fear and, laughing gleefully, the shades snatched the wand from her hand and flung it aside. Her fear increased and, for the first time, she considered the very real possibility of defeat.

But Portia was not the leader of the council for nothing. A lesser witch might have panicked, but again she imposed a modicum of serenity, this time reaching beyond the atoms, into the very tiniest molecules. As she fought to drown out the voices that brutalised her mind, a timely reminder found a tiny entrance and entered; *the dead have no power here!*

And it was true; outside the land of the dead, these images could not harm her, and she returned their laughter with such scorn and surety they began to dissolve immediately. Quickly adapting her spell, using a mind that was now razor sharp and free from doubt, she intensified the potency of the words, and again, the Sanctuary could only submit. Yet it rallied once more and for a long time the advantage was exchanged as each sought to dominate and triumph. But the

Sanctuary had one unique disadvantage, the absence of an ally. Had Morgan or Molly been present, Cornelius or Rosalind, the outcome might have been in doubt. But they were not, and it was not.

The magic resisted and fought magnificently, but ever so slowly Portia gained the upper hand. Then suddenly it was over, and a silence descended on the building, for that's what it was now, a building. The Sanctuary was just a collection of stones, wood, and glass, utterly powerless.

Chapter 45

After the majority of the witches decided to take shelter, rather than fight, it had taken another couple of days for Agnes to get them moving. Despite the mortal fiction that describes them having broomsticks, they don't, nor can they fly and she was becoming frantic at the delay. Some wanted to take the entire contents of their households before being asked sarcastically by Agnes how they planned to carry it all into the mountains. But the main problem was that witches were laid back to the point of being horizontal, and most simply didn't see the need for haste. But at last, a long line of them were headed into the mountains, and Agnes heaved a sigh of relief.

Most had already reached the safety of the caves near the summit of a snow-capped mountain when first they sensed the presence of Portia's army entering their land. Agnes hurried the few stragglers along and soon all were safe to watch the enemy begin their ascent.

The mountain paths were icy and treacherous and while they had posed no difficulty for the sure-footed witches, it was not so for the unlucky ones. Crowding together on the narrow paths, pushing past each other in their eagerness to reach their quarry, many hundreds fell to their deaths. Thousands more fell victim to the barrages of wand fire they were subjected to.

Although the older, more traditional witches didn't hold with such modern ideas, many of the younger ones favoured bows as well as wands. From the shelter of their refuge, it was easy to pick off those who did manage to get close. As for the few thousand or so who chose a different route, thinking themselves unobserved, the witches waited until they all clung to the side of the mountain before causing an avalanche that swept them away. It wasn't until his army had been decimated by at least a half, that their leader had them retreat down the mountain to regroup.

Having done her best and got the witches to safety, Agnes felt confident in leaving them, for it was clear the invading army would have no success in climbing the mountain. The witches had food and water enough to last a week and she knew the battle in the mortal world would either be lost or won by then. She gathered the thirty or so that had agreed to accompany her and began the spell that would transport them into the mortal world.

Chapter 46

Charles and Penelope were waiting for something to happen. He'd not been pleased to find Amelia back at the house until Penelope had breathlessly explained all that had happened. Having questioned Amelia in minute detail, he had to acknowledge the courage she'd shown in escaping Anarkus' clutches. Penelope hadn't needed to plead for her to stay; he'd readily agreed.

They'd returned to the lamppost at least a dozen times, only to find the way through still blocked. Charles surmised that Molly had learned of the approaching threat and put up barriers to prevent anyone from entering. Penelope pointed out she wouldn't just simply hide away in there while the mortals were attacked. Whatever was happening, Charles still retained some of the heightened wizard senses he'd been given and now he could sense magic in the air; lots of magic.

He took out his mobile and dialled Peter's number again, then listened as it rang and rang. *Where is he?* Charles thought as he cut the call and tossed the phone onto the table in frustration. Perhaps Luke's father could open the way into the Sanctuary, but so far they couldn't get hold of him.

"Maybe I'll check his house again," he announced and reached for his jacket.

"Dad," said Penelope firmly, "it'll take at least an hour to get across London and back. If he was home, he'd answer his phone."

"I can't understand why he doesn't take it with him when he goes off on holiday," Charles grumbled.

"He'll be at one of his weekend retreats again,"—she smiled—"no phones, no laptops, just a group of odd bods communing with nature and sat in a circle by the campfire, chanting mantras and stuff."

Despite his frustration, Charles smiled back. "So, Peter's an odd bod, is he?"

"I love him to bits, so don't tell him I said so. But you've got to admit —" She was interrupted by the sound of the front door crashing open as Lucy rushed in, panting for breath, panic-stricken and wild-eyed.

"Lucy!" Charles exclaimed, reaching her just as her legs gave way. Penelope rushed to help and together they guided her to an armchair.

"Mum, thank goodness you're safe! What's happening in the Sanctuary? Why can't we get in?"

But Lucy was beginning to hyperventilate, and Penelope hugged her tightly, trying to soothe the trembling body. Gradually Lucy's gasping breaths eased, and she could breathe more normally. But she was still unable to answer their questions, instead staring fixedly forward as shock set in.

"What can we do?" Penelope pleaded; somehow Lucy's silence was even worse to cope with.

"Tea." Charles said after a moment's indecision. "I'll get tea!" And despite herself, Penelope felt a flicker of amusement. Tea, the English solution for any crisis. Yet it seemed to work and as Lucy sipped the hot liquid, her trembling slowed and she began to speak, haltingly at first, then with more urgency. Charles and Penelope listened with mounting horror, their faces grave.

Chapter 47

"Follow me," Marica instructed in hushed tones. There were curious looks from some of the drinkers as she led them through the bar and to a door at the other side. Marica glared around, daring anyone to question what was happening as she opened the door and motioned them up the staircase beyond. At the end of a short corridor was a bedroom and Wallace lay Cissy gently on the bed.

"Now, what is happening?" Marica said in a low voice. "There have been rumours of a great evil befalling the mortal world."

"That's the bleedin' understatement of the century," Molly replied curtly, her anger rising again at the atrocity Portia had committed.

"Who is the girl? Is she ill?"

"We'll tell you everything soon, Marica," said an increasingly irritated Molly, "but first I need to make this room safe."

"Safe? Safe from what?"

"Questions, questions!" she snapped. "Too many bleedin' ques—"

"We thank you for allowing Cissy to stay," Wallace interjected, glaring at Molly, "and we apologise for the intrusion."

Molly had the grace to look a little shame-faced at her bad temper. "Erm, yes, thanks, Marica, this is very kind of you."

There was an awkward silence until Marica winked at Wallace. "She doesn't change, does she? Come on, let's leave her to it." She led the way back down to the bar, where there were more curious looks. "Now, what will you have?" She placed two glasses on the bar and smiled.

Upstairs, Molly was already busy making her warding spells, starting with the window, which would hopefully keep Cissy from escaping the room, all the while keeping an eye on the sleeping girl.

"Not enough bleedin' time," she muttered tensely as her wand flew, jabbing and prodding the air, creating the spell. "I hope it's going to be strong enough." Then she heard a faint giggle and spun around but, fast as she was, Cissy was faster, and she pounced on the witch, knocking her to the ground. Quick as lightning, she threw the door open and leaped out.

To quell the speculation, Marica was just introducing Luke and Wallace as two friends from 'out of town' when she heard the upstairs door slam open. As Cissy, crazed and giggling maniacally, tore down the stairs, Marica reacted instantly. Simultaneously drawing her wand and shouting for everyone to flee, she flung a barrier spell to the bottom of the staircase. It was only powerful enough to stop Cissy for a few seconds, but it was enough for Molly to recover and fire a stream of power into her back.

"Help me!" she shouted, and Marica sent her own fire toward Cissy's chest, but she was only a minor witch and Cissy batted it away contemptuously. Wallace reacted with a speed that belied his aging limbs, scooping an arm around the demented girl and raced back up the stairs. He threw her onto the bed and Molly slammed the door closed then quickly fashioned a locking spell.

Panting heavily, she and Wallace returned downstairs to face the others. There was silence for a while, each of them stunned at what had just occurred until finally, Marica spoke.

"That won't be good for business," she observed wryly, looking at the now empty inn. "Now, I think you have some explaining to do."

Chapter 48

"Where are we going?" Catrin asked excitedly. She'd never been on a train before; in her world, they were yet to be invented, but she was enjoying the immense speed at which they were moving. She and Grufydd had often raced their horses flat out across the Welsh countryside, but they couldn't run anywhere near as fast as this!

"Canary Wharf," the Conductor replied and, lowering a window, stuck his head outside, holding his cap firmly on his head. "We'll be there in no time!" he shouted above the rushing wind, just as a huge cloud of black smoke from the engine's great chimney enveloped him.

"It's not close enough!" Rosalind yelled, trying to outdo the noise of the huge steel wheels clattering over the tracks. "We need to get near the Sanctuary!"

The Conductor closed the window and looked at her, then wiped a smudge of soot from his nose. He nodded. "Well, if you're sure?"

"Yes, yes!" she responded impatiently, before adding, "I mean, please."

"Okay." He grinned happily, his teeth white against his soot-covered skin. "You asked for it."

"You do realise your face is still completely black?" said Catrin, before Rosalind could ask what he meant by that last comment. "Apart from your nose, that is. Your nose is pink."

"No time to worry about that now." He grinned as the train passed from daylight into the electric glare of the station lights. "Any second now…" And no sooner had he uttered the words, than the train veered sharply to the right and entered a dark tunnel.

Rosalind was looking a little sickly and she smiled weakly at Catrin, who grinned back excitedly. "Perhaps Canary Wharf would be okay after all?" she suggested.

"Too late now,"—the Conductor rolled his eyes—"we'll be stopping soon." He winked at Catrin. "Although when I say stopping…"

"Shouldn't we be slowing down then?" asked Rosalind, uncertainly.

"Quite the opposite," he said nonchalantly, and sure enough the train seemed to be hurtling along even faster. "Hold on tight," he warned, "this could get messy!" And the train left the tracks, just as they entered an old, abandoned station. It smashed into the wall, the enormous cow catcher on the front scattering white tiles and bricks in all directions, before it came to a juddering halt. Looking out the window, Rosalind was surprised to see they were in the passage-between-the-worlds.

"Close enough for you?" the Conductor deadpanned.

"Yeah, thanks, I think," Rosalind said, shakily. "That will do nicely." She stared at the devastation. "You've made a bit of a mess."

"I know, Molly will not be pleased," he agreed, "but once I've reversed the train and got out of here, she'll never know it was me."

"Well, thank you," she said as she and Catrin climbed down from the carriage. But the Conductor was already reversing the train and didn't reply. Instead, he tipped his hat slightly, and within seconds the train had disappeared into the gloom and they were alone in the passage.

"That was fun!" Catrin laughed loudly but Rosalind shushed her.

"Quietly now," she cautioned, "there's something wrong." She took Catrin's hand and together they walked toward the Sanctuary entrance. When she saw the door hanging from its hinges, she took out her wand. But when they stepped cautiously inside, the place was empty; all that was left was a ruin.

*   *   *   *

"She can't get out again, right?" Marica looked nervously up the stairs to the door at the top.

"Don't worry,"—Molly smiled grimly—"it's as secure as I can bleedin' make it; Cissy won't get past my spells."

"Good," said Wallace briskly, "that's sorted then. So what do we do about Portia? She's out there in the mortal world and they have no protection."

"We have to help them!" Luke exclaimed.

"I agree." Molly patted his shoulder with approval. "Come on, Wallace, stop messin' about and get your bleedin' sword!"

"And what am I supposed to do while you lot go off saving the world?" Marica said mildly, but none failed to see the steely glint in her eye.

"What do you mean?" Molly said impatiently, only half listening as she waited for Wallace to get himself organised.

"I mean, you come here, bringing a very dangerous girl with you, take over my home, wreck my business, and now you want to leave? What am I supposed to do if she gets out? Just politely die?"

"Marica is right," Wallace agreed, "we can hardly just leave her. Or I should say, you can't leave her."

"Why?" objected Molly. "I told you, the spells are strong, Marica will be quite safe until we return."

"Because Cissy still must eat, which means opening the door. And you're the only one who can do the spells, Molly," he said testily.

"Okay, you two go off and fight and I'll just stay here," she complained. "Leave the woman at home! It's just bleedin' inconsiderate, if not downright sexist!"

"And what other choice is there?" Wallace was annoyed. "Marica can't do it, can she?" He frowned at Molly, and she glared back.

"Oh, stop it, you two!" snapped Luke in a rare display of annoyance, and the others looked at him in surprise.

"I agree," Marica said sternly, "both of you need to calm down!"

"Sorry," Wallace muttered, eyes downcast.

Marica nodded. "Molly?"

"Yeah, yeah," she said sulkily.

After that, nobody knew quite what to say. But just then, there was a loud hammering at the secret door behind the bar.

Chapter 49

As she looked at the ruination of the Sanctuary, Rosalind felt her anger rising. "Portia." Her voice was low and dangerous. "She has been here recently. And she's stolen the magic."

"What?" Catrin asked as she stared around. "Who's Portia? And where are Molly and the others? What happened here?"

"I don't know." She shrugged. "Dead, captured, who can say?" Her bluntness shocked Catrin into silence, and Rosalind noticed the fear in her eyes. "I'm sorry." She hugged the girl tightly. "Molly is no pushover; maybe she and the others escaped."

"This Portia must be very powerful."

"Yes," Rosalind agreed bleakly, "she is." Unwilling to delay any longer, she led Catrin back down the passage-between-the-worlds and into the circular room, but to her chagrin she discovered that, as well as the Sanctuary itself, the portal into the mortal world had lost its magic.

"Dammit!" she exclaimed, and Catrin looked at her in surprise; in the time she had known her, she'd never seen Rosalind anything other than calm and untroubled.

"Can we get through?"

"Perhaps," she replied shortly. "Wait." It took nearly an hour for Rosalind to fashion even a basic spell, such was the damage to the Sanctuary, then she grabbed Catrin's hand. "We must be swift," she explained, "the magic will last only a few seconds. She stepped upwards as if onto an invisible ladder and they were transported through a small aperture near the ceiling and out, through the doorway of the lamppost, into the mortal world.

"That was strange." Catrin felt the need to check all her limbs were still present and in the correct place.

There was no reply and Rosalind stood for a long time, peering intently in all directions, sniffing the air and examining the ground. Catrin ached to interrupt and find out if she knew anything yet but didn't dare. At last, Rosalind nodded in satisfaction.

"The good news is that Molly escaped, along with Wallace and Luke. The scent of her magic is strong and I can follow it." She pointed along Old Kent Road. "There was also another whom I can't identify; a mortal."

Catrin breathed a sigh of relief. "You said the good news. What's the bad news?"

Rosalind's face was grim. "Portia was here too, along with her disgusting creations; lots of them. The mortal world is in grave danger." Catrin looked around fearfully as if she expected hordes of the enemy to pounce. "Come on." Rosalind put an arm around her shoulder. "Let's find Molly."

By now it was early evening and they were able to use the shelter of the lengthening shadows. Keeping a wary eye out for trouble, Rosalind followed the trail left by Molly, keeping Catrin close, and soon they reached the darkness of the alley. The witch smiled; now she knew exactly where Molly had taken Cissy.

Chapter 50

For a short while the devastation that had hit London was reported on both the BBC and ITV news networks. But now they'd gone off air and all the programs had been replaced with just a single page, accompanied by background music that soon became tedious, saying *normal service will resume as soon as possible*. The American networks were still showing pictures of the destruction, even the bodies, but curiously they had been unable to capture any images of those responsible.

Outside, the street was calm and serene; it appeared the fighting hadn't reached this part of London yet, but they knew it was only a matter of time. Charles and Penelope in particular fretted at being unable to help, while Lucy thought they should barricade the doors and windows and sit tight until it was all over. As for Amelia, she woke around midday and immediately felt Anarkus' influence tugging at her, at one moment tempting her with dreams of power that both delighted and terrified her, at others promising death of the direst and most painful kind if she didn't return to him. She said nothing of this to anyone, choosing to spend most of her time in Penelope's room, distracting herself with loud music through headphones clamped tightly to her ears.

Charles had submitted to his wife's entreaties to barricade the house and now a large, heavy display cabinet blocked the front door, the windows had been boarded up and the back door nailed shut. Lucy confessed she felt safer and neither Charles nor Penelope told her that if the creatures, whatever they were, wanted to get inside, such paltry defences wouldn't prevent them. Charles phoned Peter's number for the millionth time and left yet another voicemail asking *where the hell are you!*

After they'd barricaded the house, Charles went for a lie down while Lucy busied herself finding useless odd jobs around the house. Penelope could bear it no longer; it was claustrophobic being locked inside and she was going stir crazy.

Checking nobody was about, she wrote a hurried note and lifted Charles's keys from his jacket pocket. Then, with some difficulty, she moved the cabinet aside, unlocked the door, and stepped outside. The afternoon air was crisp and cold, and she breathed big lungsful with relief and enjoyment, then unlocked Charles's car and sat inside. When she turned the ignition key, the car jerked forward; she'd forgotten to put the gear shift into neutral. She tried again and the powerful engine roared.

Taking a deep breath to calm her nerves, she edged the car into the road, not for the first time wishing it had an automatic gear shift. She'd had a few lessons but wasn't a confident driver. Plus, she hadn't passed her driving test, but she couldn't worry about that now and suspected the police would have more important issues at the moment.

Driving slowly but without incident – there were few other vehicles on the roads, despite this being a weekday – she eventually she arrived at her workplace, worried because she'd tried ringing on and off all morning without a reply. She wasn't unduly surprised to find the building deserted and the offices where she worked a wreck of broken glass, upturned tables, and graffiti-covered walls. She noticed at once that all of the computers were missing and suspected looters had been there. She hoped desperately that her colleagues were okay; Kane, Mikey, and the others, even Tom. As she returned to the car, she wondered idly whether Mikey had ever sent that friend request.

Starting the car, Penelope set out on the next leg of her journey, nervous now as scenes of devastation became more frequent; a burned-out building here, others with their windows smashed. Occasionally she saw people walking brazenly from shops carrying TVs, computers and other valuables. As she rounded a bend in the road, a small group of people were crowding around a jeweller's window, helping themselves to rings, bracelets, watches, and any other valuables on display.

This is all I need, she thought nervously, increasing her speed to get away. *Next, I'll bump into a crowd of these monster things.* She crossed her fingers to guard against tempting fate, but as it was, she reached Peter's house without incident. Running up the drive, she banged on the door, already knowing from the absence of a car that nobody was home. Wishing she'd thought to bring something to write on, she searched in the glove compartment of Charles's car and, to her relief, found an old envelope and a pen. *Where are you!* she wrote. *Phone us immediately!* Opening the letterbox to push it through, she remembered suddenly and added, *Love, Penelope xx.*

The drive home was uneventful until she was within a kilometre or so. She turned a corner and was confronted with a large group of people walking down the road, still distant, but closing rapidly. At least, she thought they were people and not the vile creatures her mother had described. As they got closer, she was relieved to have it confirmed; she didn't think the creatures would be carrying sticks and iron bars or drinking cans of lager. She wondered if they would part and let her drive through, and decided they probably wouldn't.

Braking sharply, she slammed the car into reverse and, as the crowd surged forward, running toward her, she turned the car around, wasting valuable seconds as she crashed the gears. Her heart hammered as she saw in her rear-view mirror how close they were. A brick smashed through the back window, narrowly missing her head, and she screamed as she accelerated away, by some miracle not stalling the car. Reaching home at last, she swung the car into the drive, scraping the gatepost as she did so, and ran, almost sobbing, into the house.

Chapter 51

As Morgan was about to deliver his killing blow, the fighting around him continued. Dominic's army fought valiantly but they were depleted now and there were gaps in their circle. Some of the unlucky ones, by sheer weight of numbers, managed to break through, and the army suffered more losses.

But Aeryn and Daraproud were invincible, seemingly indefatigable, incapable of stopping, even for a second. The unlucky ones tried to avoid them, but such was the strength and speed of the sisters' onslaught, so irresistible their anger, that soon, some began to run. The rest, wary of their leader's vengeance, remained, and still the wizard's army numbered many thousands.

But suddenly, Aeryn's horse was killed beneath her, and she went down, instantly surrounded by hordes of unlucky ones, clamouring for her blood. Morgan forgot the wizard at his feet and ran toward her, his wand firing a desperate barrage of wand fire. Daraproud's horse reared, whinnying wildly as she dragged it around and charged toward her, while Dominic's army surged forward, cutting down anyone who stood in their way.

But they were too late. Aeryn fought bravely, jumping lithely to her feet the moment she hit the ground, her sword dealing death to all around her. Sensing a chance to weaken their enemy, and each wanting the glory of doing so, almost the entire army of unlucky ones converged on her. As her companions fought desperately to reach her in time, she went down at last.

Daraproud was nearest but still too far away. She could only watch, despairingly, as someone took hold of her dead sister's hair and dragged her to her knees, while another swung back his sword, ready to strike. The sword was arcing toward Aeryn's neck when an arrow, its cruel tip flashing in the sunlight, pierced the unlucky one's head, killing it instantly.

Stunned, Daraproud reigned in her horse and, staring with disbelief at her sister, was almost caught unawares as a sword came flashing down.

"Your Majesty!" the warning came just in time, and she dispatched her attacker violently.

Your Majesty, she thought dully. *Yes, I suppose I am queen now.* Her mind refused to comprehend the reality, and she thrust it aside. Now was not the time for grief; that and the tears would come later.

With a long, anguished cry of primeval pain, she lost all reason and now she fought with the mindless ferocity of the berserker. The unlucky ones broke and fled but were quickly pursued. Many were trampled to death beneath the galloping horses, while the rest, with their backs to their enemy, did not survive long.

The wizard watched the dying remnants of his army with horror, then lay down his wand in surrender, hoping for clemency; in that he was to be disappointed. Morgan looked at the body of his wife for a long time, unable to comprehend the fate that had cruelly given them only a few years of happiness, after so many years had separated them. Within him a rage burned, a rage such as he'd never felt before; he turned and walked back to the terrified wizard. Scorning his wand, he withdrew his sword.

It didn't last long and within seconds the wizard was dead, yet Morgan kept on hacking at the body. Tears streamed down his face and in the distance, he heard a visceral screaming, not realising it came from his own mouth. The body was an unrecognisable pile of bloody meat, yet still he couldn't stop. Only when Dominic reached him and dragged him away did he cease, collapsing, sobbing to the ground.

As for Dominic, there was only a sense of unreality. That morning, he had breakfasted with his mother and aunt, they had laughed at something, some silly joke he could no longer remember. When Daraproud came, she found him wandering aimlessly, the same phrase leaving his lips, repeatedly.

"My mother is dead; my mother is dead."

Chapter 52

With the Sanctuary defeated and Cornelius and Morgan occupied, Portia and her army could rampage across London unopposed, and she took full advantage. Arrogantly, she dismissed the goblins as posing little threat, which was why the wizard she had chosen to lead them was the worst of a bad bunch. Aeryn's threat was greater, but no match for the size of the army she'd sent. As for Agnes and the witches, she barely gave them a second thought. She knew Molly, along with that ridiculous wizard Wallace, would come eventually and she looked forward to it. She also knew the Sanctuary's leader – *former leader* – was insane and one of her first tasks when the mortal world was vanquished would be to have the girl executed. She looked forward to that even more.

When they had finally left the Sanctuary in ruins and entered the mortal world, it had taken several hours to organise the huge army into sections, each one to target a different area of the city. But for that, the devastation and death might have been much greater. Even still, by mid-afternoon they'd left scores of buildings ruined or on fire and many hundreds of mortals dead. It was all going as planned and she could execute the next part of her plan. She summoned one of her unlucky ones, whom she'd kept from the fighting, a huge mountain of a man, possessed of reasonable intelligence.

"You understand your task?" He nodded eagerly. "Then go, do not fail me." At once he began shouting orders, his voice booming out into the streets of London. Within an hour, he had a huge gathering of unlucky ones around him. He barked one last order, and they headed north, out of the city.

The killing continued and so far there were none to stop Portia's relentless surge for ultimate power. Many mortals tried to hide in their homes, only to be found and dragged outside to be used as sport before being brutally killed. Other more fortunate ones were quickly dispatched where they hid. Some chose other places to hide, garages, garden sheds, and the like.

The unlucky ones ignored smaller buildings like these, and many mortals survived.

Among the most vulnerable were those who tried to escape London in their cars. The streets soon became gridlocked and the air was filled with a harsh symphony of car horns that only served to lead the unlucky ones to them. The drivers and their passengers died where they sat but some people had hidden their children in the boot of their vehicles and many of these also survived.

The army Portia had sent out of the city reached Brent Cross shopping centre, next to the Northbound M1, where many were as yet unaware of what was happening further south. Mortals died in their hundreds, in shops, on escalators, and in restaurants and coffee bars.

Yet there were small miracles. The bride-to-be who cowered, half-dressed in a changing cubicle, along with her mother and the sales assistant. The elderly couple celebrating their golden wedding anniversary, out on a day trip to find something to mark the occasion. These days, finding the escalators something of a challenge, they had to use the elevators and, by keeping their finger on the 'close door' button, somehow managed to evade the marauding creatures. And the mother who'd taken her young son to the children's play area and survived by hiding them both within a pool of plastic balls.

But these were small victories and when the army drifted out at last to begin their trek north, the shopping centre was a scene of carnage and blood.

*　　　　*　　　　*　　　　*

Molly stood, wand in hand, flanked by Wallace and Luke. At a nod from the witch, Marica flung open the door and they all stood, open-mouthed, as Rosalind and Catrin burst in.

"What the bleedin'—" Molly began, but Catrin cut her off.

"We've got a cure!' she shouted excitedly. "Where's Cissy?"

"What do you mean, a cure?" Luke stared at her. "There is no cure; Molly, Morgan, everyone has said so."

"There is!" Catrin took the vial from her pocket and held it up. "Look!"

"How did you find us?" Wallace added, somewhat irrelevantly, and Rosalind looked at him impatiently.

"We followed the trail left by Molly, but that doesn't matter—"

"You left a trail of magic?" Wallace turned to Molly, incredulous. "What if Portia had sensed it?"

"You worry too bleedin' much." She punched his arm lightly. "Anyway, she didn't. Now, let me see this cure."

Catrin handed it over and Molly examined it closely, taking out the stopper and sniffing, then passing her wand over it. Finally, she nodded, her eyes shining with excitement.

"It's real," she said, and looked at Catrin. "Where did you get this?"

Impatient to get to Cissy, the girl quickly explained how the Landlord had sent her to the land of the dead, but for now at least, she didn't recount any of her adventures. Molly couldn't help feeling a bit miffed.

"So the Landlord knew of this cure, and I'm betting Morgan did too." She sniffed eloquently. "Why do they never share their bleedin' secrets with me?"

"Probably they didn't want you to be disappointed if it turned out to be false," soothed Marica, just as loud screams of rage broke out from the room above.

"Come on," urged Luke, "stop all this talking and let's use the cure." He had watched the girl he loved suffer for the past ten years, neither able to comfort her nor ease her torment, and now he was impatient. They quickly decided on a plan, making sure everyone knew what to do, then walked up the stairs. Molly took out her wand and reached for the doorknob.

"Wait," said Catrin, "there's something else."

From inside the room, the screams and cursing continued, unrelenting.

"Well? Are you coming in?" Cissy screamed maniacally. "Don't be scared, I'll kill you quickly!" Catrin's eyes filled with tears; this was the first time she'd witnessed the damage done to her friend. "Except for the fat bitch!" the tirade continued. "I'm going to kill her slowly, very f—"

Catrin clapped her hands over her ears to silence the stream of expletives that followed and retreated back down the stairs.

Indicating the others should wait, Molly followed her down. "How do you stand it?" Catrin asked, wiping away tears. "The screams, the things she says?"

"We stand it because we have no choice and because we know it is not her fault. Now, you said there was something else. What is it?"

"This." She drew out the Knife of Rai.

Molly stared in amazement at the twin to the Knife of Chiang. "That has not been seen for many a thousand year," she breathed, adding with some delight, "I bet even Morgan didn't know where it was!"

The girl nodded. "Maybe. Can we just get on with it?" she said unhappily, fraught with nerves and shouting a little over the noise which, if anything, had intensified.

"This changes things. Do you know what to do?"

"Yes, yes!" she exclaimed impatiently. "Siwaraksa explained it all! Come *on!*"

Back upstairs, Molly quickly explained the change of plan and again reached for the doorknob. As soon as they were inside, Cissy leaped forward, cackling gleefully, but the two witches halted her with their wands. Luke gripped her head while Wallace forced open her mouth and Catrin poured in the liquid. Wallace closed it quickly before she could spit it out and forced her to swallow. Cissy struggled wildly and the two men held her with difficulty, even with the power from the witch's wands.

"Quickly now," ordered Molly, and they heaved her back, flat on the bed, and held her head to one side. The scar shone brightly, a small but ugly cicatrix that seemed to offer a challenge to the trembling girl who stood, knife raised.

"I don't know how far in to push it in!" she sobbed. "Siwaraksa didn't tell me that!"

"The knife knows," said Molly gently, "just let it do its work."

"Bitch!" Cissy spat, fixing her with her free eye, hatred oozing from it. "Whore!"

Catrin's resolve strengthened at the insults and she plunged the knife down, right into the centre of the cicatrix. Cissy emitted a horrific scream, high-pitched and drenched with anguish, and from the fresh wound in her head there streamed a dense cloud of dark grey vapour. As the windows in the room shattered, she shrugged Wallace and Luke aside with ease, then leaped for the two witches, so fast she was only a blur as she knocked their wands from their hands. Then she turned her gaze upon Catrin.

It hasn't worked, the girl thought in despair as Cissy advanced. *I'm about to die.* She watched as Cissy smiled crookedly, in no hurry now. In the corner of the room hung the cloud of vapor. Molly and Rosalind were scrabbling on the floor, trying to reach their wands but getting in each other's way. Cissy raised her hands to Catrin's throat as Luke flung himself upon her. She batted him away and he flew to the far side of the room. Wallace followed close behind and received the same treatment. Rosalind had reached her wand and raised it, ready to deliver what must be a killing blow, for Cissy's clawed fingers were around Catrin's neck now, squeezing while the girl stood, transfixed, frozen.

And then Cissy's arms went limp and dropped to her sides, just as a bolt of light left Rosalind's wand. Molly sent another, deflecting it, and it missed Cissy by centimetres, instead demolishing the wall behind.

"The potion!" Molly yelled. "It's working!"

"Hi, Catrin," Cissy said, the crooked smile gone, replaced by one of pleasure. "What are you doing here? In fact, where is here?" Then she fell to the floor, unconscious. When the others looked, the cicatrix, like the cloud of grey vapor, had gone.

Chapter 53

Kamontip watched as the effects of her spell took shape, while beside her Logan stared in amazement. Kamontip had been alert, ready to quickly alter the spell if the enemy entered her land from a different direction, but she'd judged it perfectly. The portal had appeared exactly where she'd anticipated and already thousands of deformed creatures were pouring through.

Goblin towns are made mostly from magic; they aren't too fond of hard labour such as bricklaying, and why should they be when their wands are the finest it is possible to make? Their roads could be made to alter direction, walls to become higher or lower, and buildings change shape, move, or disappear altogether.

Possessed of one of the most powerful wands ever made – only the wand owned by Portia held more – it was a simple task for someone of Kamontip's skill to weave her magic. So now, instead of the usual single narrow street leading into the town, there was a wide road, skilfully crafted from perfectly formed slabs of stone and, crucially for her plan, nice and wide; perfect for an invading army.

The terrain around the town was already rocky and uneven and had been made even more so by Maisey and Myla, who'd spent a happy afternoon with their wands, causing small explosions everywhere. Now the ground was littered with craters and quite unsuitable for marching upon. As Kamontip had planned, the unlucky ones naturally gravitated onto the beautifully smooth road, and that was their mistake.

Confident of victory – after all, it was only a few goblins they had to defeat – there was an almost carnival atmosphere as the army marched along. Excited at the prospect of an afternoon's killing and pillaging, there were smiles on faces, jocular banter, and even the occasional bout of raucous singing. At their head, the wizard general strode, proud and confident in the responsibility he'd been given. The least able of all the wizards on the council, he didn't know that Portia had given him what she believed to be the easiest task.

At first, nobody noticed the road becoming subtly narrower; their focus was on reaching the goblin town which, although still distant, grew steadily larger every minute. Soon they could clearly see the high walls encircling the town and their excitement grew. It was then that Kamontip enacted the next part of her spell. On either side of the road the air began to shimmer, so faintly it was almost unnoticeable. The road continued to narrow, so gradually that the army marched on, unheeding.

As they neared the goblin town, its walls, which had appeared tall and imposing from a distance, proved to be only about head height. Strangely, perhaps because of the sense of hysteria that pervaded the entire army, none thought to question why. But now there were occasional murmurings of puzzlement as the narrowing of the road forced them closer together so that soon, their shoulders were pressed together as they marched.

Then a soldier tripped over the feet of the one next to him, stumbling into the one in front. He spun angrily around and thrust his sword into the belly of the unfortunate offender. Soldiers nearer the front faltered as further progress became impossible, and those further behind, where the road wasn't quite so narrow, didn't yet understand the problem and crashed into them. Soon they were falling beneath the feet of their companions to be trampled to death. At that moment, the shimmering air solidified into a high stone wall and the army began to panic.

As some unlucky ones clambered onto the shoulders of others in a desperate but vain attempt to scale the wall, more swords were drawn. Fighting broke out and they killed each other with abandon. Panicking, their wizard leader sent bolts of wand fire into his army in a desperate attempt to restore order. Those nearest to him stopped fighting each other and turned on him, growling and baring their teeth in fury at his apparent betrayal. Desperately he blasted his wand fire into them but there were too many. They fell upon him and tore him limb from limb, before turning once again on each other.

The whole debacle took less than an hour. As she watched the last of the unlucky ones perish, Kamontip glanced across the valley to where two small figures stood, high upon the mountain, and shook her head in frustration. "Come on,"—she led Logan further up the hill—"we need to get into the mortal world."

"Shouldn't we tell your people that the battle is won?" asked Logan, in rare consideration for others. "They will want to return to their homes."

"Oh, they will know soon enough." She sighed, unsure whether to feel annoyed or amused. "Maisey and Myla, *particularly* Myla, don't know the meaning of following instructions to keep well away." She took his hand and they trudged up the hill. "At least they can be trusted to make certain everyone returns home safely."

"What are we going to do about them?" Logan looked down at the mass of corpses which could still be seen from the top.

"There are too many to get rid of now, we can worry about it later. If these creatures are here, you can be sure they're at the other dimensions too, and in the mortal world." She took out her wand and said the words that would summon the door into the corridor of dimensions. It appeared, but rather than the solid door she expected, this one was faint, and when she grasped the knob her hand passed right through.

She tried again, increasing the power a little. The door looked more substantial but still she couldn't open it.

"What's causing this?" Logan asked and she shrugged.

"I don't know, but I suspect it's nothing good." She increased her power further until she was straining to maintain it. At last, the door opened, and they hurried through before it could fade again.

Chapter 54

Because she suspected the way through the corridor of dimensions would be unavailable, but mostly because they were stuck high up a mountain and couldn't reach it anyway, Agnes was compelled to create a portal of her own. It wasn't an exact science, and her knowledge of mortal geography was sketchy at best, so all she could do was specify south. They ended up in a small town called Penzance. After shoplifting a map, it told her they were a long way from London and she scratched her head, wondering what to do.

Numerous holiday coaches entered the town, bringing fresh supplies of tourists eager to visit places like St Ives and Land's End. Agnes was watching one now, its engine running and smoke belching from its rear. Mortals spilled out, heading for the nearest of the ubiquitous gift shops, full of expensive tat, or the equally numerous fish and chip shops that are a must for British holidaymakers. Agnes had heard of coaches although she'd never seen one and certainly didn't know how to make one move, but how hard could it be?

Suspecting it was something to do with the chair the big, fat mortal had vacated, the one with the enormous wheel in front of it, she motioned her fellow witches and they crept forward. She climbed up into the seat while the others entered via the side door, somehow still undetected, and looked at the array of buttons and switches that confronted her. Helplessly but hopefully, she pressed them at random.

First, the hazard warning lights switched on, but fortunately the driver was engaged in assuring an elderly lady that the seven suitcases she'd brought for the weekend trip could be safely left while she went in search of a nice cup of tea. Then the doors *swooshed* closed and he turned, puzzled, just as another elderly mortal, a man this time, tugged his arm and requested urgent directions for the nearest loo.

But when the stereo began belting out *Abba's Greatest Hits,* he abandoned his passengers and banged on the door of the coach, staring in amazement at Agnes and shouting increasingly panicked expletives which, fortunately, she didn't understand.

"It's not working!" she wailed. "I can't get it to move!" It was then that Clarissa made her first contribution. Clarissa had always been fascinated by two things; mortals and machinery. Unfortunately, there wasn't much scope for either in the witch's world and that was why, slightly unbelievably but nevertheless true, she owned a stack of car magazines gleaned from goodness knew where.

Clarissa had never seen a coach either, or driven one, but at least she'd seen pictures. She had an inkling it was something to do with that stick positioned to Agnes's left, the one with 1-2-3-4-5-R stamped on it, and the pedals beneath her feet.

"Here," she said impatiently, "let me have a go." Within a minute they were lurching, stop-start, from the car park, the astounded driver jumping up and down, his triple chins bouncing furiously, shaking his fist at the rapidly retreating vehicle and shouting more expletives that made the old-aged pensioners in his charge cover their ears in horror.

There were hoots and yells of triumph within the coach and, although both its previously pristine bodywork and the walls that lined the unfeasibly narrow Cornish roads took a beating, they were soon hurtling up the A30 into Devon and beyond until they turned, going the wrong way around a roundabout onto the M4, bound for London.

Chapter 55

As the last of the unlucky ones fled, Morgan, Daraproud, and Dominic surveyed the battlefield, barely able to comprehend the terrible cost of what had just happened. As well as Aeryn, twenty of their army had lost their lives. The anger and need for revenge would come later, but for now, there was only sorrow.

Slowly, they dismounted and walked reluctantly to where lay the body of their queen, mother, and sister. There were no tears and no words, just a silent melding of their thoughts as they shared their grief.

Daraproud summoned one of the soldiers. "Organise your men to carry the fallen into the castle," she ordered quietly. "Handle them gently, with respect; they have earned it and more today."

"Yes, Your Majesty, it will be done at once."

Daraproud had been turning away but at his words she spun round, spearing the unfortunate man with a ferocious look. "Do not call me that!" she hissed.

The soldier flinched, then hovered, uncertain what to do until Dominic took pity on him. "To your task, soldier. Once the bodies have been removed, tend to the wounds of the men, then seek refreshment. Tell the cooks to feed everyone."

"Sire,"—the man hesitated still—"their families, who will…"

"I will do it," Dominic confirmed. "Thank you. That will be all, Aeneas." Surprised, the soldier wanted to ask how the prince knew his name but thought better of it, wary of inciting Daraproud's anger again, and scurried away to carry out his orders.

Dominic smiled to himself, without mirth. He knew the names of all his men, as well as those of their families. He knew their strengths, weaknesses, quirks and foibles, the names of their children, their grandparents, and even some of their ancestors. He recognised every single one of the dead who lay scattered across the battlefield, bodies torn, limbs twisted in the undignified poses of violent death.

That one there, he thought, looking at a large man who lay on his back, face serene, hair blowing gently in the breeze, *he was the father figure of the group. Older than the rest, always there to counsel the younger ones, ease their fears, and give advice.* Dominic sighed. *He will be missed by us all.*

For a moment he didn't recognise another who lay nearby, such were the terrible wounds inflicted on him, his face cleaved down the middle so that the two halves had fallen apart, exposing his brain. *Ondrej,* he thought, *I never really liked you, few did.* Truthfully, the man had been a bully, slyly terrorising those weaker than he, whenever he thought no one was looking. *No, you weren't popular, but you fought well, and you didn't deserve a death such as this.*

None of you did! Anger coursed through him as he observed the decimation of his army. Silently he spoke the names of those he could see; *Alain, Chatri, Owen…* Owen, was it only two days ago they'd wagered on the outcome of a horse race between Daraproud and one of the men? He was young, a boy really, and had been thrilled to have the attention of his prince. Dominic had purposefully kept the wager small, knowing there could be only one outcome; none could truly challenge his aunt's skill on a horse. He'd even tried to write off the debt, small as it was, but Owen had insisted he would fetch the money when his next soldier's pay was due a few days hence. The young man had known his wife would be displeased at the loss; they were newlywed and trying to save all the money they could, but a wager was a wager he'd told Dominic earnestly.

"Keep it, Owen, with my blessing," he muttered, drawing a curious look from Daraproud. He shook his head and looked down at the body of his mother. *How can you be gone?* he wondered with a sense of disbelief. *You were indomitable, indestructible.* He felt tears fill his eyes and said, gruffly, "Come on, we must carry her home. Morgan, will you help?"

For a moment, Dominic thought his words hadn't penetrated; the wizard's eyes were haunted, his shoulders bent so that for the first time since Dominic had known him, he seemed diminished. But then he straightened and nodded, and together the three of them lifted her gently and they began the slow walk home.

Morgan stayed only a moment to gaze down at the woman he'd loved for more than three hundred years. Then the anger returned and, quite unable to manage emotions he'd not had to face for a long time, not since Logan had murdered their father, he quickly left the room, leaving the two of them alone.

"You'll have to get used to it, you know," Dominic said mildly. "That soldier was right, you are the queen now."

"I know," she acknowledged, "I just don't want to face it quite yet. Somehow it will make this real." He nodded, understanding. "Damn, I'm going to have to apologise to him, aren't I?"

"Well, he certainly didn't deserve it," Dominic agreed, "he was only doing his job."

"I know." She flushed, embarrassed.

"You were very harsh."

"Okay, Dominic! You've made your point!"

"Thank you… Your Majesty."

For a moment she was furious, but then recognised his attempt to ease the tension. They'd always been more like siblings than aunt and nephew and their teasing and practical jokes, each vying to beat the other, had often driven Aeryn to distraction. For the first time that day, Daraproud smiled.

Just then the door crashed open and Aeryn's two younger adoptive children rushed in. Both were teenagers now, stuck in that awkward place between child and adult. Sebastian, too young to completely hide his desire to weep, yet too old to allow himself to do so. He stood, rigid, as he stared at his mother, his body trembling as he fought to keep from breaking down. Daraproud's heart ached for him and silently she moved to his side and took his hand in hers; he did not resist. Angelina had no such reservations and flung herself onto the supine body, sobbing hysterically until she had no more tears and her voice was hoarse. Only then did Dominic, gently but with some difficulty, prise her away and hold her close.

Chapter 56

"Hush," Kamontip hissed, "something's wrong."

"What is it?" Logan looked around; the corridor looked the same as the last time he'd been there. That was when he'd been imprisoned in the Chasm of Nothingness by his brother and the Landlord. He shuddered at the memory.

"There's no magic," she answered slowly, "something's happened."

"I don't—"

"Logan, the Sanctuary is so steeped in magic you can smell it,"—she shook her head—"but now there's nothing." She took his arm and stepped cautiously onward. "Come on, but stay alert." Wands held before them, they walked softly into the passage-between-the-worlds, wondering at the massive hole in the wall until they reached the ruined door of the Sanctuary. Then they stepped into a scene of utter devastation.

Logan looked curiously around; of course, he'd never entered the Sanctuary, and it felt strange to stand where his brother had lived and worked for so many years. "This'll take some fixing," he said, without irony. "What happened here?"

"Portia!" the word spat viciously from her mouth. "That's what happened!" The place was in ruins. Every door hung from its hinges or had fallen off entirely. Huge chunks of plaster littered the floor where Portia had blasted holes in the ceiling and in the lounge, the sofas were burned-out skeletons and the large plasma TV a distorted mound of melted plastic.

Moving cautiously into the hallway, they encountered more destruction; part of the grand staircase had been blasted away, its wooden banisters in pieces, and a sweet, sickly stink of rot was already beginning to pervade the place.

"Come on." Kamontip had seen enough, and she led him back into the passage-between-the-worlds and to the circular room. There she spoke the spell that would take them through the lamppost, much as Rosalind had the previous day, but nothing happened. She tried again and again but still nothing, and she uttered a rare curse.

"The magic is gone," she said at last. "Even with the Queen's Wand I cannot get through."

"So what do we do now?"

"I don't know!" she snapped. "Let me think!" She took his hand apologetically and tried to think of another way into the mortal world, but it was Logan who eventually spoke.

"There might be a way…" he said, hesitant.

"Yes?" she said, but still he hesitated, blushing.

"When I… when I attacked the Sanctuary with my lost souls…" His eyes were cast downward and he felt an unfamiliar sense of shame.

"Go on, Logan!" Kamontip had no time right now for sensitive feelings or hesitation; time was of the essence.

"My brother and the witch,"—Logan still couldn't quite bring himself to say their names—"they used a different exit to this one."

"Where is it?" she said excitedly, gripping his arm. "Do you know where the portal is? Perhaps there is still magic to be found."

"No," he admitted, "but my sense is that it is inside, possibly higher up."

Within minutes they were back inside the ruined Sanctuary, wands alert and searching for any residual magic. They explored downstairs first, but there was none, and then they climbed, with some difficulty, the shattered staircase. They explored the upstairs rooms, Logan in particular curious to see what it was like. He recognised Morgan's room immediately, kept just as he had left it although he was no longer the leader, for it was furnished and decorated much like the one he'd had when they were boys. Logan remembered, again with a sense of shame, when Morgan had left that room with his sword and how they had fought after he, Logan, had stabbed their father. How Morgan could have killed him that day but had shown mercy.

Lost in thought, he hadn't noticed Kamontip going up another, smaller staircase, and had to hurry to catch up. So far there had been not a hint of magic, and he was starting to think he'd been mistaken. Together they stepped into the training room and Kamontip was momentarily distracted by the array of weapons displayed there.

"Look at these swords," she breathed in wonder, "some of them are truly ancient." She lifted one from the wall and stroked its smooth metal, polished so brightly it hurt to look at. She tested its keen edge with her finger; it was extremely sharp and she playfully placed the tip against Logan's chest. "Got you," she said, smiling.

Logan smiled back, enjoying the moment, then moved the sword gently away. "Come on," he said, "we have work to do, remember?"

She nodded, replaced the sword, and they continued their search around the room. All at once, the Queen's Wand began to thrum gently. It led them to a small door near the back of the room and, when Kamontip flung it open, vibrated wildly. Excitedly climbing yet another staircase, this one short and cramped, Kamontip pushed the door at the top and, relieved, they stepped into the mortal world.

It was dark and they looked around cautiously, but there was nobody to be seen. But as they approached the city centre, they came across evidence of Portia's presence; destroyed buildings and dead mortals became increasingly apparent. The hours passed and still they came across none of the enemy. But Kamontip had extremely acute hearing, much like some animals, and she could hear sounds of shouting and triumphant laughter, far in the distance.

Fatigue overcame Logan, and he yawned widely.

"I'm tired too," admitted Kamontip. "Let's find somewhere to sleep." She made for the nearest building. "It will be an uncomfortable night, but at least it's sheltered from the rain."

"No,"—Logan pointed across the road to a budget hotel—"in there, it will have beds." Kamontip looked at him quizzically. "I know," he said, laughing, "but you have to remember mortals are strange beings. They actually leave their homes just so they can sleep in a different bed, *and* they pay money to do it!"

Inside, they went to the top floor and opened the first room they saw. Then they curled up together on the bed and within minutes they were asleep.

Chapter 57

When Cissy slipped from unconsciousness into a deep, restful sleep, the first she'd had in many years, Rosalind said her goodbyes, unwilling to say where she was going, only that she had business to attend to. Wasting no time, she returned to the narrow corridor that was the boundary between the London of Marica's time and that of the present day. But instead of jumping down into the alleyway beyond, she turned instead to one of the doors that stood opposite each other in the narrow room. Being a former member of the witch and wizard council, Rosalind was privy to many secrets; even Molly, Morgan, and Cornelius didn't know of this particular portal. Not that it was a secret, just that it had long been forgotten. The door was locked – indeed it had no visible lock or doorknob – but Rosalind knew the spell and it swung inward at her touch.

Even running much of the way, the night had become morning by the time she reached the portal. As she ran, her imagination worked overtime and she imagined Cornelius lying dead and mutilated, while those hideous creatures fought over his body. At last, she came to a window, quite small, with four square panes of glass. Holding her breath, hardly daring to look, she pushed it open.

*   *   *   *

The road was clear. Nobody was going into London, they were all trying to get out, and the coach sped happily along. The other carriageway was at a standstill and cars beeped constantly, no doubt trying to warn them to turn around. Luckily for the witches, thanks to that inherent reluctance to break the rules that most mortals have, particularly British ones, none had yet thought to break through the central barrier and drive the wrong way down the motorway, thus easing the congestion and increasing their chances of escaping.

But things were about to go wrong. Clarissa might well have had a stash of car magazines that she read avidly, but still, she was no expert and she'd forgotten one vital thing; vehicles need fuel. So when the little red light appeared on the dashboard display, she ignored it and kept the gas pedal pressed hard to the floor. A few minutes later, the engine coughed and spluttered a few times, then the coach shuddered to a halt. Clarissa sat there for a long time, trying to figure out what had gone wrong, her companions offering helpful suggestions to pull this lever or press that button. Eventually, they realised they were going nowhere and piled out of the coach to consider their options.

Although they weren't dressed in black cloaks and pointy hats – another mortal fiction – they were still an odd-looking bunch and it wasn't long before comments were being shouted from the windows of the stationary cars. All came from men, obviously, and none were as funny or clever as they thought they were, even more obviously. "The fancy dress party's been cancelled!" shouted one. "You auditioning for the new Harry Potter movie?" yelled another. It wasn't until someone shouted another suggestion, equally unfunny but infinitely more helpful, that they knew what they had to do. "Need a push, darlin's?"

They were still fifty kilometres from London and the prospect of pushing the huge vehicle all that way was not appealing. Even though there were thirty of them, it would still be a struggle. Some wanted to use magic, but Agnes wouldn't hear of it; she didn't want to alert Portia to their presence in the mortal world any sooner than was absolutely necessary. The first few kilometres were okay and they made good progress, the next few not so much. By the time they'd covered twenty, they were exhausted, and it was with relief they saw a sign offering food and drink. With difficulty, they heaved the coach up the steep incline that led to the service station and allowed it to roll to a standstill. Looking around for help, they saw the place was deserted.

A few of the group went in search of food while Clarissa tried to figure out what was wrong with the coach, which by now they were all sick of the sight of. Casting her mind back to the magazines, something tugged at her memory, but it wasn't until her companions had returned with a mountain of pasties, sausage rolls, chips, and the most wonderful thing they'd ever tasted, chocolate, did she remember you had to put fuel in.

It didn't take long for her to locate the line of fuel pumps, but it took another thirty minutes to work out how to use the machine and then only because one of them had entered the shop to get more chocolate and, noticing the button that suddenly started flashing and beeping loudly, pressed it. Then there was the problem of how to actually put it into the vehicle, but at last they figured it out and were ready to leave. After a couple of failed attempts, the engine fired and, not realising they should actually pay for the fuel – or the food and chocolate – which would have been impossible anyway, they sailed happily out of the service station and back onto the motorway.

Chapter 58

Charles and Lucy were too relieved to be angry, but Amelia was torn between wanting to shout at her or hug her.

"What possessed you?" she yelled, hugging her anyway. "How could you be so stupid!"

"I needed to go check on my workmates," Penelope countered defensively, "to make sure they were okay." To Amelia, who'd never had any friends, this was unfathomable.

"Well, it was still stupid," she said, but more gently. "We were all so worried." Unconsciously, she allied herself with Charles and Lucy, taking the first step toward being part of a family for the first time since she'd been a child.

Although Penelope was relieved the inquest into her disappearance hadn't been more severe, there was little talking for a while until Lucy had had enough. "Come on," she said, taking charge, "you've not even had lunch. You too, Amelia, sit at the table. Charles, you make the tea."

"Could I have coffee, please, Mrs. Hamilton?" asked Amelia, a little shyly, and the older woman smiled.

"So long as you call me Lucy, dear," she said, giving her husband a pointed look.

"What?" he said, wondering what he'd done wrong, and she inclined her head slightly.

"Oh, right, of course. And I'm Charles." He smiled at Amelia. "I can't be doing with all this Mr. Hamilton malarkey; makes me feel about ninety."

Amelia was embarrassed and, seeking to smooth things over, Penelope announced, "I put a note through Peter's door, asking him to ring us urgently." And seeing the protest forming on her mother's lips, she continued, "I know, I know, he'll ring us anyway when he sees how many times you've tried to get hold of him."

"Anyway," said Charles firmly, also seeing the look on Lucy's face, "we can drop the subject now."

They finished the meal and prepared to face a boring day filled with worry, but under the circumstances, it turned out better than they could have hoped. After a few games of Scrabble, which Amelia turned out to be unexpectedly good at, they played Uno, which Lucy couldn't get the hang of at all.

So this is what it's like having a family, Amelia thought, deciding she kind of liked it and hoping she wasn't making too bad an impression. That night when they went to bed, Lucy kissed her daughter as usual, then turned to Amelia.

"Goodnight, dear." She kissed her also, and although Amelia's instinct was to turn away, she managed not to do so. But her guard, which had begun to slip, was reinforced once more.

Don't get too comfortable! her senses screamed. *They are not your family!*

Unaware of her inner turmoil, Charles hugged Penelope and then turned to her. "Goodnight, Amelia." He touched her arm briefly. Later, when he and Lucy went to bed, he took his car keys with him, just as a precaution.

The next day, breakfast was a silent affair. Afterward, they tried playing board games again, but nobody was in the mood. The pressure of being trapped indoors was telling on them all and they felt bad-tempered and fractious. Charles and Lucy snapped at each other constantly, which Penelope hated – it was so rare. Amelia, deciding family life wasn't so good after all, wondered what she was doing stuck inside when she could be free. She made the mistake of saying as much to Penelope and neither of them spoke much until the silence was broken by a loud knocking on the door.

Chapter 59

It had been a battle to test even the Landlord's great power and skill, but at last, the unlucky ones had been decimated by his rage, and around him lay a thick sea of bodies. The remainder, only a couple of thousand, were in flight, and Suluhura was long gone. Exhausted, for the night had fallen long ago, he lowered his wand and sat, weeping with sorrow and guilt at the slaughter around him. It was a long time until he stood finally and walked wearily back to the old inn, anxious, although he didn't think the enemy would return, to repair the barrier and make sure it was sound.

Satisfied, he turned to look at the devastation of Portia's army, wondering with despair what he was going to do with all the bodies. He sat for a long time, but at last his head lolled and he dozed. The moon was high in the clear night sky; it would soon be dawn when he was jerked awake by a noise. To his astonishment, a window appeared in the air before him, several meters in the air, and there was Rosalind, gesturing frantically.

"Cornelius!" There was joy and relief in her voice. "Come on!" Without hesitation, he leaped up and she caught his arm, pulling him through until he landed in an ungainly heap on the floor of the passage beyond, with Rosalind sat on top of him.

"Rosalind!" He laughed as they got to their feet and, holding her close, said, "Where did you spring from? And where's Catrin?"

Rosalind was still laughing with relief at finding him alive. "She's with Cissy now, they're at Marica's, and Cissy has already been given the cure."

Although her words came as a relief to the Landlord, something caught his attention. "Why are they at Marica's?" he asked with a sense of foreboding.

"They're all there, Molly, Luke, Wallace. Cornelius,"— she took his hand and squeezed—"the Sanctuary is destroyed."

"What do you mean, *destroyed?*" he demanded, staring at her, and she could barely meet his eyes.

"I mean destroyed, its magic is gone," she answered bluntly, and it was like a hammer blow to his heart.

"Then we must hurry," he said as he ran ahead.

DAY TWO

Chapter 60

Maisy and Myla continued to follow their orders conscientiously and it wasn't until all their people were safely back in their homes that Myla reverted to mischief mode.

"Kamontip went to the mortal world!" she said excitedly. "Let's follow!"

"We can't! She will sense it."

"We won't go that way." Myla grinned. "I know a better one."

Maisey looked at her sister, wondering why she insisted on telling such enormous fibs. "There are no other portals to the mortal world."

"There is one! Honestly!" She hopped from one foot to another gleefully as she led them out of the village and along a path into the mountains. "You remember when we were children and you used to visit the old folks and drink tea and act all polite?"

Maisey nodded. "I am polite, and yes, you were supposed to come with me but you could never be found."

"*Exactly!* I used to wander the mountains and one day I came across this portal, quite by chance. While you were chatting away being *polite,* I was nipping into the mortal world!"

"Why did you never tell me?" Maisey felt outraged and a little disappointed.

"Ha!" Myla laughed. "Because you'd have told someone. And then there'd have been trouble."

"I would not!"

"Would."

"Wouldn't!"

"You absolutely know you would have."

"Oh, shut up, Myla," Maisey said in disgust. "So where is this portal, then? Probably another of your lies."

"You're wrong, as usual," her sister taunted, "it's here." At first, Maisey couldn't see it, the crack in the rock was so small, then she looked at Myla, incredulous.

"We're supposed to fit through that?"

"It'll be a tight squeeze," Myla admitted, "that's why I had to stop using it. But if we hold in our breath for about,"—she nearly said five minutes but quickly amended—"a minute to make ourselves thinner, we can just about make it."

"Oh alright." Maisey was still convinced this was one of her sister's pranks. "Let's do it."

Five minutes later, they were in the mortal world.

* * * *

"We're going to be in so much trouble for this," Velveteena hissed, but Moth merely shrugged.

"I don't see why; we *are* allowed to go outside." They were sneaking along the deserted pathways of the faerie palace gardens and had already eluded two sets of guards in getting there.

"But probably not at night, and *definitely* not when we're planning what we are."

"So what? We can worry about it later." She was starting to irritate him; he didn't like being faced with unpalatable truths.

"It's forbidden to leave our world without a very good reason," she persisted, "and without the permission of the Lord and Lady."

"Yes, Velveteena," he snapped, "I know!" There was a long pause before he added, "Perhaps they won't find out." He sounded suddenly less sure of himself.

"You know they will."

It was dawning on him that this wasn't just a bit of mischief – something for which the pair were well known – this was serious. But Moth had always been able to shunt such things aside, to be considered only if they couldn't be avoided. "Yeah," he agreed and grinned, "but I'm going anyway. You stay if you want."

Shaking her head, Velveteena tried to disapprove, but secretly she was as excited as he was. No way was she missing out on such an adventure! "No, I was just pointing out the consequences if we're caught. One of us has to be the sensible one," she added primly.

Watching from one of the palace windows, the faerie queen sighed. She supposed she should have stopped them but really, what was the point? Except, perhaps, to save them the heartache that was surely to come.

"You are far too lenient with those two, Ana." Her husband walked into the room, trying to look stern but betrayed by the sparkle in his eye.

"Probably," she agreed, "but they grew so fond of those who inhabit the Sanctuary the last time they were there."

"Those who are about to be slaughtered by the renegade witch's army, you mean?"

To this, Ana had no answer.

When Velveteena and Moth had gone before to the Sanctuary, they'd quickly grown to adore the irritable old witch Molly who'd summoned them (or so she thought). Having revealed Cissy to be the one who fulfilled the prophecy, they had helped her and the rest of the Sanctuary narrowly defeat the might of the demons.

They'd had such fun popping demon eyeballs that it had become a competition between them and having escaped the rather formal restrictions of the faerie world for a while, they'd been sorry to say farewell, particularly to Molly, after the battle was won. Molly, although she had a soft spot for the pair of them, couldn't help feeling relieved when they left; they were extremely mischievous.

The queen watched as her two faerie children snuck out of the garden and hurried along the lane beyond, casting furtive glances all around. She shook her head sadly, having no doubt their friends among the Sanctuary were about to die. That the two young faeries would be devastated at their loss she was certain of, but then she turned away, dismissing them and setting her mind to other, more lofty concerns.

Chapter 61

Her eyes flickered open and as consciousness returned Cissy was aware of a heaviness in her limbs and an unwillingness to move. It was a nice feeling, like realising it's the weekend and you can stay in bed. Her gaze moved to the window – and through a chink in the curtains she saw the light of early dawn – then around the room until it rested on the figure of someone dozing in an armchair. *Catrin,* she recognised. *What's she doing here? And where am I?* She smiled, unable to remember when she'd last seen her friend, then the effort of keeping her eyes open was too great and she slept once more.

When she awoke again, Catrin had gone. She lay for a while until curiosity got the better of her, then swept the bedsheets aside and swung her legs out. The sudden movement made her feel woozy and she sat for a few minutes until it passed, then stood and opened the curtains, flooding the room with the morning sunlight.

Where am I? Cissy wondered again. *And whose are these pyjamas?* She was confused; something was different, missing. She sat on the edge of the bed and thought for a long time until she realised what it was. *I'm not angry,* she thought in wonderment. *I've been angry for so long, but now it's gone.* The fuzziness in her mind cleared a little and she remembered her friends, wondering where they were. *Luke,* she thought, and an intense longing enveloped her, *and Molly, dear, dear Molly.* Cissy didn't realise it then, but this was the first time in a decade she had thought of her friends with anything other than suspicion and paranoia.

She looked out over the rooftops of London and thought of her parents, wondering what they were doing and whether they thought of her sometimes. A fleeting memory flashed through her mind, that she'd been ill, and of her mum sitting at her bedside, stroking her hair while she slept. *But this isn't my room at the Sanctuary,* she thought, and then remembered she'd seen Catrin. Her puzzlement deepened.

There was a wardrobe in the corner of the room where she found a couple of pairs of jeans and a few tee-shirts. She dressed quickly, then opened the door and crept silently down the stairs, wondering who and what she would find. At the bottom, she saw she was in the bar of a pub.

"You're awake!" She spun at the sound of a voice she knew so well. Molly was already halfway across the room and Cissy let out a cry of delight and ran to meet her. Molly folded Cissy into her arms, and they stood there hugging tightly, neither able to find the words they wanted so badly to say. Her old friend looked just the same, and smelled the same, a combination of wildflowers and magic that was impossible to describe, but wonderful and comforting.

Then she saw Luke and let out another cry. She detached herself from Molly's arms and walked slowly to him and there they stood, facing each other, both shy and unsure what to do.

"Go on, lad," Molly interjected finally, "give her a bleedin' kiss!" Suddenly the ice was broken and they were in each other's arms, kissing and talking at the same time, their exuberance overflowing. With a diplomacy nobody would have expected, Molly quietly left the room, smiling and wiping away a tear.

When she returned, they were chatting animatedly, Catrin too. She'd been in her room and had heard the commotion downstairs. Marica was out and Rosalind had left, rather mysteriously, the night before. Cissy motioned for her to sit with them. "They wouldn't tell me what's been happening, why we're all here instead of at the Sanctuary." She smiled at Molly. "My memory is still a little vague."

"Right," she said carefully, giving Luke a warning glance, "well, it's a long story, love, and one perhaps best left for another time, when you're stronger." Seeing she was about to protest, Molly took a small rectangular box from her pocket and placed it on the table. Cissy picked it up and held it reverently before opening it.

"My wand," she whispered, and her eyes glistened with tears. "I thought it was lost forever." Just then, there was another loud knocking on the door.

"Not again!" Molly complained as they each took up their wands and swords. "It's like Piccadilly bleedin' Circus around here." But before anyone could reach the door, it clicked open and two familiar figures walked in.

"Landlord!" yelled Cissy, flinging herself into his arms. "I've missed you so much!"

Overcome with emotion, he couldn't speak, but tears trickled down his cheeks as he held her tightly, as if he'd never let her go.

"Careful, you idiot, you're squeezing the life out of her," Molly said at last, "and we've only just bleedin' cured her."

He let go finally, still hardly able to speak. "Wonderful… wonderful!" He grabbed her again and spun her around, only letting go when she begged for mercy. Just then, the door to the inn opened and Marica walked in. She stood for a moment, too stunned to move, then she too hugged him tightly, her eyes shining.

"Quite the attention grabber, aren't you, Cornelius?" observed Molly, but without heat. It was an open secret that Marica had long loved the Landlord, but in kindness to her, it was never talked about. It was Marica's cross to bear; the Landlord was very fond of her but there'd only ever been one love in his long life.

Later, when everyone had calmed down and they'd brought each other up to speed, it was time to plan their next move. It was simple really – they needed to get to the mortal world immediately.

"I'm coming too," announced Cissy. "I'm feeling much better and—" She interrupted herself with a wide yawn.

"No, you must rest awhile longer," Molly insisted, "and you must reacquaint yourself with your wand, do a few spells, get used to it again; it's a long time since you both last met."

"But…" She looked at the Landlord for support, but he shook his head.

"Molly is right, Cissy, your strength must return fully. You will know when the time is right."

Secretly relieved, she didn't argue further; she was too tired. She said her goodbyes and hugged everyone in turn, then wearily climbed the stairs and collapsed thankfully into bed.

"Maybe I should stay behind too," said Molly, to nobody in particular, "make sure she's okay." She said it so half-heartedly that Marica bit back a smile.

"It's fine, Molly," she said, a little sad at the thought of Cornelius leaving again so soon, but it had always been that way, "you should go too. Cissy is cured now and Catrin and I will look after her."

They left soon after, and when the secret door behind the bar clicked shut, Marica straightened her shoulders, breathed deeply, then opened the front door of the inn. She had a business to run and it was time to get the punters back in. She stood, enjoying the sunshine as the first of them approached.

Chapter 62

Morgan spent the night sitting quietly beside the body of his queen, holding her limp, cold hand. Then as dawn approached, he gathered the few things he would need and prepared to sneak from the castle.

"You're going to the mortal world." Daraproud had also spent a sleepless night. "I'm coming too."

"Yes," he agreed, "I go to the mortal world, and no, you are not." He turned and faced her. "You are queen now; your duty is to your people." He strode away and she hesitated before running after him. "Daraproud, you must stay—"

She placed a finger on his lips. "I know," she said softly, "it's just—"

"I will avenge the deaths of our loved ones," he promised.

When she had gone, he thought for a while about how he would travel to the mortal world. The obvious way was the portal into the corridor of dimensions, yet he hesitated. He presumed Molly, Luke, and Wallace would be out fighting Portia's army, but if anyone was there, he didn't want them to sense his presence; this was a personal matter.

There was a spell that would take him to his former study within the Sanctuary; it seemed an age since he'd used it to follow the young Penelope into Aeryn's world. He decided to go that way; with a little adapting it would be perfect. Soon he stood, not in the Sanctuary, but in the mortal world.

Morgan had witnessed many dark things but even he was shocked at the death and destruction he found. By now Portia's unlucky ones had spread throughout London and his presence didn't go unnoticed for long. Soon he was surrounded by several hundred of the creatures and he raised his wand eagerly, waiting for the attack. When it came, it was short and bloody; Morgan fought with a single-minded ferocity that his enemy was powerless to resist.

Afterward, with the absence of people or traffic, it was curiously quiet, almost peaceful. A slight noise made him spin around, but almost immediately he realised he could sense no threat.

"Come out of there, now!" But even he was surprised at the two small figures who crept from their hiding place, fear written on their faces. "What are you doing here?" he demanded. "Does Kamontip know?"

"She's already here somewhere, fighting."

Morgan looked at them, surprised.

"Yes," Myla went on, "she came with—" She yelped as Maisey dug her hard in the ribs.

"With who?" he asked suspiciously.

"Oh, just a friend; nobody you know," Maisey improvised, knowing she would be in such trouble when the wizard found out she'd lied. Just then, a group of unlucky ones came around a corner and stopped, eyeing Morgan warily.

"Idiot," Maisey hissed as the wizard killed them, swiftly and brutally, "he doesn't need to know his estranged brother is here!"

"You need to return to your world right now," Morgan said, turning his attention back to them. "As you can see, it's hardly safe for you here."

"Do we have to?" Myla knew it was useless to argue, merely stalling for time enough to put her hands in her pockets and cross her fingers. Maisey put hers nonchalantly behind her back and did the same.

Morgan had no patience for two goblin children who'd been stupid enough to put themselves in danger and just glared.

"Okay." Myla smiled winningly and squeezed her crossed fingers more tightly. "We promise."

Chapter 63

Molly, Wallace, Luke, Rosalind, and the Landlord jumped from the portal and into the mortal world. They left the alleyway and were met with an apocalyptic vision; London was a ghost town, with no sign of life anywhere.

It was a nightmare of partially destroyed buildings, abandoned vehicles, some overturned, others wrecked and burning. Most of the shop fronts were destroyed and the sun reflected brightly from the carpet of broken glass that littered the pavements. The air was hazy with dust and smoke and the rank stink of gasoline made them gag. Fallen streetlights crisscrossed the road like a giant game of jackstraws.

A small dog ran from a nearby doorway and, seeing them, it growled, shaking with terror, its tail tucked tight between its legs. Rosalind crouched and tried to tempt it to come, but it took a few tentative steps then ran away, barking loudly.

"Where is everyone?" Luke whispered.

"Gone, love." Molly put an arm around his shoulder.

"Perhaps they all escaped the city," he muttered.

"Perhaps," the Landlord spoke gently, knowing the boy was about to witness things that would haunt him forever more. They walked warily down the street, feet crunching the glass, a musical sound but eerie and loud in the silence.

The nightmarish scenes were replicated in the next street and the next until at last they found the first of the bodies, those who'd tried to run but had been too slow. They were an elderly couple, both their heads lying in a pool of blood. They'd died together and lay now with arms outstretched, their fingers almost but not quite touching.

There was nothing to be done for them and the group moved on, soon encountering more dead mortals, most with vicious stab wounds, often limbs missing, occasionally a head. They had all died horrifically and Rosalind blinked back angry tears. "What has happened here?" she asked hoarsely.

The question was rhetorical, but the Landlord answered anyway. "Something terrible has been created, beyond our understanding." There was no reply from his sombre companions. Turning another corner, they saw smoke billowing from the entrance to a tube station.

"There'll be people down there!" Luke was already running. "We should help them!"

"No, love!" Molly shouted, but he was already running down the steps to the platforms below, only to reappear minutes later, tears streaming down his face. Nobody thought these were caused by the smoke.

"Where are we heading?" Wallace asked at last, but Molly shrugged. "Cornelius?" The Landlord looked at them without reply. They reached the Thames embankment and stared in horror at the dark green water of the river. Except now it wasn't green but red from the blood of scores of corpses who sped along its surface, jostling each other in a macabre race to reach the estuary and the open sea.

Moving more urgently now, they approached Westminster Bridge. Across the river, the London Eye lay on its side, half submerged in the water so that many of the floating bodies had become entangled in the wreckage. Most of its pods were smashed, those inside mostly dead, except for the few fortunate to be near the bottom of the rotating wheel when it toppled over. These wandered dazedly in varying states of injury, wondering what had just happened.

To his horror, Luke saw that one of the pods was almost intact, the family inside fighting to open its door as water flooded in, promising to drown them within minutes. "Help them!" he cried. "You have to help them!"

The Landlord rushed to the riverbank and sent a stream of argent fire across the river. It hit the top of the pod and smashed it to pieces. Moments later, the occupants had scrambled to safety.

"Run!" he shouted. "You must find shelter!" But the wandering mortals either didn't hear or chose to ignore him and continued their dazed meanderings. The Landlord tried again but with no success. Forced to leave the mortals to their fate, he and the others continued on their way.

As the bodies multiplied, so more buildings lay in ruins, some blazing fiercely. The Houses of Parliament looked intact, as did Westminster Abbey, but as they walked along Whitehall, they passed the gates that had protected Downing Street, now torn from their hinges. Number 10, along with other buildings, was alight with flames. They didn't bother to enter; the dead were strewn across the street and there was nothing they could do to help. And there was no time as, finally, they heard sounds of life – raucous, triumphant screams.

*   *   *   *

Portia had already sensed Morgan's appearance in the mortal world. No doubt he was causing great loss to her army but that didn't matter; there were plenty to replace them. But for now, she was distracted and still unaware the Landlord had entered the fight.

She was still awaiting news of his death, the thing she craved most, and her heart leaped with delight when one of her lieutenants came hurrying towards her. But when he began gasping tales of fighting a few kilometres distant, Portia was puzzled. *Who?* she wondered. *Not Morgan.* She knew from her spies that he was in a different part of the city. *Not the mortals, obviously.* More intrigued than concerned, she gathered a large force around her, summoned Anarkus, and followed the lieutenant.

It wasn't long before they encountered the first of her unlucky ones. Death eliminates all discrimination and there were many lying among the dead and dying mortals. *How?* Portia wondered. *Surely the mortals couldn't have done this.* Suddenly a man staggered dazedly from a nearby doorway, blood streaming from a head wound, and she blasted him viciously, leaving a gaping hole in his chest. Soon her dead became more numerous and at times they had to clamber over them. As the sounds of wand fire became louder, she saw the reason why. Ahead were two figures, their wands dispensing death, *murdering* her army.

Portia was unconcerned for the dead, they were only the tiniest fraction of the force she commanded, but for the first time, she felt a seed of doubt, for she had recognised one of them. *The goblin queen! Why is she here and not fighting for her own world? And who is that with her?* On cue, the man turned slightly, and Portia erupted with anger. *Logan! The filthy goblin must have freed him!*

"Anarkus," she screamed, "deal with him!"

Obligingly, Anarkus sent a bolt of fire, so fast that Logan was slow to react. Luckily Kamontip was not, and she nudged him from its path.

"Concentrate, dear," she said calmly. "Do try and not get yourself killed." She ducked as Portia sent her own bolt whizzing toward her.

Logan grinned; he was many things, not many of them good, but he was no coward and could fight. Soon he was engaged in deadly combat with Anarkus, who was really more interested in preserving his own skin than fighting, and soon began to retreat.

But Portia had the most powerful wand ever made and even though Kamontip was the more gifted fighter, even her Queen's Wand couldn't keep up. Soon she was spending more time dodging than attacking.

"Tactical retreat?" she said calmly, dancing as yet more wand fire dug deep holes around her feet.

"If you like," Logan agreed, "it is getting a little hot out here. You go first."

"No, we go together. Now!" They sent a barrage of wand fire, forcing Portia and Anarkus to throw themselves to the ground, and then they were gone.

Chapter 64

At the top of Whitehall, Nelson's Column had stood in tribute since 1843. Now it lay toppled, broken into three large pieces, the statue itself just a scattering of stones. Only the lions remained, proud but unseeing and unable to help. Here they saw the first of the unlucky ones.

A few were splashing in the fountain's water, seemingly oblivious to their companions who screamed joyfully, the bloodlust still upon them. There were about a hundred and their celebrations stopped abruptly when they spied the intruders. Quickly, they gathered into a group.

The Landlord and his companions formed a circle. Up close, the creatures were barely recognisable as once human, their faces distorted horribly, limbs twisted grotesquely. Saliva poured from their mouths in anticipation of an easy kill, yet they eyed their prey warily until one, bolder than the rest, attacked.

At once, Wallace stepped forward and swung his sword, killing it instantly. Immediately, another took its place and this time it was Luke who dispatched it. The rest backed away, muttering uncertainly; perhaps their prey wouldn't be so easy to kill after all. But then an order was barked from somewhere within the mass, then repeated forcefully. The unlucky ones attacked again, this time *en masse* and with intelligence. Some targeted the rear, others the flanks, so that within seconds they surrounded the group and leaped forward, eager for the kill.

Luke and Wallace fended them off while the witches and wizard sent swathes of wand fire in great sweeping arcs. It didn't last long; less than a minute had passed and now Trafalgar Square was carpeted with bodies.

"What are they?" Rosalind breathed. "They're the same creatures who attacked your world, Cornelius."

"And the bleedin' Sanctuary."

"Abominations," he replied sadly. "They are mortals turned into abominations." He could only hope Oscar had reached Aeryn in time.

As yet, the Landlord and his companions were not facing such odds, and after the short but victorious battle of Trafalgar Square, they stood while the Landlord tried to determine their next move.

In nearby Greek Street, Morgan had come across a large crowd of mortals taking the opportunity to loot its many shops and restaurants. Angry at their stupidity, he sent bolts of fire above their heads and they scattered and ran, terrified. Further along, he encountered more mortals, dead ones this time, most with their throats ripped out or limbs dismembered, some still grasping the spoils of their looting.

Suddenly a group of unlucky ones crashed through the window of the famous *L'escargot* restaurant, clutching large slabs of meat, huge cheeses, and casks of wine. Many were already drunk, all were intent on eating the food, tearing at it violently and fighting each other when their own was finished. None of them noticed Morgan until it was too late.

As he moved cautiously onto Shaftesbury Avenue, the Landlord and his small company left Trafalgar Square and, with no particular direction in mind, continued along Charing Cross Road. As they made their way past Strand, Luke saw a large monument lying broken in the road and recognised it as the *Eleanor Cross* that had stood outside Charing Cross Station. Although he knew this one was a replica of the original, it saddened him to think how many other famous treasures, like Nelson's Column, might already have been destroyed.

From behind the church of St-Martin-in-the-fields, yet more of the enemy emerged. There were more of them this time and they were hard-pressed to fight them off. The sounds of wand fire and the smell of magic reached Morgan's ears and nose and he paused, wondering, before heading in its direction.

Molly dispatched the last of the unlucky ones and as they passed the National Portrait Gallery, flames and smoke poured from its windows. Luke remembered a school trip there and it seemed so long ago, in another lifetime. Now they could hear shouting, laughter, and even harsh, guttural singing interspersed with piercing screams.

"Leicester Square!" Luke shouted. "They're in Leicester Square!"

They had already passed so many dead mortals they had almost become inured to the sight, but now they were shocked at the sudden increase in their numbers. Hundreds littered the pavement and road, mortals laden with shopping bags, others sitting at roadside cafes, the remnants of their meals still on the tables. Some died inside their vehicles, one had smashed through the windshield of his black cab, almost decapitating him, and blood still pumped from his severed trunk. In the back were two teenage girls who'd looked forward to their day out in London for so long. They huddled together on the floor of the cab, sobbing quietly; miraculously, the unlucky ones had missed them.

Leicester Square resembled a disaster area, littered with glass from the huge neon signs, vehicles overturned, fires everywhere, and it was packed with unlucky ones. They were soon embroiled once more, fighting for their lives.

Suddenly more wand fire entered from across the arena.

"Morgan! What are you doing here—" The Landlord stopped as he saw the expression on his friend's face; he knew instantly what had happened. "Morgan, I'm so very sorry," he said quietly.

In response, Morgan slashed an angry arc of fire, killing several dozen of the enemy with one sweep. He completely ignored the Landlord and the others.

"We should fight in a group," said Molly, who'd also realised Aeryn had been killed, "so we can protect each other."

"You fight in a group if you want to," Morgan replied, tonelessly, and his eyes were terrible. "I don't care what happens to me."

"Don't be stupid." The Landlord winced at his own choice of words. "We need to—"

"Leave me alone!" Morgan rasped, and suddenly he ran, putting as much distance between them as quickly as he could. As he ran, his wand swung viciously, leaving a trail of death behind him.

Nevertheless, the Landlord knew they stood a better chance by staying together and they moved with him, always keeping a short distance away.

*　　　　*　　　　*　　　　*

The unlucky ones had now infested most of London and the mass exodus of vehicles continued. Some who'd acted quickly had made it out of the city to the motorways and Portia ignored them; they could be picked up later. For those stuck in central London, crowding the bridges, the enemy found a new sport. They had taken to lifting the cars, their terrified passengers still inside, and tossing them into the Thames until it was no longer a river of water, but of twisted, mangled metal. Many mortals drowned as their vehicles quickly submerged, while others managed to scramble out, only to find themselves forced back underwater by the sheer weight and number of vehicles. But many hundreds climbed onto the roofs and sailed away, unwittingly finding a quicker path to safety.

Portia, from her vantage point on the Skydeck of The Shard, high above London, could see the progress of her army. With her keen eyesight, much sharper than that of a mortal, she could even see those making their way North toward other towns and cities. But it was the flashes of wand fire not too far away that caught her attention and she smiled.

At last, she thought, *they have arrived.* Skipping lightly back down the stairs, she fervently hoped Cornelius would be there.

Chapter 65

Lucy looked at her husband, her eyes big and frightened. "Who could it be, Charles?" she whispered. "Best just ignore it!"

Instead, he carefully moved the cabinet, taking care to make no noise, and peered through the keyhole. Then he gave a cry of delight and flung open the door.

"Peter!" he exclaimed. "At last! Where on Earth have you been?" He ushered him inside and rushed to put the kettle on while the girls careered downstairs to see what was happening. When she saw him, Penelope flung herself into his arms and burst into tears.

"We only returned late last night," he said, bewildered. "There are fires and broken shops everywhere. What's going on, have there been riots?"

"Worse than that, we've been trying to get hold of you for ages!"

"Really? I hadn't noticed," said Peter drily, thinking of the 378 missed calls on his phone. "What do you mean, worse?"

"Is Luna with you?" Charles asked.

"Yeah," he replied, with sarcasm born from sudden worry at what he was going to hear, "I left her outside on the doorstep." Peter's wife had wanted to come but he'd refused, thinking she'd be much safer at home with the doors locked.

"Sorry, of course." Charles took him into the sitting room and began to talk. When he had finished, Peter sprang to his feet again.

"I must go!" He ran to the door and shoved the cabinet aside, waiting for Charles to unlock the door. "The others will need my help!"

"Do you have your wand?" said Charles, a little wistfully, wishing he had the power to rush off and fight evil.

Peter drew it from his pocket; it was shining a little with the prospect of being useful once more. "Yes. I don't usually carry it these days but with the unrest outside..." He kissed

Lucy's cheek and hugged Penelope tightly. "Stay safe," he whispered hoarsely, "all of you." He nodded at Amelia. "Nice to meet you," he said with a crooked smile. "Well, almost meet you." Then he shook Charles's hand and was gone, returning seconds later, opening the door before it could be locked and shouting, "Let Luna know where I've gone!"

*   *   *   *

Lucy rang Peter's wife and listened to half an hour of her panicking and crying on the phone, barely able to get a word in. At last, she ended the call, sympathetic but relieved; she had her own family to worry about. Minutes later, it rang again and this time Charles answered.

"Charles!" Luna screeched. "Peter hasn't got that knife! I don't know if he'll need it! Oh, God, let him be safe! I can't bear it!"

"Knife?" Charles's brain was slow to catch up.

"Yes!" she exclaimed impatiently. "That knife of Ch… Cha… something…"

"The Knife of Chiang." Charles groaned, trying to think if Peter would need it. *What would Morgan do?* He dithered for a moment while the others looked at him curiously, then made up his mind. "I'll be there soon, don't worry. Luna, everything will be fine." With that, he slammed down the receiver.

"What?" asked Lucy, her voice rising.

"What is it, Dad?"

As he quickly explained, he grabbed his coat and turned to the door.

"No. Charles, you can't leave us!" Lucy snatched the coat from his grasp.

"Lucy, I must! I think Peter will need—"

"I'll go, Dad, I'll get the knife and give it to Peter."

"No you will not, young lady," Lucy exclaimed. "You're going nowhere!"

"Dad, they're my friends!" Penelope knew he was more likely to fight her corner. "I have to do something!"

As they all argued, trying to decide what to do, nobody noticed Amelia had gone completely silent and moved away to the other side of the room.

What do I do now? she wailed inwardly. She knew she couldn't let Penelope go alone into danger but if she went with her… Anarkus' pull was strong and she was having trouble keeping him at bay. *How much worse will it be when I get closer to him?*

"Mum," Penelope was saying, "I'm not a child and you can't stop me." It was a card she rarely, if ever, played because she knew it was unfair, but she was desperate. "Anyway," she continued artfully, "what if something happened and Dad wasn't here?" She reached into Charles's coat pocket, withdrew the keys, and looked at Amelia. "Coming?"

"Don't worry, Mrs. Ham… I mean Lucy." Amelia jumped to her feet. "I won't let anything happen to her."

Penelope went to them both and hugged them tightly, while Amelia hung back. "I love you," she said quietly, and they turned to leave.

"Amelia," Lucy said, and held out her arms. Startled, she allowed herself to be hugged, unable to remember the last time that had happened. She turned away, *really* hoping Charles wasn't going to do the same. He wasn't, but he patted her shoulder awkwardly. "Good luck, Amelia. Look after her, and yourself."

Chapter 66

By the time the witches re-entered the motorway, dusk was already falling and they were all tired. It wasn't long before most of them, replete with too much fast food and chocolate, were asleep. In the driver's seat, Clarissa felt her own eyes drooping and after she'd hit the central barrier for the third time, terrifying the drivers on the other side and jolting her companions awake, they thought it prudent to pull over and rest for the remainder of the night. Early the next morning, they were back on the road and approaching London.

Ketsara, one of the younger witches, had badly wanted to be of use and volunteered to read the map. Agnes, who found such things tedious, was happy to let her. So far Ketsara had done a good job, although to be fair she'd only needed to direct them onto two big roads. But then, as they entered the edge of the city, she inexplicably directed them off the motorway, and unknown to any of them, they were now headed in the wrong direction.

It wasn't until they saw a sign saying M1 North that they realised their mistake, but they were puzzled because all around there were signs of the enemy having been there. Appalled, they looked from the windows at the many burning vehicles and dead or dying mortals. At Agnes's request, they pulled over for a quick conference.

"I thought the enemy was fighting in the middle of the city."

"I think they are," agreed Agnes, "but maybe… I don't know, let me think." Apart from the rumbling of Maymea's stomach – she was always hungry – there was silence until Agnes spoke again.

"It's obvious," she said quietly. "Portia has sent some of her army to conquer the other cities. The question is, do we turn around or do we follow?"

"Follow," said one, immediately.

"Follow."

"Yes, follow."

Decision made, they set off again. It was trickier now the road was littered with vehicles, and soon Clarissa gave up trying to weave around them, choosing to shunt them aside instead. It wasn't long before the coach was in a rather worse condition than when it had left Leeds the previous morning. A few hours later, they came upon stragglers from Portia's army and Clarissa simply ran them down. When they became more numerous, the witches piled out of the coach and quickly dispatched them.

After a quick stop at a service station, where they refuelled themselves and the vehicle, they were back on the road and nearing the first town. Already they could see the smoke rising from burning buildings.

Chapter 67

"We don't have a chance!" Luke looked despairingly around. No matter how many of the creatures they killed, it seemed like another ten stepped in to replace each one.

"There is always a chance, my boy." Wallace lay a steadying hand upon his arm. "Do not abandon hope yet."

"Yet?" a voice tinkled merrily behind them. "You are wrong, Wallace, we will *never* abandon hope."

They spun around, wand and swords raised, except for the Landlord, who'd already realised who it was. "Well, this is a lovely surprise," he drawled, turning slowly and smiling. "You come to lend a hand?"

"Oh, you know me, Cornelius, always a sucker for a lost cause." Kamontip pirouetted, and her wand fire removed the heads of several creatures who'd thought to offer a challenge. "By the way, I've brought a friend." She pointed to where a tall figure could be seen cutting his way through a wall of unlucky ones, attempting to reach Morgan, who was almost engulfed.

Luke didn't recognise him at first but Molly and Wallace certainly did. Wallace was too busy swinging his sword in great sweeping arcs to do anything other than splutter his outrage, but Molly couldn't contain hers.

"Well, that's marvellous." She glared at the goblin queen. "Honestly, Kamontip, I like and respect you, I really do, but you've gone too bleedin' far this time." Several unlucky ones, perhaps sensing her distraction, ran at her quickly from behind. Without looking, she sent a bolt of power over her shoulder, incinerating them.

"I don't think she's happy," Kamontip whispered to the Landlord, just loud enough for Molly to hear.

"You think?" He smiled, shaking his head. "You're so naughty, Kamontip, how do you get away with it?"

"Charm, my dear." She smiled sweetly as she lopped off yet another creature's head. "Pure, unadulterated charm. As well as a shocking disregard for rules."

"You've got that bleedin' right," Molly agreed sourly.

Unaware of Kamontip's appearance, Morgan swung his wand with complete abandon, hardly caring where his streams of fire went, so long as they killed as many of the vermin as possible. He fought in a blind, all-consuming rage, with total disregard for his own safety.

"One would almost think you're trying to get yourself killed, brother," Logan said casually, at the same dispatching a half dozen unlucky ones as he forged a path to his brother's side.

Morgan's head whipped around, and he stared at him in amazement. That brief pause should have cost him his life, as a spear came hurtling toward his chest, but at the last second Logan flicked his wand and it swerved, missing by mere centimetres. The irony of him saving Morgan's life was not lost on either of them.

"What are you doing here?" he rasped. "How did you escape?"

"Now, now, dear brother." Logan, as always whenever they encountered each other, couldn't help adopting his usual mocking tone. "Aren't you pleased to see me?"

In answer, Morgan swept a particularly vicious arc of fire, killing at least fifty of the enemy. The rest backed away from the two wizards and the first ranks broke and ran, soon followed by the rest. Within seconds, Morgan and Logan were alone, apart from the scores of dead that littered the ground at their feet. Catching their breath and stretching their aching muscles, they looked at each other.

It was what Morgan had dreamed about for so long, a rapprochement with his brother, but he could take no pleasure that it might suddenly be possible at last; his grief at Aeryn's death was all-consuming. And there was still the question of trust. Logan might appear to be throwing himself into the fighting, and he *had* saved his life, yet Morgan still couldn't help questioning his motives. Logan never did anything that wouldn't benefit him.

"Why are you here?" he repeated. "Who set you free? It can't have been Cornelius; he'd have spoken to me first." Logan was ready with a stinging retort when something else occurred to Morgan. "And where did you get such a powerful wand?"

"Oh, stop with the holier-than-thou attitude," Logan snapped. "If you must know, it was Kamontip!"

"What?"

"Kamontip freed me and gave me the wand."

"You're lying!" Morgan was incensed. "If you're Portia's lap dog, I'll—"

"You'll what? Kill me?"

Suddenly the gulf between them was infinite. Unconsciously, both had raised their wands, but then Logan's shoulders slumped, and he lowered his.

"Go ahead," he said softly, "I dare say I deserve it."

Morgan had been ready to unleash his full fury at his brother but now he paused. For the first time since he could remember, Logan's words held a ring of truth. *He seems different*, he thought. *What's happened to him?* He looked down the slope to where the battle was still raging.

"Come on," he said softly, "we're not done yet." He walked away and was soon embroiled in the fighting once more.

Logan watched him for a moment, then followed. Soon, with the addition of Kamontip, the group, at least briefly, began to gain the upper hand.

*   *   *   *

From the edge of the battlefield, careful not to get too near the actual fighting, Portia and Anarkus watched the progress of their army, not liking what they saw. Some were running away and the rest, like sheep, were starting to follow. She'd howled in triumph when she sensed Aeryn's death and made a note to reward the wizard she'd sent to conquer her world. Well, reward him before she got rid of him, of course. But when Suluhura arrived and told of his failure, her rage was black, and she'd killed him immediately.

Now, as she watched the decimation of her army, she smiled. *Let Cornelius and his merry band think they are winning.* Moving into a nearby building, where she wouldn't be observed, she began her spell. Minutes later, a portal appeared and the third of her army she'd kept in reserve poured through.

Chapter 68

Penelope started the car while Amelia ran to open the gates. As they drove out, there was a soft *shplatt* and a slight bump beneath the wheels and Penelope braked sharply. The pavement was littered with apples and oranges, potatoes and carrots. Beyond lay the body of an elderly woman.

Oh no, Penelope groaned silently, *not Mrs. Mitchell.*

On the same day each week, Mrs. Mitchell made the short trip to the local shops to buy fruit and vegetables. Walking was difficult for her these days and she couldn't go far or carry heavy shopping bags. Her daughter did most of her shopping for her online, but Mrs. Mitchell wouldn't give up altogether and was determined to make her weekly trip for as long as she could.

Only a few evenings ago Penelope had gone round and read to her, as she often did. She knew the old woman had lived in the house two doors down for many years, and that since the death of her husband, she was lonely. Now, with her failing eyesight, she was unable to read easily, her favourite thing, and she and Penelope had grown very fond of each other.

There was nothing to be done right now and their mission was urgent. Penelope pulled out into the road and immediately saw dozens of people further up. There was no doubt they were the enemy; many were horribly deformed and she watched in horror as they dragged people from their houses and brutally murdered them. She sent a quick text to Charles, warning him to stay inside, but made no mention of the old lady, knowing he'd probably rush out and try to help.

"We have to turn round!" she yelled, but Amelia was already looking in the rear-view mirror.

"No! There are more behind us! Drive!"

Penelope rammed the accelerator pedal to the floor and the powerful car shot forward. She covered her face as they approached the unlucky ones and screamed when the first of them bounced over the bonnet of the car onto the roof, to lie broken and bloody on the road behind. And then they were through.

Penelope heaved great, anxious breaths, her heart hammering. Amelia was no less shaken, but she placed her hand on Penelope's thigh and squeezed.

"You were amazing." She smiled, leaning over and kissing her on the cheek. "I'm so proud– Watch that one!" The car swerved as Penelope narrowly avoided another of the enemy, though Amelia wondered why she hadn't just run it down.

They continued in this way until, eventually, Peter's house came into view. By now the car was covered in dents and scrapes, one headlight was smashed, and steam was seeping out from under the bonnet. Not bothering to stop at the wooden gates, Penelope crashed right through, screeching to a halt at the front door, which immediately opened.

"Oh, my dear, I was so worried!" cried Luna. "Here, it's here!" She passed the knife through the open window then leaned in and hugged Penelope, who briefly hugged her back before slamming the gearshift into reverse.

"Go back inside and lock your doors! Don't come out for anything!"

Luna nodded. "Be careful!"

The journey toward central London was even worse as the enemy became more numerous. And now there were worrying noises coming from under the bonnet, as well as much more steam.

Amelia had gone quiet, and Penelope presumed she was frightened, but that wasn't it. Anarkus was strong in her mind now, taking over. *Come, you belong to me,* his voice said, *come now.* She was able to resist at first, but as they drove further into London, Amelia began to realise he spoke truth, she did belong to him. *Kill the girl.* But she shook her head; that was too much. *Kill the girl!* Anarkus insisted, and now it seemed a reasonable request. She took out the knife and held it hidden by her thigh. She looked at Penelope for one last time, dispassionate, more than ready to do Anarkus' bidding. But then Penelope turned and smiled at her, and for a second, Anarkus' voice became fainter.

"Stop the car!"

Startled, Penelope hit the brakes, and they skidded to a stop. "What? What happened?"

"I have to get out!" Amelia pushed open the door and threw herself into the road. "I'm sorry," she sobbed, "I'm so sorry!" And then she was gone, swallowed up by the crowds of unlucky ones.

Bewildered, wondering what had just happened, Penelope began to cry. *Amelia is already dead,* she thought. *She wouldn't have stood a chance. What just happened?*

Despite her shock, she knew she couldn't just sit there and soon she was back on the move. Presently, she saw flashes of wand fire and headed toward it. Steam was obscuring her view; the car wouldn't last much longer. It was making a loud screeching noise and juddering violently, protesting at the abuse it was suffering.

When Penelope turned into Leicester Square, she was confronted by thousands of unlucky ones, and she groaned, wondering what to do. All at once, she spotted a familiar figure and sped toward him, sliding to a stop and almost running him down.

Chapter 69

Buoyed by the influx of new fodder into her army, Portia soon had the small company of witches and wizards retreating again.

The Landlord was filled with pride at the way his companions continued to fight, even though they must know, as he did, that it was hopeless. *Some of us could still live,* he thought, looking round at his companions. He knew Molly and

Morgan would insist on staying until the end, and he looked at Rosalind.

"No!" she said, anticipating him, accurately reading his mind. "I won't abandon you!"

"But we can't win!" he tried arguing, but she ignored him, sending more of the enemy to their doom instead.

Suddenly, a wall behind them was demolished by a bolt from Portia's wand. Luke skipped nimbly away, but Wallace, with his dodgy leg, was not so fortunate and he lay there, trapped, grimacing and stifling a cry of pain.

"Wallace!" Luke dragged him from beneath the pile of bricks, while the others protected them.

"You need to get to safety!" shouted the Landlord above the noise of the snarling unlucky ones who'd edged closer, sensing a kill.

"Not a chance!" Wallace limped forward, preparing to fight again, but the Landlord took his arm and leaned in close.

"Think of Luke!" he whispered. "He shouldn't die like this!"

Wallace looked at him and then nodded. He gripped the Landlord's hand in farewell, then shouted, "Luke, we're getting out of here."

Luke was no coward and had fought bravely, but he couldn't help feeling a sneaking sense of relief. Before he could reply, the Landlord cast a glamour over them and Wallace pulled him away.

Suddenly, two tiny figures emerged from nowhere, emitting high-pitched squeals of excitement. In their hands they carried swords, each no longer than a fingernail, and began stabbing the eyeballs of the unlucky ones, jumping from one to the next in a blur of speed.

"What are those two bleedin' doing here!" yelled Molly to nobody in particular as the intervention gave them a brief but welcome respite.

When Velveteena and Moth had entered the mortal world that morning, they'd been astonished at the devastation they'd found, and at the sheer number of Portia's army. They immediately set to work and within an hour hundreds of unlucky ones were blinded. Within two hours they numbered in the thousands. Stumbling blindly around, these were easy prey for those who coveted their weapons or armour, and soon mass brawls broke out everywhere, resulting in many hundreds more deaths.

"Shame we didn't invite a few friends to come along," said Moth when they'd stopped for a brief rest, "they'd have loved this!"

"This is not a party," his sister responded sarcastically, "that's why we didn't *invite* anyone!"

"Oh, shut up! You know what I mean—" Moth was always ready for an argument, but Velveteena poked him in the ribs.

"Not now, Moth, look!" Running from around a corner was another huge group of the enemy, and she grinned.

"Back to work!" they said in unison.

Anxious as they were to reach Molly and her companions, the appearance of yet more of the enemy on every street they flew past was too much temptation. Thus, it wasn't until late afternoon they spotted the small circle, about to be overcome.

"We're too late!" cried Velveteena, but Moth shook his head.

"No, we're not! Quickly! Come on!"

As they zoomed into the plethora of eyeballs, swords in one hand, wands in the other, Velveteena spotted Molly and waved, but the witch was too surprised to wave back.

"Who cares!" Morgan yelled back. "Keep attacking!"

At first, Portia couldn't understand what the delay was; she was anxious now for it to be over so she could gloat over the bodies of her enemies, Cornelius in particular. Then she saw the faeries and screamed in anger, directing her fire at them instead so that now, as well as popping eyeballs, they had to dodge her deathly power. But then, when one narrowly missed Velveteena, it was Moth's turn to scream.

"How dare you!" he shouted, sending his own bolt of fire, which, more by luck than skill, shaved across the top of Portia's head.

"My hair!" she screamed, outraged, putting her hand on her head. "You've ruined my hair!"

"Serves you right!" Moth grinned, popping yet another eyeball while at the same time making a rude gesture.

But despite the aid of the faeries, the small company was doomed. Urged on by Portia, those that had shields held them above their heads and slowly they closed in once more.

Chapter 70

"They are losing." In her mind, Siwaraksa could see the battle as surely as if she were there.

"Yes." Mitra knew there was no point in denial. "Where is Cissy? Surely the potion should have worked its magic by now?"

"If the girl managed to get it to her," she agreed, glumly. "The battle is fierce."

"She will prevail," said Mitra, thinking, *she must*. When there was no reply, she persisted, "You were determined she would reach it, weren't you? The potion, I mean."

"I have no idea what you mean." Siwaraksa avoided her eyes. "Catrin found it on her own merit, I had nothing to do with it."

"Oh hush." Mitra smiled. "You foresaw this battle, as did I. You knew they would need the Sanctuary's leader if they were to have even the slightest chance of victory."

"Where do you get your courage, Mitra?"

Mitra stared at her, confused at the change of direction. "What do you mean?"

"I'm talking of Cornelius," she replied quietly.

Turning away so that Siwaraksa wouldn't see the tears in her eyes, she took a deep breath before turning back. "Many have tried to end his life," she said, "and none have yet succeeded." There was a hint of pride in the statement but there was no denying the hopeless look she gave her friend.

Siwaraksa smiled and squeezed her arm. "Catrin will get the potion to Cissy, you said so yourself. There is great strength and determination in her."

"I know," agreed Mitra. "She'd have made a fine witch, wouldn't she? But do you think Cissy will have the power to defeat these creatures if she is cured?"

"*When* she is cured," Siwaraksa corrected, "I think Cissy will…" She paused. "Well, let's wait and see."

"It won't make any difference." Racine sneered. "Your friends are all going to die!"

Not for the first time, Siwaraksa regretted freeing her from the web, but it was Mitra who reacted. Rarely angry, she let out a cry of rage and waved her wand at Racine. The vile old witch had power, but she was far too slow to prevent the spell from taking root. Instead, she could only stare, cross-eyed, as the skin of her lips melded together, unable even to give a cry of protest as her mouth was firmly closed.

"Don't say a word," Mitra warned Siwaraksa, seeing her friend about to speak. "She deserves it and I'm tired of hearing her vitriol."

"Oh, don't worry,"—Siwaraksa smiled—"I was only going to say how peaceful it suddenly is around here."

Chapter 71

It was with mixed feelings that Amelia watched Penelope drive away; part relief but also despair. She wondered whether they'd ever see each other again. But her thoughts were fleeting, almost consumed by the presence of Anarkus in her mind. As she walked slowly toward the fighting, she tried to resist but her feet kept walking and she had no control.

Soon she was walking through Portia's army, only vaguely wondering why they left her alone instead of tearing her to pieces. All too soon, she stood before Anarkus, who grinned maliciously and then spun her around to face the small, almost defeated company of the Sanctuary, holding her in an iron grip.

"Now you can watch as your friends die."

"They're not my friends," she snapped. "I don't know them."

"Nevertheless, you will watch and then you will find your dirty, mortal girlfriend and kill her too."

"I will not!" She struggled to release herself, but his hold was far too powerful. She knew that Penelope was trying to reach Peter, and she sent a silent prayer, possibly the first time she'd ever done so, that Anarkus wouldn't find out she was so close.

* * * *

The battle was lost, and they were surrounded. Miraculously, they still lived, but as they saw Portia striding between the ranks of unlucky ones toward them, they knew it wouldn't be for long.

"Cornelius!" Portia smiled, holding out her hand to be kissed. "How nice to see you again, it's been so long!"

"Oh, not so long really." He ignored the hand. "An eternity would've been better."

"Tut *tut,* Cornelius!" The anger flashed through her eyes so quickly the Landlord would have missed it had he not been watching. "You were always ready with a quick retort. Even as a child, you were the same; I didn't like you then, either."

He clapped a hand to his chest. "I'm wounded," he parried. "My heart is filled with pain." Then he yawned widely, wishing she would get on with it.

"Well now," she continued, "you boys really shouldn't have defied me, you know." She clapped her hands merrily. "But never mind, I've decided to forgive you." She beamed round at them all, as if expecting thanks.

"Forgive us for what?" Morgan drawled, knowing full well.

"Morgan,"—she shook her head sadly—"you should never have stolen your brother from me, it was very naughty. But, to show there is no ill feeling, I've decided to make your deaths quick!"

"How very charming," he murmured, "we can't thank you enough, Portia."

"I know!" She gave a graceful curtsey. "Never let it be said I'm not munificent in victory."

"Bleedin' idiot," muttered Molly.

"And, Molly,"—Portia couldn't hide her satisfaction—"you thought you'd escaped me, didn't you? Yet here we all are."

"You haven't bleedin' won yet, you silly woman."

"Oh, but I have!" She looked at Rosalind but said nothing; the hatred in her eyes was eloquence enough. "But you…" She turned to Logan. She hadn't forgotten the humiliation of his escape from her courtroom, and she had special, extremely painful plans for him. "I will give you power, riches!" Portia's eyes burned with an intensity that couldn't be ignored and Logan found himself entranced. Suddenly she seemed to him the most beautiful woman he'd ever seen. "Join me now, Logan." She held out a hand and he took an involuntary step forward. "We will rule this land of mortals together, you and I."

"You do know she's enchanting you," observed the Landlord, mildly. "That this is all a trick?"

"Be quiet!" She flicked her wand and knocked him several meters backward, where he landed with a thud. He got to his feet gingerly, rubbing his backside.

It was what Logan had always craved but never quite been able to achieve. And here it was, offered on a plate should he choose to accept. The temptation was unbearable and impossible to resist. Around him, his allies looked at him impassively, none trying to dissuade him. They looked, if anything, merely curious to see what he would decide. He knew this was a line that, once crossed, could never be uncrossed, and suddenly he heard a roaring inside his head, urging him to take Portia's hand. *Take it,* the voice told him, insistently, *take it!* He took another step forward.

Another step and he knew he was about to receive the power he wanted. A surge of triumph surged within, only to be replaced quickly with another emotion, one he didn't immediately recognise. *Sorrow?* he wondered. *What have I to feel sorrowful about?* He looked at his brother, trying to gauge his feelings, but Morgan's face was closed. Next in line was Molly; a hint of contempt in her eyes, nothing he wouldn't have expected.

Logan took another step and now Portia's hand, still outstretched, was within touching distance. He continued to look around the circle. Wallace; Logan remembered him from their childhood – they'd never been friends. The one called Luke; not a boy anymore, he realised, but a young man. It seemed a long time ago that he'd once wanted to capture him, believing him to be possessed of incredible power. But no, that had turned out to be the girl. *Where is she?* he wondered. *Why isn't she here?*

His gaze met that of the Landlord, and they stared at each other for a long time. Logan sensed that this wizard would know whether he was about to make a huge mistake, but the eyes were, for once, devoid of emotion and Logan could read no clue within them. In his peripheral vision, Logan saw that Kamontip was next in line but that was one pair of eyes he could not search. His sorrow was joined by a sense of shame, and he turned quickly to look at Portia.

The voices, which had lulled slightly, were back in full force. *Take her hand!* they screamed, and all at once, he acquiesced. He knew now that this was pre-ordained and that it was useless to resist. *And why should I?* he thought. *I deserve this!* Slowly, his hand rose toward Portia's.

"Logan," a voice behind him said softly, and his hand wavered and ceased moving. "Logan, don't."

Ignore her! his mind screamed.

"Logan," the voice said again, "look at me." The word held a note of command that was irresistible, and he turned slowly.

"Logan!" Portia snapped. "Come here!" This was also a command, but he found it easier to dismiss.

"Look at me," Kamontip said, and this time it wasn't a command, but a request. Reluctantly, his gaze met hers. The shame he felt was almost overwhelming, and he caught his breath in astonished wonder. Kamontip's eyes were filled with such love and understanding that he was speechless.

It's not possible, he thought, incredulous. *It is not possible for me to be loved.* In this he was mistaken; his father had loved both twins with a deep, fierce passion. Loved them equally and without reservation or preference. His brother, despite the centuries of ill will and betrayal, loved him still. But Logan, so long deluded after so many centuries of hating everything and everyone, including himself, had found it easier to deny than embrace. But now, the evidence couldn't be denied and this time the step he took was toward Kamontip.

"Logan!" Portia shouted again. "Don't be a fool!"

The voices in his head made one final attempt, but he dismissed them with ease, like swatting a troublesome fly. Yet he turned and looked at Portia, seeing her now for what she was; a woman who was not loved, one who had only ever craved power by any means, who had only one weapon in her arsenal, that of fear. He took a moment to wonder what it would be like if he accepted her offer, but it was an idle thought, for he realised he would only be allowed to live at her whim.

He turned once more to Kamontip and suddenly, with his facial muscles almost having to practice, so long was it since he had done so, Logan smiled. Kamontip took only the time to breathe a sigh of relief before she ran forward into his arms.

"How very noble of you, Logan!" Portia spat, disgusted. "Perhaps I will spare your new friends after all, make them my subjects. They will lose their power, of course – I know a very useful spell to make that happen. Accept my offer or you will all die." She was met with stony silence, apart from Molly.

"No bleedin' chance." She spat on the ground, aiming perfectly between Portia's feet. "I'd rather stick pins in my eyeballs,"—she tapped her pocket, warning the faeries to be ready to fight—"or even miniature swords."

Portia decided not to rise to the bait, somehow understanding she could never win an argument against Molly. "Very well." As she raised her wand, there was a surreal silence, the air heavy with a mixture of triumph and defeat.

Yet they weren't quite beaten yet; would not be until they lay dead on the ground. The Landlord, Rosalind, Morgan, and Logan still had their wands, but in her supreme arrogance, Portia didn't really care. She pointed her wand at each of them in turn, mocking them, savouring the moment as the silence continued.

It was broken by the faint sound of glass breaking, but nobody took notice – such sounds had become common over the last few hours. Then her hand was hit by a bolt of fire that knocked the wand from her grip and sent her crashing to the ground. It was followed by more rapid bolts that tore into her army.

Chapter 72

As they drove into the first town they encountered, it was soon evident that, apart from a few of the enemy who'd lingered and who were quickly killed, the rest of them had moved on. Following, they soon saw more smoke rising in many different places and Agnes wondered how the enemy was moving so fast. It didn't take long for her to realise the answer.

The enemy had split into mini armies, each one still huge, and Oxford, Birmingham, and Derby had all quickly fallen prey to Portia's monstrous plan. Before the witches could reach them, Leeds and Manchester had followed. They kept going, watching out for the enemy until they approached the city of Liverpool and, for the first time, encountered a large segment of Portia's army. Already, much of that army was moving further up the country, through the Lake District on one side, towards Newcastle and Northumberland on the other. It wouldn't take long before they were headed for Scotland, with Edinburgh and Glasgow first in their path.

Suspecting this, Agnes considered splitting her own tiny band into even smaller groups to follow the enemy here and there in a desperate attempt to stem the tide. But there was safety in numbers. What chance would a group of four or five witches have against such odds? Anyway, they only had one vehicle and only Clarissa could drive.

Now at last the witches could really do something to help. As they came to the end of the motorway, the road divided and the enemy divided with it, some to the left, others to the right. Agnes tossed a mental coin and sent Clarissa to the right. There they encountered hundreds of unlucky ones, but these were no match for the witches, who, by stopping, fighting then moving on again, quickly made progress. Agnes sensed they'd not yet reached the heart of the enemy, and so it proved.

Driving alongside a large area of grass, they saw thousands of unlucky ones running up the hill to a huge building at the top. Smashing through the iron railing, they followed, mowing down all in their path until they reached the top and the famous Anfield Stadium. There they encountered thousands of the enemy, all trying to get inside.

The witches had no idea what this place was, but they could sense the presence of many mortals inside. Unknown to them, these had been trapped overnight, since the football match had been abandoned. At half-time, news of the atrocities in London had begun to show on the TV screens displaying the half-time results. It soon became apparent that whatever this was, it was quickly spreading north and the stewards had closed and barred all the iron gates leading into the stadium. Then they'd hustled everyone back into the arena itself, football teams included, and barred the numerous entrances too. Sure enough, the enemy had eventually arrived, but so far had been unable to gain entry.

When the coach was finally unable to move forward, the witches leaped out, sending colourful streams of wand fire all about them. Normally, wand fire tends to be white, occasionally blue, but witches are known for their style and each had adapted theirs to their favourite colour so that now the air was filled with clouds of technicolour smoke. Soon they'd forged a path and made their way up the wide steps that led to the main stand entrances. From there they could direct their fire onto those below as well as prevent the unlucky ones from following up the steps at either side.

The enemy died in their hundreds, and then thousands, but still Agnes despaired, knowing they were failing. After a couple of hours, they'd killed tens of thousands, and yet still they came.

Chapter 73

Peter had no difficulty in finding the site of the battle, for the air was filled with magic that intensified as he drew closer. A dozen times he was forced to stop and fight as the enemy crowded around his car, baying for his blood. On one occasion, they were so numerous he couldn't open the door and he was forced to climb through the sunroof and fight from there.

But at last, he spun round a corner, tires screeching, and almost cannoned into the back of Portia's army. Before they could react, he flung himself from the car and dashed into the nearest building, running to the second floor to gain a clearer view. What he saw made his blood run cold; he couldn't make out who Portia was aiming at but someone was about to die.

He wasted precious seconds trying to open a window, then frantically grabbed a chair and threw it, shattering the glass. His bolt of fire was perfectly aimed and, pausing only to send a barrage of staccato-like bolts, and scorning the stairs, he leaped through the window and landed, sure-footed, on the pavement. Sending more bolts of lethal power into the unlucky ones, he was about to charge forward when a car screeched to a stop in front of him, almost running him down. Peter stared in amazement as Penelope hopped out and ran to him.

"Peter!" She gasped, overwhelmed with relief at having found him. "You forgot the Knife of Chiang!"

"What are you doing here!" he yelled, appalled at the danger she had put herself in.

"There's no time! Take the knife!"

He took it and stuck it into his belt, then hustled her through the doorway of the building, telling her to take shelter. Then he was gone, his wand creating violent death as he forged a path through the unlucky ones, toward his companions.

But Penelope knew Amelia was among them somewhere and she ignored his instructions. She followed the path he had taken, firing her wand as she ran. It was in no way powerful

enough to kill, but it flashed and banged a lot and the unlucky
ones didn't realise it.

*   *   *   *

"It's Peter!" the Landlord yelled as he sent his own
terrifying swathe of fire tearing into the unlucky ones.
Kamontip sent her own bolt hurtling toward Portia, but with
the speed of a cat, she reached her wand just in time and
deflected it, sending it whizzing into her own army. Anarkus,
terrified to be in the midst of the fighting, backed away, pulling
Amelia, who was less resistive now, with him until he was
enveloped by the army. For a mad moment, he considered
simply running away, but then his mind cleared, and he knew
he would face the wrath of Portia if he did. There was nowhere
he could hide, not in any universe or dimension. And anyway,
he wasn't about to give up on the prospect of power and riches.
He gathered the little courage he possessed and returned, still
gripping Amelia, thrusting her before him.

Amelia had tried so hard to resist, and for a time
managed to retain her memories of what it was like to be free,
of the short time she'd spent with Penelope and her family. But
really, it was all too much, so much easier to stop resisting. *It's
not so bad,* she thought, almost drowsily. *When Anarkus wins,
he'll teach me lots of things; I'll have so much power…* She was
too tired to realise that the thought gave her no pleasure at all.
Nor had it occurred to her that when she had outlived her
usefulness, he would discard her like a broken toy.

Peter reached them and, with renewed vigour, the small company resumed their assault on the impossibly huge army. Behind him, Penelope had somehow managed not to get herself killed and, so far, none of the company had noticed her. But someone else had.

Penelope, what are you doing here? thought Amelia, wondering if she was dreaming. *You need to leave before you're killed. I don't want you to die.* Suddenly the voices were back; *You do want her to die,* she heard, and now that seemed perfectly reasonable until the other chimed in, *you must fight, Amelia, you must resist.*

Suddenly a man was running toward them, brandishing a knife, and she recognised Peter who Charles had been so desperately trying to reach. He was still too far away and Anarkus had seen him, already raising his wand. With a huge effort of will, she banished both voices from her mind and bit down hard on his other arm, which still gripped her around her neck.

With a scream of pain, Anarkus backhanded her viciously and she crashed to the ground. Peter was drawing closer and Anarkus ran toward him, blind with rage. Rosalind saw his intention and levelled her wand at him, ready to save Peter.

"No," Morgan warned, placing a hand on her forearm, "it must be the knife. History has decreed that Anarkus, if he lives, will be a far greater threat than Portia ever was. Wand fire will not kill him, only the Knife of Chiang."

"But—" Rosalind tried to object, but Morgan interrupted.

"This is Peter's destiny, it has been for thousands of years, ever since the creation of the blood moon. He may live or he may die, but you must let destiny take its course."

Amelia, of course, knew nothing of this as she lay there despairing, knowing she was too far away to do anything. Her mind was clear now and she was enraged that Anarkus was about to kill yet again – *and* kill someone who was a friend of Penelope's.

She had little skill with magic, but she had listened intently to Anarkus' lessons and, though she no longer had her wand, she still knew some words. She uttered one now and it held barely enough magic to raise the leg of the dead unlucky one, just enough for it to lift slightly as Anarkus stepped over, sending him sprawling. He was instantly back on his feet, but off balance, and it gave Peter enough time to reach him. This time there could be no failure, and as Anarkus raised his wand despairingly, Peter thrust the Knife of Chiang deep into his heart.

The unlucky ones howled with rage at the fall of one of their leaders, and their attacks intensified. But Portia smiled as she saw Anarkus was dying; it wouldn't alter the outcome of her battle, and his death saved her the problem of killing him herself.

As he lay there, quickly becoming weaker, he looked at Amelia. *She is the cause of my downfall!* he thought wildly. *It was her betrayal that caused this!* He knew he was dying, could feel the darkness crowding in, along with the spectres of all those he had murdered over the centuries. Almost too weak now, he lifted his wand and aimed at her, summoning the strength to make one last kill.

"No, you *don't!*" Penelope, panting heavily, had only just caught up, and she kicked the wand from his hand.

Defeated at last, and as the light faded from his eyes, he gave Amelia a puzzled look, unable to understand why she had betrayed him. In his arrogance, Anarkus had assumed everyone was like him at heart; evil. But Amelia was not evil, she was damaged and that, he had failed to realise, was a different thing.

Chapter 74

While Agnes fought a losing battle in the North, in London the end was very close now. They'd fought bravely and would continue to do so until the very last second, but there could only be one outcome. The faeries again created havoc, flying intricate paths between the heads of the enemy, jabbing and stabbing. But now there was no fun in it, for they too understood there was little hope; soon they would return to their land and their friends in the Sanctuary would be no more.

Spurred on by Portia, who contributed her own power from the middle of her army, safely beyond reach, they were again surrounded, with the enemy creeping ever closer. Their dead were piled high but those next in line simply walked over them, unintentionally gaining a height advantage from the heaped bodies of their companions.

So far, they'd managed to shield Penelope and Amelia, but now there was little time left. The Landlord quickly enveloped them in a glamour and pointed to a shop about fifty meters away. Outside was a big sign saying *Lego Store*. The Landlord knew there'd be places to hide in there; he only knew of it because he'd gone himself from time to time. The models fascinated him although he would never admit it to anyone.

"Run, as fast as you can, and don't stop until you reach it," he urged. "There are huge, tiny buildings in there," he added, somewhat confusingly. "Get inside them if you can, but stay beneath the glamour!" When Penelope tried to object, he pushed her gently. "Go now! Don't worry, we'll be fine."

It was a lie, for the Landlord had long accepted his fate. It didn't concern him much; he knew he'd be joining Mitra in the land of the dead. His only sadness was Oscar, but he knew Catrin and Gruffydd would look after him. Anyway, he was sure he could persuade Siwaraksa to let the little dog visit once in a while.

Molly, despite her propensity for complaining about some things – most things, really – was an eternal optimist. The odds against surviving were overwhelming, yet she refused to believe she was about to die and would continue to do so until… well, until she was actually dead.

As for Morgan, he didn't care either way. Peter fought with a sense of unreality, unable to comprehend that less than a day earlier he'd been sitting in a woodland paradise, meditating and drinking herbal tea. But Rosalind was neither optimistic at their chances nor pessimistic, she simply refused to die at the hands of the woman she despised so much.

"This is no good!" she shouted. "We need to get higher!" Without waiting for a response, she leaped up onto the ever-increasing pile of bodies. She was closely followed by the three wizards, leaving Molly on her own.

For a mad moment, she considered clambering up after them, but the thought of dying on her hands and knees, backside stuck in the air, probably with her knickers on display for all to see, put that idea firmly from her mind.

Well, that's bleedin' inconsiderate, she thought, as the unlucky ones surged closer. "Did you forget someone?" she yelled sarcastically.

The Landlord looked at Molly, then at Morgan. "Oops." He grinned, and they jumped back down, quickly linked arms with her, then leaped with some difficulty back up, dragging her behind them.

"Thank you, boys," she said, adjusting her bosom, which had become slightly askew, "much obliged." She raised her middle finger at the enemy below, who'd almost reached her, before incinerating them with a sweeping arc of power.

Suddenly much higher up, they could see for the first time the full extent of their problem; Portia's army was simply enormous.

"Oh, well that's bleedin' marvellous," Molly observed.

"Quite," agreed Morgan. "Looks like we're done for, old friend."

"Oh, be quiet, you're always so bleedin' pessimistic."

"Er, Molly? Less chat and more wand waving, perhaps?" The old witch stared at Rosalind, an acerbic reply already forming, but it was stilled as she saw Portia was approaching again.

"It's time to make an end!" Portia shouted, the gleam of triumph in her eyes visible for all to see.

"Oh, for goodness' sake, I'm getting really tired of that bleedin' woman," Molly muttered. "Who says!" she shouted, and Portia grinned.

"You were always such a fool, Molly!" she countered. "Oh, and, Cornelius, those two dirty, *disgusting* mortals you've just sent away, they won't get far."

The Landlord felt his anger rising; he would do anything he could to protect the lives of those *dirty* mortals. As one, the company sent their streams of fire, this time at Portia alone, but she fended them off easily.

She held out her wand and uttered one single word. "Goodbye."

Then the whole area was lit by an intense blue light.

Proud and tall, Cissy walked slowly through the back of Portia's army, her wand held high, sending out pulsing waves of blue wand fire. She was magnificent as, at last, the ancient prophecy was fulfilled. Never had any witch or wizard held power as potent and strong as this.

Each pulse felled hundreds of the unlucky ones in its path. Those few who tried to fight back simply died where they stood. Portia watched, fascinated, as the edge of the light came ever closer until it was almost touching her. Then she hopped backward with a yelping sound, quite unbecoming for a warrior witch.

All around, her army were running, suddenly uncaring of Portia's wrath, and though she screamed and berated them, she was ignored. Most didn't get far, only a few hundred managed to reach the shelter of the close-knit London streets before the pulsing blue fire caught them. As for Portia, although she didn't know the light's source, she sensed this was one enemy she couldn't defeat. Ducking down, she ran, blasting any of her army who got in her way. Unfortunately for her, she also wouldn't get far.

Chapter 75

It took a long time for the excitement of reunions to settle down, for there were tears and laughter, hugs and kisses, thanks and explanations. All the while, Velveteena and Moth stood on each of Cissy's shoulders, nibbling her ear fondly. Only Logan sat apart at first and the others, sensing his discomfort, left him alone for now. But he deserved his share of the congratulations and eventually his brother motioned him to join them.

As for Amelia, there were so many new people to meet she was feeling overwhelmed. At the Landlord's urging, they'd reached the store and, by breaking a few of the bricks, hidden inside a huge model of Elizabeth Tower and the Big Ben clock. Now, for someone who'd lived a solitary life with nobody to care for her, the kindness she was being shown was alien and uncomfortable. And here was another; a pretty woman, young-looking yet ancient.

"Greetings and thanks." The woman bowed low and Amelia took a step backward in surprise. "My name is Kamontip, queen of the goblins, and we all owe you a great debt."

Debt? Amelia wondered. *What does she mean?*

"The part you took in the death of Anarkus," Kamontip said, noticing her confusion. "He was a blight on the universe for millennia and it is a safer place now he is gone."

Penelope took her hand proudly, but Amelia had no time to dwell on the goblin's words as she saw someone else approaching. He was very tall, slim, and dark-haired. His features were so similar to Morgan's she knew they must be brothers, yet this one was the more handsome of the two. But as he drew closer, Amelia stared at him, transfixed for long seconds, her mouth gaping. Then something shattered within her mind and her screams rang out across London, shrill and terrified.

Logan stared, his brain refusing to compute what he was witnessing, but he'd recognised her instantly. Now, as she shrank away, her eyes wild and terrified, he took a step toward her and she ran, still screaming. When Penelope caught up, Amelia collapsed into her arms, shaking uncontrollably, casting fearful looks to where Logan still stood, unmoving.

Why did I do it to her? Shame settled deep in the pit of his stomach, but he knew the answer. *It was for my own amusement.* Not for the first time recently, he felt a strange out-of-body experience, as if the person who'd done so many terrible things over the centuries was someone else, not he.

The others had quickly reached the girl and were talking to her urgently. After a few minutes, she seemed calmer, and Kamontip gestured him forward. As he approached, Amelia leaped to her feet and withdrew her knife, pointing it at him threateningly, although her hand shook so much she could hardly keep from dropping it. He stopped, not yet able to look her in the eye, part shame, part reluctance to risk frightening her further.

"I no longer wish you harm," he said softly. "You have nothing to fear from me." He looked at the knife. "If you wish to use that, I will not stop you."

"That's twice in one day you've offered your life, brother. Perhaps you have changed after all." Morgan was sceptical. *He probably knows we won't allow her to kill him.*

But for once in his life, Logan was sincere. "Nevertheless," he said, his voice clear and proud, "it is hers to take, should she so wish." He looked at them all in turn.

"Nobody is to prevent her." He spoke with complete authority and his gaze rested on Kamontip. "Nobody."

"Logan," she began, but he shook his head.

"Not even you, love."

And she nodded, understanding that he needed to do this thing.

"Nothing can atone for the harm I did you." He faced Amelia again. "If you desire my life, it is yours." He lay his wand on the ground, then stood tall and erect, with utter dignity, looking beyond her and suddenly aware of the sounds of birdsong, returning now that the battle was over. The sun was still warm, and he turned his face to meet it. For the first time in his life, Logan felt at peace as he waited, fully expecting to feel the brief sting of the knife at any moment.

"Why did you do it?"

Why indeed? He thought long and hard, wanting to give her the honesty she craved and deserved. But how to explain the corrosive jealousy of his brother that had shaped him from an early age, made him first seek out Kanzser and then the Necromancer? How to put into words the harm that had been done to him by the demon king, damage that had made him uncaring of others, desiring only to cause hurt and chaos? *And for what?* He smiled cynically, knowing now how foolish he'd been. *Merely because Morgan was born a few minutes sooner than I?*

"What are you smiling at?" Amelia raised the knife higher. "You think what you did to me is *funny?*"

"No," he denied, "I do not." And the sincerity in his voice stayed her hand for a few moments longer.

"You still haven't answered my question."

"I know." He nodded. "It is difficult…"

"Amelia, please." Penelope couldn't bear it any longer, but she was ignored.

"You know, Amelia," he said, almost conversationally, risking the use of her name for the first time, "we are alike in many ways."

"No!" The word tore from her mouth.

"Yes," he insisted. "The experiences of my childhood determined the man I became, just as yours have determined the woman you are now."

"We are nothing alike!" she screamed. "You are evil!"

"That's not what…" He stopped, realising she was too young and too disturbed to understand. "It is too late for me"—he indicated the knife—"but you are young, you can change."

"Logan, you don't have to do this," urged Kamontip.

Molly, unusually silent so far, agreed. "Anytime in the last few hundred years, I'd have been wanting to stick the bleedin' knife in myself. But now, somehow it doesn't feel right." She looked at Amelia, trying to convey that it was time to forgive, time to set her life on a different path.

"Stop it!" he snapped. "All of you!" Logan looked at Amelia and smiled regretfully. "Make an end to it," he said calmly, "your friends are suffering." He stepped forward slowly, until his chest was only centimetres from the knife.

Amelia looked at him and saw the honesty there, then looked at the knife she'd kept with her for so many years. Suddenly it disgusted her.

"Aaargghh!" she shouted, a lifetime's anger in the cry, and she flung the knife aside.

AFTERMATH

Chapter 76

After the initial celebrations, Morgan moved away and sat alone, thinking. Soon he would return to Aeryn's world. *Aeryn's world no longer*, he realised. There he would have to witness the grief of her family, her people. He would have to stay strong when all he wanted was to lie down and die himself. And then there was the funeral…

He looked up at the sound of footsteps.

"Morgan," said Mitra softly, "once again the Sanctuary has saved the mortal world. I wish we were reunited in happier times; I know you have suffered a great loss. Aeryn, she was…" She stopped, unsure what to say next, appalled by the grief she saw in Morgan's eyes.

He nodded, unable to speak, and there was silence until he saw Siwaraksa walking toward them. Suddenly excited, he rose and gripped Mitra's arm. "She was brought back once; it can be done again!"

Mitra shook her head, sadly. "No, Morgan, that was different. This is beyond any power to heal." She looked involuntarily at Siwaraksa.

Morgan nodded. "But not beyond yours."

"No, it is not beyond my power," Siwaraksa agreed, "but highly irregular and out of the question." She couldn't quite meet his eyes, nor those of Mitra's.

"What," he urged, "you've never broken a rule? Not once in your life?"

"That is irrelevant," Siwaraksa snapped.

"In all the centuries I gave service to the Sanctuary, never once did I ask anything for myself. Now I do ask, no, I *beg*. Not only for me but for her and for her children." His words were eloquent, spoken calmly, and the two witches could hear the anguish behind them. But still, Siwaraksa shook her head. "You did it before, during the fight with the demons!"

"That was different, that time Aeryn gave her life in a selfless act to save the Sanctuary and thus the mortal world."

"Didn't she just do the same?"

"It's not the same, and you know it." For the first time, Siwaraksa looked uncomfortable. "Your soldiers also lost their lives, yet you don't plead for them. And the mortals who have perished; thousands of them!"

Morgan felt a stab of guilt. It was true, he'd barely given them a thought. "Perhaps you could also—"

"No, I could not. Morgan, do you realise the trouble I'll be in when I have to explain myself to the older dead? The ancient wizards who died not thousands, but tens of thousands of years ago. They will not be impressed."

"But you could do it."

Siwaraksa sighed. She could feel Mitra's eyes boring into her; it was clear what her views were on the matter. But it wasn't she who'd have to do all the explaining. "She can have one century, and no more," she said at last. "And only then because I like you." Despite the severity of her tone, her eyes twinkled.

A hundred years! It was more than he'd hoped for, and when that time drew near, he could negotiate more!

"And you won't be able to renegotiate."

He nodded, grateful beyond measure. "Thank you." He stepped forward and kissed Siwaraksa's weathered cheek.

Just then, the Landlord approached and, seeing the broad smile on Morgan's face, guessed what had happened. He was pleased for his friend, and for Aeryn too, of course, but right now he had eyes for only one person.

The light in Mitra's eyes danced as she looked at the man she had loved for so long. Her hair, still a vibrant russet red even after so many years, blew across her face in the gentle breeze. She had never looked more beautiful, but for a moment, the Landlord saw a different vision; of her hair wild and bedraggled, her clothes torn, and insane vitriol pouring from her lips.

"Stop it, Cornelius." Mitra sensed where his thoughts lay. "That was a long time ago."

"And yet that day is still as fresh in my mind as if it were yesterday. If only I had—"

"Hush." She put a finger to his lips. "It is the past, my love."

The Landlord thrust away the image of her falling, *letting* herself fall from the cliff edge, down into the crashing waves far below. "Can't you stay this time?" He brushed away the strands of hair, and she shook her head sorrowfully.

"You know I can't." She reached up and stroked his cheek. Then, her voice full of the old mischief and merriment, she added, "but Siwaraksa and I were thinking…" Then, without finishing the sentence, she skipped away, laughing, much as she had the very first day they'd met, when he didn't even know her name or where she lived. He remembered how desperate he'd felt that he might not see her again, only to realise she'd only been teasing him. This time she came back, kissing him softly and tenderly, holding him like she never wanted to let go.

They were interrupted by a shout of anger from Kamontip as she saw two small figures walking toward them. They were taking their time, eyes downcast, trying to look inconspicuous.

"What are you two doing here!" For once, neither Maisey nor Myla had an answer.

"Yes," agreed Morgan, frowning, although they couldn't fail to see he was trying not to laugh, "you promised me you'd go straight back home."

Kamontip looked at him questioningly, but it was a story for another time.

"I… I know," stuttered Myla, "but we *did* have our fingers crossed."

"Oh!" And now the laughter came. "That's alright then!" Seeing Kamontip about to speak, he nudged her. "Oh, come on, all is well now; give them a break."

The goblin queen looked at the two sorry-looking figures for a moment, then broke into a smile. Kneeling, she held out her arms. "Very well, just come here, you two!"

Chapter 77

Wallace and Luke weren't far away when they saw the strange blue glow in the sky, followed by the sudden flight of their enemy. The older man had refused to leave the battle completely and abandon his friends, and instead they'd fought in the nearby streets. Now the reunion between Luke and Cissy was wondrous to see.

For the longest time, they stood and stared at each other, not from shyness, but rather a sense of disbelief that this could be happening. Then they were in each other's arms, each touching the other's face to make sure it was real, and then they kissed. That kiss lasted a long time, and the others turned away to give them privacy; more than one had tears in their eyes.

The Landlord and Mitra had finally *stopped* kissing, just for the moment, and they walked over to where Siwaraksa stood.

"Did Portia escape?" he asked softly, and she looked at him coolly.

"Hardly. She is being well guarded."

He nodded. "Somewhere safe, I hope." It wasn't really anything to do with him, but as always, he was incurably nosey.

"Somewhere safe," she confirmed, adding, "I never trusted her. Even as a girl she was a sly little thing. I was astounded at the stupidity of those who allowed her to become leader."

"Why did you never join the council, Siwaraksa?" he asked, curious.

She chuckled, her eyes sparkling. "What, me? Join that band of reprobates? No, too many rotten apples for my liking."

"Cornelius," said Rosalind, as she and the others joined them, "it has come to my ears that Portia sent much of her army to overcome the towns in the North."

"Then we must go North," announced Cissy.

"The enemy is too widespread," objected the Landlord. "While we concentrate on one city, thousands more mortals will die in the others."

"There may be a better way." Morgan looked at Kamontip.

"No!" she said sharply, knowing exactly what was in his mind.

"You must," Morgan replied quietly, deep sympathy in his eyes, mirrored in the faces of the Landlord and Rosalind.

"Could someone tell me what's bleedin' going on?" Molly looked from one to the other. "Keeping me in the dark again. You've always done that, Morgan, ever since we were kids!" Morgan blinked at what was a gross exaggeration. "You might be the one with the brains, Morgan, more than me anyway,"—again, not true, and he opened his mouth to argue—"but it's... well, it's bleedin' inconsiderate!" She was red-faced and breathing heavily now. "Wallace, do you have any idea what this clown is talking about?"

Before either Wallace or Morgan could respond, Siwaraksa laid a hand on her arm. "Calm yourself, Molly, you'll have an aneurysm or something. Nobody is keeping secrets. Morgan refers to Portia's wand, it must be destroyed." She reached within her robe and withdrew it.

"I won't do it!" Kamontip cried, snatching the wand from Siwaraksa's grasp. "It is too much to ask." Her pretty face was a mask of anger. "Never, *never*, has a goblin destroyed a wand, any wand. It would be sacrilege and against our laws!"

"All this talk about rules and laws!" exclaimed Siwaraksa, frustrated. "How many do you think I have broken recently, Kamontip?" She breathed deeply and said, more quietly, "Resurrecting Catrin when she was murdered by Racine. Aeryn also, and my very presence here, absent from my rightful place, breaks at least a dozen laws of the dead."

"And those were your choices!" Kamontip raged, close to losing control. "I should never have given my help in fighting your war. Goblins do not get involved in mortal matters; why did I forget that!" She stormed off without a backward glance and the others stared after her, open-mouthed, until Morgan made to follow. But Logan gripped his arm, and in his expression, there was something… Morgan couldn't quite read it, but something different in his normally mocking eyes.

"Leave it, brother," he said, and his voice was almost gentle, "let me deal with it." He caught Kamontip easily, for she had slowed to let him do so. They spoke for a long time, before returning to the others.

"I understand now." Her anger had gone, and she looked lost and bewildered. "The necessity, I mean. Logan has reminded me the wand has been compelled to do many evil things, to do so time and again." As if to confirm her words, the wand glowed softly. "He reminds me that no wand should be made to suffer such things and that it may wish to end its life here, to be reincarnated elsewhere by our master wandmakers."

The glow became brighter. "But I can't do it, Siwaraksa, can't you? Mitra? Cornelius?" She turned to Morgan. "You do it, it was your idea!"

But Siwaraksa shook her head. "One wand isn't enough." It was stating the obvious, for they were talking about the most powerful wand ever made, but Kamontip was not thinking clearly. "It must be all of us. It may, at the final moment, still resist."

But Siwaraksa was wrong, the wand did not resist. Instead, it emitted a groan, but not one of pain. Instead, it sounded like a release, a freeing from pain. Goblins do not make wands to be used for evil, yet, for millennia, this one had been abused, used to do unspeakable things in the name of Portia's ambition. Kamontip understood that when something is in great pain or is broken beyond repair, it can be a mercy to end its suffering.

Chapter 78

In Liverpool, the witches were unaware of what was happening in the south and continued to fight, and so far all of them still lived. The dead stretched way beyond the stadium, into the streets beyond. Agnes sent yet another bolt of fire into their midst and then stared sin amazement. The unlucky ones had fallen *before* the fire hit them. Suddenly they were all falling, bodies everywhere just collapsing, laying there and not moving. Soon, not a single one stood. Clarissa and Agnes approached cautiously, suspecting trickery, but there was no trick; they really were dead.

"I guess that means the Sanctuary has defeated Portia." Agnes grinned triumphantly.

"Thank goodness for that." Clarissa slumped to the ground as exhaustion set in. "What happens now?"

"Food?" said Maymea, hopefully.

"I suppose we go back to London."

"I am not driving that thing all the way back down that tedious path."

"It's called a road, dear," another witch chimed in.

"Whatever; I'm not doing it."

Nobody argued and they began trudging through the streets, still wary of coming across signs of the enemy, but all they encountered were dead ones. As they passed, people stared at them through windows, some even opened their doors and made tentative steps outside. At last, they reached the centre of the city and, looking for somewhere to rest, entered a large building, not too far from the river. The sign outside said *Liverpool Lime Street.*

Inside they paused at a booth selling chocolate and, having got a taste for it, helped themselves. They moved further inside until Agnes stopped, smiling.

"What about one of those?"

Clarissa's eyes gleamed as her eyes feasted on the shiny engine, complete with several carriages behind.

"Now you're talking!"

Chapter 79

For the mortals of London, the threat that had so suddenly appeared had just as quickly gone away, and among the funerals for the thousands who had died, there were wild celebrations at the city's deliverance. Family ties were strengthened and petty feuds forgotten, street parties sprung up everywhere and several leading rock and pop stars organised a benefit concert to be held at Wembley Stadium in aid of the families who'd suffered losses.

On TV, experts speculated on the causes of what had happened; church leaders blamed the modern tendency to turn from God and urged a return to old values they believed had been lost. A celebrity scientist, often seen on the telly, took the opportunity to exacerbate the arguments between science, which was 100% in the right, and religion, 100% in the wrong, gaining new supporters by the bucketload while alienating just as many others who were sick of the whole thing and weren't really bothered either way.

A former politician called Toni Thewlis, ousted from her party after selling a story to one of the more popular red-top tabloids, stating the government had ironclad evidence of a flying saucer (complete with aliens) having been captured on the Isle of Man some years ago, had managed to get herself on TV. It was not so much the story of the UFO that had got her ousted, but rather her attempt to force the Prime Minister into admitting the aliens had been living there, tax-free, for the last thirty years. In Toni's opinion, only the rich (and English) should pay less (or zero) tax; the rest of the world could go to hell in a handbasket for all she cared.

When news of the attack on London emerged, Toni, ever quick to seize an opportunity, had quickly formed a new conspiracy theory group called T-i-T (Trust-in-Toni), with membership an eye-watering £5000 per year (hopefully to become six-monthly should the group prove popular).

Now, from the comfort of her country manor in the Dominican Republic (chosen for its lack of an extradition treaty with the UK), she was appearing live on a studio debate via Zoom – despite her well-publicised aversion to all things American – and was earnestly (with her most trustworthy, well-practiced face on) assuring her adoring public that the whole London thing had been engineered by the Chinese. Or possibly the Russians, with definite (or possibly maybe) some collaboration with the North Koreans. She went on to assure her adoring public that, in her opinion, she'd have made a great Prime Minister, if only the government hadn't been so thoughtless as to sack her.

Things wouldn't end well for Toni, who would soon find herself kidnapped, allegedly by that same government – although everyone knows they would never sanction such a thing – and charged with tax evasion. Following a suspiciously speedy trial, she found herself in prison, ironically on the Isle of Man.

The rumour and speculation continued for a while, and quite typically for mortals, everyone had an opinion. But in the absence of any concrete explanations, interest soon waned and, apart from the ardent few who still insisted the Earth had been visited by some kind of alien force, attention moved to more important topics. It wasn't long before the majority were again debating which 'celebrity' would be victorious in the jungle, the desert island, or that strange, sterile, made-for-television house.

Meanwhile, Siwaraksa and Mitra worked tirelessly to return the tens of thousands of unlucky ones back to their eternal rest, but they were unable to do so in complete secrecy, so widespread the carnage had been. So Molly and Cissy were on hand, creating glamour's and altering the memories of those citizens who saw what they were doing and were a little too curious for comfort.

Each corpse was treated with dignity; after all, they had not asked to be dragged back into a semi-alive state and infused with evil – that had all been Portia's doing. The spell the witches used compelled the evil to dissipate from their flesh, allowing them to fade gradually away, each spirit able to rest, never to be disturbed again.

"Do you think anyone will remember any of this?" Cissy fretted.

Molly was of the opinion that most mortals had the attention span of a fish and told her to stop bleedin' worrying.

*   *   *   *

"I believe you want to be a healer, my dear?" asked Siwaraksa. "Cornelius has said as much." And when Catrin nodded eagerly, she went on, "Then you'd best come and stay with us for a while."

Seeing her doubtful look, Mitra laughed. "Don't worry, no traps are awaiting you this time. Racine has been quite… subdued."

If Racine could have heard, she would have cursed her into damnation. Unable to stand her constant carping any longer, and tired of the complaints from the other residents of the land of the dead, Siwaraksa had acted. Temporarily, just for a little peace, it was necessary to zip her mouth closed, much to her fury. And what was worse for Racine, no matter how hard she tried, she couldn't break the spell.

"But how will I get there?" Catrin was thinking of the portal and the trip through the forest.

"Oh, I imagine Cornelius will be paying us a visit quite soon." She winked at Mitra. "You can come with him."

Their task in the mortal world complete, Siwaraksa and Mitra moved on through the other dimensions, completing their grisly work. The witches left their mountain retreat and returned home, as did the goblins and their families. Queen Aeryn recuperated in her castle and showed every sign of recovering fully, while in the goblin world, Maisey and Myla delighted in regaling a firsthand account of the destruction of the invading army to anyone willing to listen. The Landlord returned to the peace of the old inn, where he and Oscar were reunited, while Catrin returned to her home village in the 17th century, where she and Gruffydd had much to talk about.

In the land of the dead, the trees had been outraged at first when the woman had been sent to live among them. But soon they were having a fine time leading her astray down dead-end paths or leaving their roots lying carelessly around so that she often tripped and fell flat on her face. A favourite trick was for the wind to be particularly strong at night, making their leaves rustle so loudly she couldn't sleep. Not that the forest was particularly malevolent, they were just trees, albeit magic ones. But still, life could get a little boring just standing there day after day, so a little fun was very welcome.

When Siwaraksa and Mitra returned home at last, it was to find they'd forgotten to unzip Racine's face so that she'd endured weeks of being unable to complain to Liias about the blatant rule-breaking that had been going on. The dead couldn't just choose to wander back into the land of the living whenever they felt like it, it was simply not allowed!

But much to Liias's relief, Racine was unable to utter more than constant grunts which, although mildly annoying, was much more acceptable than her usual, high-pitched whining. In truth, Liias could have undone the spell quite easily, but who was he to interfere? The two witches were most apologetic at their oversight, although Mitra's sparkling eyes and her need to turn away lest Racine see her trying not to laugh, cast some doubt on their sincerity.

Not long after they'd settled back home, there was a heightened buzz around the place, quite at odds with its usual state – being quietly dead. Mitra could barely contain her excitement and, unable to sit still or apply herself to anything useful, found herself spending most of the morning going in and out of the entrance door to gaze into the forest. Even though she knew it was still a few hours from the appointed time, she hoped he might be a little early, at least.

Going outside for the umpteenth time, she peered into the trees, far in the distance, and listened for the tread of his feet, still familiar after so many centuries. But it was the sound of angry protests that heralded his arrival.

The Landlord had entered the land of shades with Catrin, Oscar trotting happily by his side and making quick progress through the forest. He was welcomed by the trees and unhampered on his way, for he was Cornelius the wizard, respected by all. He had not expected to see Portia, and at first didn't recognise her; the woman blocking his path was old and wizened, her face displaying only traces of its once fine beauty, still evident in the delicate lines of her bones. *But of course,* he'd realised, *she has been stripped of the magic that kept her young!*

"You," she'd screeched in fury, "are responsible for this!"

That wasn't true at all, the only person to blame was Portia herself, but the Landlord had no time to protest as she launched herself at him, hands bent into wicked claws, ready to scratch and maim.

"I have nothing to say to you, Portia," he'd said, calmly fending her off, and the sly old witch had become immediately penitent, a pretence of course. She'd tried to tell him how sorry she was, that it had all been a mistake.

"Free me and I will change my ways," she'd begged.

It was not in the Landlord's nature to be cruel, and even now he could feel a measure of sympathy for Portia's plight. But nor was he easily manipulated, and when, without answer, he tried to pass, she had jumped at him again, consumed by rage, subconsciously seeing in him the values she'd never managed to attain, resenting the love and respect he seemed to command without effort.

But before he needed to protect himself, the nearest tree had bent, wrapped a slim branch around her waist, and lifted her high out of harm's way, and her angry screams were what Mitra had heard.

Seeing the tall figure of the man she'd loved for so many centuries, she ran across the bridge, laughing with excitement, and flung herself into his arms.

Chapter 80

Back in the mortal world a few weeks later, Charles and Lucy were hosting a barbecue, and to Penelope's amusement, it appeared they'd invited half of London. She, Amelia, and Cissy had retreated to a more secluded part of the huge garden, while Luke had gone to help Charles and Peter, who were in charge of the cooking. They'd been getting in each other's way and so far the food was turning out rather more blackened than their guests would have preferred.

Amelia felt a little out of place, not yet used to being among crowds, so she kept missing many of the social cues, reacting awkwardly whenever anyone spoke to her. She was also in awe of Cissy, who had displayed the power that she, Amelia, had once dreamed of. As for Cissy, she understood something of what the girl was going through; she didn't particularly like meeting new people either. Over the last few weeks, Amelia had begun to share a few details about her childhood and later years, and Cissy, protective of others as she'd always been, found herself warming to this strange, troubled girl.

Kane, from Penelope's workplace, had called in briefly and then dashed off, on his way to a festival, but Mikey and his new girlfriend, Patricia, were there. Typically, they were too shy to mingle and had found a quiet spot where they sat, holding hands and gazing at each other. Even Tom had been invited and Penelope was pleased to see he'd lost much of his swagger; even he couldn't fail to see how happy she and Amelia were together and had finally given up his doomed pursuit.

Just then, Luke delivered a pile of food to share. Amelia, not wanting to cause offense, picked up a sausage and bravely tried to nibble it but gave up with a grimace. The others laughed and Penelope took it from her, tossing it into the flowerbeds. They were still laughing when Cissy's iPhone heralded a WhatsApp notification; it was from the Landlord.

There'd been a distinct lack of enthusiasm when Cissy suggested they all have mobile phones, pointing out that it would have been much easier during the recent attack if they'd been able to contact each other. Even Luke, who usually supported her in everything, including her more outlandish ideas, had been sceptical.

Kamontip said she had no idea what one was and that she'd managed very well for the last few thousand years without, thank you very much, and Rosalind was of much the same opinion. Wallace, as was his way, said very little, while Morgan, although he was aware of their existence, was reluctant to put too much faith in what was, after all, not magic, but merely a mortal invention.

As for Molly, she'd muttered something about new-fangled mortal bleedin' technology, and Luke had pointed out that phones wouldn't get a signal in the other dimensions anyway. Disappointed, Cissy had snapped that they could use magic to make them work, but Luke had just grinned at her in that infuriating way he sometimes had. When he'd asked where she planned to get the money, seeing as each one would cost about a squillion pounds, she'd shrugged and guiltily muttered something about using magic to kind of multiply the tenner she had in her purse. Luke had simply looked at her and the idea was dropped.

But the Landlord, who loved gadgetry – he had a 1950s jukebox in his kitchen, after all – surprised her by saying he'd like one anyway, just for the fun of it. He always carried odds and ends in his pockets and, fishing deep inside one, he drew out a handful of coins. Discarding the ones from several centuries ago, he scraped together about five pounds and presented it to her, asking if she would mind buying one of those iPhones she'd mentioned, as he had no idea how to go about it. Cissy had winced, realising she'd dug herself into a deep hole; she'd just have to delve into her savings, she supposed.

As for Penelope, she still felt guilty about the time she'd laughed at Amelia for not having a phone and offered to buy her one too. Amelia's first instinct was to reject it as charity, but she held her tongue, knowing deep down that the intent behind the gift was sincere. When it arrived, she was secretly delighted with it, although she tried to play it cool.

As for the Landlord, he'd been like a child with a new toy and insisted right away that Cissy show him how to use it. Amelia, although she had more of an idea, having watched Penelope with hers, did the same, mostly so she could spend a little time with the Landlord. She had immediately sensed the goodness in him and gravitated toward it; she'd rarely known good in her life. Sensing this, once they'd been shown the basics, he'd shooed Cissy away and he and Amelia had spent a happy hour taking photos of each other and messing about with the filters, laughing at how ridiculous they both looked.

Now, at the barbecue, the food had improved with Luke's input, alcohol was flowing, and everyone seemed to be having a good time. Lucy and Luna, Peter's wife, stood watching the three young women as they laughed together. "You must be so relieved she is well again," observed Luna, "and so proud."

Lucy nodded; it would be a long time until the nightmare of the last ten years began to fade. It was remarkable that Cissy seemed completely back to normal after her ordeal. What she didn't know was that much of it was just vague memories and feelings in her daughter's mind. The suspicion and paranoia, the attempts to harm her mother and Molly, or anyone else who'd tried to get too close, were forgotten. Countless times in the ten years or so she had been insane, she had pulled out her hair in clumps or, disliking the pretty face she saw in the mirror, had raked her nails across it, leaving deep, bloody gouges that would certainly have scarred her had Molly not used magic to prevent it. All of this was gone from Cissy's mind; the potion had done its job well.

"They make a nice couple, don't they?" Lucy looked over to where Cissy and Luke were busy throwing inedible food at each other. "If a little silly at times," she added primly.

"Yes, they do," Luna agreed, and said mischievously, "Penelope and Amelia too." She was amused to see the slightly uncomfortable look on her friend's face.

"How is Peter faring?" Lucy said at last. Since the battle had ended over a month ago, Luke's father had been noticeably absent, avoiding their phone calls and being unusually quiet and withdrawn on the few occasions they'd seen him. He'd taken an awful lot of persuading to attend today's event, only repeated pleading from Luna and Luke finally getting him there.

"Oh, he's fine," Luna replied, her face darkening. "Actually, he's not really. He still hasn't come to terms with killing that horrible man. He still thinks he did a terrible thing, even though everyone keeps telling him he's a hero."

Lucy nodded, thankful that her Charles was no longer involved with the affairs of wizards and witches. She looked across the garden to where her husband had given up incinerating the food and was ordering pizzas.

Cissy looked again at the message from the Landlord. Typically, it was filled with the text speak she'd taught him, telling her all the latest news from the village, where Catrin had been busy rekindling her relationship with Gruffydd. The message was packed with emojis and Cissy could tell he'd had great fun sending it.

Aside from all the waffle, the message was simple; a meeting was needed and she, Cissy, should suggest a time and place for it to happen. She thought for a while but was unable to come up with anything. She supposed they could all meet here, but she doubted her mother would be keen on the idea. She took the problem to the others and immediately Penelope and Amelia looked at each other and laughed. "We know just the place!"

Chapter 81

It was a strange bunch who piled into Starbucks a few days later. Cissy and Luke were there, of course, Molly, Morgan, and Wallace also. The latter was staring into his drink in bemusement; for someone who only ever drank tea, it looked rather exotic and suspicious. The Landlord, on the other hand, sipped his chocolate-mint Frappuccino with relish; it was his favourite, and he often slipped secretly into the mortal world to buy one. He grinned at Peter, who was perfectly aware of the fact and often met him there.

Kamontip had not come – she was busy with Maisey and Myla, looking after the welfare of their people – nor had Agnes, for similar reasons. But the Landlord had insisted Catrin be there, for none would ever forget her heroic actions in curing Cissy. Rosalind sat by her side, the two having become firm friends following their journey. Gruffydd, too, had been persuaded and was shyly accepting his share of praise for warning Aeryn of the approach of the unlucky ones. The warrior queen was still recovering from her death but, seeing how Morgan had really wanted to be there, she had insisted, despite his half-hearted protests. Before leaving, he rewarded the woman who'd fired the arrow that prevented Aeryn's beheading with one of her own, made from solid gold.

Penelope and Amelia were delighted with their choice of venue and if Amelia felt a little awkward in the presence of so many witches and wizards, she hid it well. She was thankful though that Logan had chosen to stay with Kamontip, despite his brother's invitation. She had hated him for so long and, although he had repeatedly protested his sorrow at the harm he'd done, she was not yet able to put it behind her. For sure, she would never forget, but perhaps one day she could forgive. She was not yet ready to trust he had completely changed his ways and thought the others a little stupid for doing so.

The arrival of so many strange characters had quickly emptied the café, and the manager thought of protesting, but these didn't look like the kind of people he could challenge easily. Then, as he placed an insincere, sickly smile on his face and tried to pluck up the courage to approach them, the big fat woman complained loudly.

"Just look at the price of these drinks! Don't they realise I'm an old-aged pensioner? Bleedin' inconsiderate, I call it!" Molly winked at Morgan, who stifled a grin. He supposed his friend could loosely be called old and wondered what the poor man would say if he knew she'd been born 400 years ago.

And anyway, Cissy had insisted on paying and absolutely forbade anyone to use their wands to magic the money, because that would be dishonest; a bit of a U-turn considering her previous plans to fund the mobile phones. Molly had grumbled about *new-fangled bleedin' ideas,* saying she and Morgan had never had qualms about doing it before Cissy came along. The manager decided to keep quiet and simply shrugged to the trainee barista by his side and put a finger to his lips. She nodded, thinking that was probably wise.

Suddenly, Moth appeared from Molly's pocket and, sensing the opportunity for mischief, dove headfirst into the Landlord's Frappuccino (his third) and emerged seconds later, coughing, spluttering, and grinning broadly. Velveteena jumped lightly onto the table and looked at him disapprovingly while secretly wishing she'd thought of it.

Molly looked at the unfortunate restaurant manager's name badge and winked. "Don't worry, Norman," she said in a side whisper, "this is all just a dream."

Understandably, Norman was quite unable to reply.

Just then, the door to the restaurant opened and, to Morgan's delight in particular, in walked Charles and Lucy. Cissy's mother hugged everyone lavishly, her eyes shining with happiness, but Charles hung back, reserved and shy. This would be the first time in a decade he'd spoken to Morgan, since the day he'd left the Sanctuary, blaming the wizard for the devastation of his daughter's mind. Penelope, understanding his reticence, took his hand firmly and led him to where Morgan sat, but the wizard was already on his feet, hand outstretched and trying to keep the huge smile from his face.

"Charles," he said quietly, "it's wonderful to see you again."

Hesitating only fractionally, Charles took the hand. "I was wrong," he began quietly, and when Morgan tried to interrupt, shook his head. "No, I shouldn't have said the things I did; should have trusted you." He looked at Cissy, whose eyes were shining with tears. "Thank you for keeping her safe, and for curing her."

"Ah, well," said Morgan, embarrassed, "you have Catrin here to thank for that; it was she who faced great peril to obtain the potion and take it to Cissy's hiding place."

Charles turned and nodded to the girl, who was blushing furiously. "Thank you," he said quietly, while Lucy hurried over and hugged her for the second, or probably third, time.

"Marica," said Cissy suddenly, "she should be here. Why didn't I think to invite her?"

"I did," said the Landlord, "but she wouldn't come. She's really rather a private person, you know, and quite at home in the dimension where she lives. Anyway, if anyone else were to join us, I think that poor fellow would have a breakdown." He nodded at Norman, who was now literally wringing his hands in despair, wondering if they ever planned to leave.

Right on cue, the door crashed open and Agnes ran in breathlessly. "Hi, everyone." She grinned. "Sorry I'm late, those damned witches just cannot stop arguing about everything!" She sat on one of the few remaining chairs and eyed Amelia's ice cream with interest. "What have I missed?"

"Agnes!" the Landlord hurried over to hug her. "We didn't think you were coming."

Oscar, who had already raced around the room a dozen times, thoroughly licking the hands and faces of everyone present, did so again, then jumped up at Agnes, barking excitedly. The witch held a special place in his heart, having rescued the Landlord from Racine's prison centuries ago and helped him escape with Mitra.

Agnes picked him up, laughing, and was subjected to more licking until, exhausted at last, he jumped down and settled at Amelia's feet, much to Cissy's chagrin. She loved the little dog as if he were her own and felt a little jealous. But Oscar had the wisdom of many centuries and could sense Amelia's discomfort. Plus, she was surreptitiously feeding him marshmallows under the table.

The Landlord rose and wandered to the counter, eyeing the array of machines with interest. "Do you mind?" He smiled reassuringly at the trainee barista. "I've always wanted to have a try."

"Go ahead," she invited, smiling back. This was certainly more interesting than the average Friday night, and unlike Norman, who looked as if he were about to have a coronary, she was having fun. Twenty minutes later, having made a round of drinks that only vaguely resembled the ones advertised, and having created a great deal of mess, he sat down at Agnes's table and handed her the drink, rather proudly.

"So,"—he watched her take a long, delighted slurp—"you were saying?"

"Honestly, Cornelius," Agnes said, grinning, "I had to come, I was going crazy. You should be glad you're not a bloody witch. Anyway,"—she eyed him curiously—"what's occurring?"

Oscar chose that moment to investigate the mess the Landlord had made and soon he was completely covered in ice cream, chocolate sprinkles, and the rest. Norman again opened his mouth to protest that dogs weren't allowed, but just as quickly closed it. *What the hell*, he thought. *Hopefully they'll drink up and be gone soon.* But his hopes were in vain as the group settled into reminiscing about the past and, as he tried to listen without making it obvious, he heard some very strange things. Something about demons and necromancers, witches and wizards; clearly this lot was on a trip out from the local asylum.

"Anyway, you still haven't told us how you managed to escape the clutches of Portia's evil band of cutthroats back in your world." The Landlord pitched his voice deliberately so Norman, who was staring wide-eyed at Agnes, could hear. That story took another hour to tell and when she had finished, the excited chatter dwindled suddenly.

All at once, they sensed the time had come to pay their final respects to the Sanctuary.

"We will go through the lamppost," Morgan said softly. "Rosalind tells me its magic has all but gone, but with our combined power, I think we can do it."

She nodded, and they stood, thanked their hosts, and headed out as Morgan muttered a simple spell that would erase any memory of the last few hours.

Amelia was silent and hadn't moved, thinking of how she'd threatened Penelope, trying to get through the lamppost. Inwardly she cringed, scarcely able to believe she'd been that person and worried in case part of her still was. She still got angry or suspicious sometimes, her paranoia not something that could abate overnight, so long had she lived with it. But she was no longer filled with hatred for her fellow human beings, and no longer had a desire to destroy anyone who crossed or threatened her. Still, she doubted she'd be invited to go with the others and wished she could slip away without anyone noticing.

"Would you like to come?" Intuitively, Penelope was aware of the turmoil of Amelia's thoughts. "You are welcome to. In fact, I'd like you to be there, we all would."

Amelia didn't know how to respond; it was possibly the nicest thing anyone had ever said to her. She couldn't remember ever being welcome anywhere. To her surprise, Charles squeezed her hand briefly under the table. After a rocky start, they were becoming accustomed to each other and she smiled at him gratefully.

The others had already left, and they ran to catch up. Penelope cannoned into the Landlord's back when he stopped suddenly. "Wait! How rude of me!" He hurried back to the door, popped his head inside, and waved his wand. Norman and the trainee barista, now having no recollection of the last couple of hours, stared in astonishment as the mess, made mostly by the Landlord himself, was erased and normality returned. The wizard took two steps back down the street then went back, waved his wand again, and they promptly forgot that as well.

*   *   *   *

The lamppost wasn't far away, and they walked slowly. It would be the last time they entered the Sanctuary, and none were looking forward to witnessing the destruction. Since her recovery, and the defeat of Portia and Anarkus, Cissy had pushed the reality of their situation firmly to the back of her mind, but she could do so no longer.

Her magic, more powerful than that of the others, would take longer to fade yet fade it would. Until now, she had not realised the full significance, that without magic, they would be forced to remain in the dimension in which they chose to live. The thought of never seeing Molly or Morgan again was anathema to her. And the Landlord! How could she never see him again? Tears welled and she fought to prevent them from falling. Molly noticed and drew the young woman close, barely able to prevent her own tears.

"I can't believe I won't be a witch anymore." Cissy sniffed. "I know it's selfish, but I'd kinda got used to it."

"Don't be so bleedin' daft," said Molly softly, "you'll always be a witch, one of the finest I've ever known."

"But I'll never see you again." Now the tears did fall, and Cissy let them. For once, Molly had no reply and Luke stepped forward and took her into his arms, trying to give comfort but unable to find the words, for there were none to say. Still, she was grateful to him for trying, and looking into his clear, green eyes, she thought she had never loved him more.

At least I'll always have Luke, she thought, and that at least was some comfort. Her mind shied away from knowing that, as a witch, she would live much longer than he; that he would eventually grow old and frail while she remained strong, with years of life ahead of her. *Maybe now the Sanctuary is finished I won't be a witch anymore,* she thought, *despite what Molly says.* Deep inside, despite her fears for her and Luke, she hoped it wasn't true.

"Will you come too?" Morgan asked, and Charles nodded. Not all his memories of the Sanctuary were bad. There were plenty of happy ones from his boyhood, before he had failed his wizard exams, so to speak.

"Yes," he agreed, "I'll come. It feels important to see it for one last time."

One last time. Morgan's mood soured. *Never did I dream this day would come.* Seeing the grim set of his features, Molly took his hand in hers.

"We've had a good bleedin' run at it, haven't we?" She smiled unconvincingly, and he nodded, not trusting himself to speak. "I'm not sure where I'll go now though." She left the unasked question hanging.

Despite his mood, Morgan smiled faintly; his friend had always been as subtle as a brick. "You'll come live with us, of course, at the castle," he said. "I couldn't bear to lose you too. Wallace has agreed already."

Molly nodded. She'd hoped he would offer but had been too proud to ask. "Thank you, I'll probably consider it." She shrugged as if it were of no great importance, as always shy of revealing her emotions. Anxious to change the subject, she turned to the witch beside her. "What about you, Rosalind, what will you do now?"

For many centuries, Rosalind had felt the intense burden of her place on the council. Now it had ended, she felt liberated. "I will go home," she said. "There is a place in the village for me. I suppose we need a new name for it now," she added, laughing. "Land of the witch and wizard council was always a bit of a mouthful, and it doesn't seem appropriate anymore."

"I hear the castle is already in ruins." Agnes shuddered, thinking of her own experience of that bleak, stark place.

"Good," Rosalind said.

"Well,"—Morgan pointed—"there's the lamppost. I guess it's time—"

He paused at the sound of singing drifting toward them faintly on the breeze, a mournful, haunting sound of many voices joined in harmony. Deep, sonorous baritones mixed with melodic tenors and sweet sopranos. As it grew louder, it sent shivers down their spines; the words, even though they were in a language now forgotten, spoke of pain and sorrow, of outrage and despair.

"Come," Morgan said softly, "it is the end of an era; many eras. Now we say our farewells."

Chapter 82

Across the mortal world, humans heard it and marvelled. For a short time at least, they ceased their wars and their greed, more at peace with each other than they'd ever been.

In the land of the witches, the woodland creatures halted their labours and their play and listened, enthralled. The witches ceased arguing about the refusal to aid the mortals in their time of need and returned to their previous, harmonious existence. In Aeryn's world, the villagers and those who lived in the palace stood and bathed in the beauty of the sound, although only Aeryn and Daraproud understood its significance.

Kamontip heard it and sighed regretfully at the passing of an era and wondered what the future held for the mortals, before turning once more to the care of her people. Goblins, as has been said before, had little dealings with those from other dimensions and her recent adventures had served to remind her why that was.

But Logan was confused. He'd felt a brief surge of delighted spite, knowing instinctively what the music meant. But why? Hadn't he changed? Wasn't he a reformed character? Suddenly he doubted himself, wondering if the rapprochement with his brother was real. And worse, he knew that Kamontip had sensed his delight. But she merely smiled at him; she knew that nobody could completely change overnight. For Logan, it would take time.

The music even reached the Chasm of Nothingness, though there were none there to hear it, and in the land of the dead, Siwaraksa and Mitra smiled a little sadly. Even Liias left his solitary place among the labyrinthine passages to join them, as did Eloise. Only Racine was unmoved.

In the former world of the witch and wizard council, the villagers paused their tearing down of the castle walls – the stones were already being used to expand and improve the village – and listened with awe, wondering where it came from.

The man who'd saved Agnes' pigeon was there too. He'd found the portal between the two worlds open one day; the pigeon had not forsaken him and had ensured Agnes' return to save him.

The music was irresistible and determined to be heard. Through the dimensions and beyond it went, past the few planets not stolen by the witch and wizard council so long ago, and out into the cosmos. And back in London, on Old Kent Road, the two faeries emerged from Molly's pocket, silent and well-behaved for once.

"What is it?" Velveteena breathed, voicing the thoughts of everyone. "Where is it coming from?"

But Morgan shook his head, unwilling to disturb the music.

"Look." Penelope pointed to the sky, where an enchantment of nightingales swooped and dipped in time to the sound, silently and with graceful vigour, as if protesting the atrocity visited upon the Sanctuary. Across the globe, birds of every kind were doing the same. Gradually they moved lower until they weaved in and out of the group who stood, entranced. Occasionally their wings brushed the lips of each one in a brief kiss of tribute. Somehow, they all knew it was a message of hope.

Then they sang, in perfect harmony with the chorus, and suddenly they were high in the sky again, still dancing and singing until they were lost from sight. The music continued but faded gradually, becoming muffled as if moving to another place, and Morgan knew exactly where it had gone.

"Come," he said as he led them to the lamppost, "we must be quick." With the combined power of each of them, it was easy to force open the portal. Soon they'd entered the circular room, hurried along the passage-between-the-worlds, and were standing once more inside the Sanctuary. Rosalind and Catrin had been prepared, for they'd already witnessed the devastation, but even they were astounded at the deterioration in such a short time. As for the others, they could only stare in horror.

The walls were rotting, stones laid thousands of years past dissolving into grey-brown sludge, and big black termites munched greedily upon the few areas of wood that remained. Permeating everything was the cloying aroma of decay, but worse than anything, the absence of magic was oppressive, weighing each of them down, challenging them to keep from running, abandoning the place forever.

Suddenly frantic, Morgan ran to the huge, old front door and flung it open. With a groan of sorrow, his suspicions were confirmed as, instead of looking out onto the streets of old London, he was met with a black, inky void. "The building is breaking away from the dimensions," he said softly. "Soon the Sanctuary will die."

Wallace, who had followed him, could only nod. "What about the other dimensions, along the corridor?" he asked quietly, wondering whether they should check, but Morgan shrugged.

"I suspect if they are not already gone, they soon will be," he said. "The end will not be long, my friend."

As if to deny his words, or perhaps to delay their truth, the music began again.

"But I don't understand," Wallace persisted. "What do the dimensions have to do with the demise of the Sanctuary?"

Morgan sighed; he thought his friend would have realised it by now, after all these years. "Wallace, what do you think the passage-between-the-worlds actually is?"

Wallace frowned, thinking. "Well, it's the passage that leads to the Sanctuary, obviously," he began, but stopped, unsure what Morgan was getting at. The wizard shook his head, frustrated.

"Portia needed to link the dimensions together so she could watch over them and exert control if she wanted to. Her recent attacks were an attempt to do just that."

Wallace nodded slowly, still not understanding.

"The passage-between-the-worlds is what links them together!" Morgan was exasperated. "But she needed to disguise her reasons for creating it. That's why the Sanctuary was made. Not to do good, Portia didn't care about that, but to provide an excuse for the witch and wizard council to continue their quest for ultimate power! Some of the old wizards, Cornelius included, understood this and used the Sanctuary to help protect the mortal world. Portia didn't like it, but she could hardly protest without revealing her true plans."

"But didn't the council object? They can't all have been evil, surely?"

"No," Morgan agreed, "just blindfolded. Only Suluhura, I think, was truly evil, but he was just her puppet.

The others followed blindly, apart from Agnes and, later, Rosalind, who did what they could to sow subversion and challenge Portia."

He was filled with a rare anger at the thought of how the two witches had endured centuries of being despised. They had fought against suspicions that, if proved, might have ended their lives – for Agnes it almost had. He forced his breathing to calm before adding, "Anyway, in a sense, Portia has won. The dimensions will move far apart, back to their original positions in the solar system. They will cease to be dimensions and become planets again.

"But what would be the point of destroying the Sanctuary if it separated the dimensions, taking them beyond Portia's control?"

Morgan forgot his frustration and looked at Wallace, impressed. It was an insightful question. "Do you know what true power is, Wallace? It is the ability to destroy that which you have created. Portia made the Sanctuary and only she really had the power to unmake it. I have no doubt she planned to rebuild it after her victory, into something abominable, to suit her desires and machinations."

"Well, at least that won't happen now," Wallace mused, "but I suppose it means we are finished; as wizards and witches, I mean."

But Morgan shook his head again. "Cissy believes our magic will fade altogether, but it's not true. We'll still have power, but without the catalyst of the Sanctuary, it will be less effective. And with us separated onto far away planets, our ability to aid the mortal world will be no more."

Saying nothing of what they'd found, they rejoined the others, to find the music had soared, louder and even more vibrant in the confined space.

"These are the voices of the dead, of the living, and of those yet to be born," said Morgan in hushed tones, answering Velveteena's question at last.

"It's beautiful," Cissy breathed, awestruck at the sound.

They were silent as they listened, entranced by its beauty and each immersed in their own memories, some brief, some thousands of years old.

So, the story of this place has turned a full circle in time, thought the Landlord, who'd been just a boy when the Sanctuary was created at the behest of Portia. He remembered his boyish, naïve excitement and was saddened for a while, wondering how she could have deceived everyone for so long, wishing he'd done more. But then his thoughts turned to Mitra, and he felt a surge of hope. For so long he had suffered the burden of guilt at her death, the cause of which had taken root in his creation of the blood moon. But now there was redemption; he knew she didn't blame him and there was the promise of seeing her again.

"What are you smiling at?" whispered Penelope, and he temporised, not wanting to explain.

"The music," he said, "it's getting closer." And so it was, as if a vast choir approached, singing its mournful, yet lovely, dirge.

"Morgan, what's happening?" Luke asked, and the wizard looked at him, his eyes wet with tears.

"It is a requiem," he said, "a requiem for the Sanctuary."

The anthem surged, now almost unbearably loud. As they looked around at the ruined building, the shades of witches and wizards, some from hundreds and thousands of years past, others from the future, passed silently by. Each one bowed first to the Landlord, then Morgan, and lastly to Cissy, its latest and final leader. It took a long time, for there were many, but at last, they faded and disappeared, and the requiem dwindled into silence.

Nobody spoke for a while, awed by what they had witnessed; never throughout history had such a tribute been paid. At last, in a tone that was almost pleading, Cissy asked, "But we can mend it and start again, can't we? It *can't* be the end."

Morgan, the music still ringing in his ears, felt the hopelessness of the last few days disappear, replaced by tiny seeds of determination. He looked at Cissy, who seemed suddenly so young and vulnerable, then at each of his friends. They returned his gaze with serenity, waiting. Then the old wizard smiled and, as one, they each took out their wands.

The End

431

Acknowledgements

So, time has passed and suddenly I've written three novels; how did that happen!

I have always imagined the *The-Passage-Between-The-Worlds* as a trilogy and that it would end there. Well that's fine in theory but I didn't account for Molly, Morgan, Cissy, Luke, et al becoming so real to me, so important that I now find myself reluctant to let them go.

More of that in a moment but first, as always, there are many people who have given me their love, expertise and support through my writing of the Passage-Between-The-Worlds.

Fi Marks, whose friendship is beyond compare. Her understanding of me during the darker days has enabled me to hold onto the thrill of writing, to feel joy at each new idea and keep going, even when the words aren't coming easily.

Paula Telizyn, another good friend whose knowledge of writing and publishing and whose common-sense, no-nonsense practicality is fundamental in getting my books to print. She will be relocating from Canada to the UK soon, which is perfect. Instead of emailing her then waiting hours for a reply, I'll be able to nip down the road and just ask her!

Jess Lawrence my wonderful editor who continues, in her gentle but firm way, to point out my errors and notice things I've missed despite my reading and rereading of the text. She is never harsh, never lowers my confidence as a writer when I do something really stupid, even though I sometimes sense, perhaps an element of 'what on earth are you doing!' Jess is wonderful and, for me the perfect editor.

Jacqueline Abromeit who is responsible for the wonderful artwork on all three novels. Supremely talented she knows instinctively what will work. She has an uncanny ability to take out the primary themes from each novel and meld them into the incredible images you have seen. I'm delighted that we have further collaborated on the Passage-Between-The-Worlds colouring book, packed with more of her stunning artwork and available now on Amazon.

And finally, as always, my good friends at the Horizon Centre. Their enthusiasm for my novels never wanes, neither does their interest in asking about my writing process, or the characters, who is their favourite one etc. Thank you, my friends of many years. You are all simply wonderful.

And so, back to what's next?

I have purposely included back story in my novels, I find this gives characters more depth and interest. After all, none of our lives are just about the present; we all have a past. And as my characters are generally ridiculously old, they have an awful lot of it.

I'm often asked things like, 'what was Molly like as a girl?' or 'was Logan always bad?' 'What happened when the Landlord and Mitra were together, before …'

So my next project will be a series of novellas about the early lives of the more prominent of those you've already met in *The Passage-Between-The-Worlds* and you can expect the first (perhaps even the second) to come your way in 2025.

At the end of the third novel, Cissy asks if the Sanctuary can be mended. *"It can't be the end,"* she pleads. Well, the old friends of the Sanctuary have taken out their wands, so we will just have to wait and see.

With love, Michael.
November 2024

www.ingramcontent.com/pod-product-compliance
Lightning Source LLC
Chambersburg PA
CBHW010315100726
47906CB00006B/993